Redeemed:

Redeemed Series Book 2

Redeemed:
Redeemed Series Book 2

Patricia Haley & Gracie Hill

URBAN CHRISTIAN

Urban Books, LLC
97 N18th Street
Wyandanch, NY 11798

ISBN 13: 978-1-62286-818-6
ISBN 10: 1-62286-818-8

First Trade Paperback Printing November 2015
Printed in the United States of America

10 9 8 7 6 5 4 3 2 1

*This is a work of fiction. Any references or similarities
to actual events, real people, living or dead, or to real
locales are intended to give the novel a sense of reality.
Any similarity in other names, characters, places, and
incidents is entirely coincidental.*

Distributed by Kensington Publishing Corp.
Submit Orders to:
Customer Service
400 Hahn Road
Westminster, MD 21157-4627
Phone: 1-800-733-3000
Fax: 1-800-659-2436

Redeemed:

Redeemed Series Book 2

Patricia Haley & Gracie Hill

Redeemed **is also available as an eBook**

Redeemed Series
Relentless
Redeemed

Also by **Patricia Haley**

No Regrets
Still Waters
Blind Faith
Nobody's Perfect
Let Sleeping Dogs Lie

Mitchell Family Drama Series
(Listed in story-line order)
Anointed
Betrayed
Chosen
Destined
Broken
Humbled
Unforgiving

Also by **Gracie Hill**

Where the Brothers At?
Sorrows of the Heart
The Kitchen Beautician
Saved, Sanctified and Keeping My Secret

Patricia Haley

I dedicate Redeemed *to my loving grandparents and to those of my husband, Jeffrey Glass. We're blessed to have grown up with grandparents who believed in family, integrity, hard work, discipline, and faith in God. They left a wonderful legacy and laid a solid foundation, which I hope to emulate.*
Clifton, Sr. and Mary Ballard Tennin
Will and Jennie Watts Haley
Eldridge and Geneva Moorman
Reuben and Mary Logan Glass

Gracie Hill

I dedicate this book to my mother, Pauline Warren. She was a strong woman who loved her children and gave each of us a wonderful sense of family and showered us with love. The greatest gift she gave me was the knowledge of Jesus Christ. She would be overjoyed to know that the seed she planted in my life about the love of God has manifested into the salvation in my life.

*I care very little if I am judged . . . by any
human court. . . .
My conscience is clear, but that
does not make me innocent.*

—1 Corinthians 4:3–4

Chapter 1

Activity inside the law firm, nestled in the heart of downtown Philadelphia, was often hectic, but today it seemed manageable.

"Make no mistake about it, he's a snake, just like the rest of them," Maxwell Montgomery declared as he reared back in his favorite chair, comfortably situated in his private office.

Garrett, his lead private investigator, didn't respond immediately.

Maxwell carried on with his tirade. "You know I'm telling the truth." The infamous civil attorney leapt to his feet and approached Garrett, who was sitting across the room. "Name one honest preacher that you know." Not allowing Garrett ample time for a response, Maxwell continued. "See? You can't think of one, not a single one," he said, pointing at Garrett and bursting into a flurry of laughter. "Not one."

"Whatever you say, boss."

"Because you know I'm right," he said, throwing a right jab into the air. "A bunch of self-righteous, money-grubbing, power-hungry hypocrites, every one of them." Maxwell sailed back to his chair in an animated fashion. "When you think about it, I shouldn't complain. They've all been good to me."

"How?" Garrett asked, seeming confused.

"Heck, look at this." He tapped on a stack of files on his desk. "Case after case, they've made me a boatload of cash," he said, rubbing his index finger and thumb together briskly.

Garrett's head tilted to the side, and his lips tightened. "Can't deny that."

"I know you can't. Man, these cats are a gold mine. Uncovering their sin is as easy as taking candy from a baby. I have more work than I can handle, going after these weasels." He plopped into his seat and began tossing a foam stress ball into the air. "Some of these cases blow my mind. Remember the priest in Allentown who secretly had three sets of children and wouldn't agree to pay child support for any of them?"

"I remember. One mother was a nursing student who was struggling to stay in school."

"Yeah, and he wouldn't pay her the measly five hundred dollars a month that she needed," Maxwell said.

Garrett leaned forward and rubbed his head. "I bet if he could do it all over again, he'd gladly pay the five hundred. Heck, he'd probably be willing to pay five thousand a month."

"I bet he would too, because once I found out about his other two sets of children, who he'd conveniently hidden from the archdiocese, paying that skimpy child support was the least of his worries. Staying out of prison for messing around with a seventeen-year-old girl took precedence."

"And the church wasn't too happy about the kind of publicity you were threatening to send their way."

"That's right." Maxwell chuckled. "I did put some heat on them." He spun a little bit in his chair. "I love my job, and what's great about it is that there are plenty more creeps out there begging for me to come after them. Take Bishop Jones. He practically dared me to bring him down, and that whole cast of characters at Greater Metropolitan Church."

Satisfaction washed over Maxwell as he recalled the case. He'd practiced law for fifteen years, and every single day throughout his career, Maxwell had dreamed of bringing down the mighty bishop Ellis Jones, the man who'd single-handedly destroyed the Montgomery household. Nearly three decades ago, his parents had been a cog in the mighty preacher's wheel of deceit. The mere memory used to be painful and would ignite extreme disdain in Maxwell, but that was before the bishop was sent to prison last year. Now Maxwell reveled in the bishop's predicament. Jones had lost his church, his freedom, and most importantly, his reputation.

Maxwell's parents had suffered a similar fate when they blindly served as loyal church members under the pastor. Little did they know back then that their senior pastor was running a get-rich-quick scheme, which ultimately sucked money from the congregation. Instead of Jones taking responsibility when the scheme was exposed, he let Deacon Paul Montgomery, Sr., and the church secretary, Ethel Montgomery, take the fall. They paid a high price. Besides losing their house and their money, Maxwell and his sister were left orphaned when their parents had to spend time in prison for fraud, while Jones spent every night with his family. Worst of all, as soon as Maxwell was old enough, he left home, intent on never returning. So far he'd been very successful with not having to interact with his family in person, except on extremely rare occasions. Unfortunately, he hadn't been as successful with avoiding their periodic calls, which had become more frequent since his father had a heart attack last summer. The situation wasn't ideal but necessary. Knowing that Bishop Jones was experiencing his own form of family separation was beyond comforting. For Maxwell, it was justice.

He squished the ball extra hard, feeling vindicated. "They all got exactly what they deserved. They're locked up in hell."

Garrett eased to the edge of his seat as his gaze plummeted to the floor. "Everybody, including Deacon Burton?"

Maxwell's adrenaline careened through his body. He sent a searing stare in Garrett's direction. "Yes, Deacon Burton too," he said with such a jagged edge to his voice that it seemed to slice the air.

"If you say so."

Garrett's reply didn't give Maxwell the validation that he would have appreciated, but it wasn't required. He was at peace with the outcome. Maxwell had taken down a despicable clergyman who'd gotten away with so much for so long that he deserved a lifetime behind bars. If his staff was guilty by association, so be it. There were no regrets. Neither Garrett nor a band of church runners was going to change Maxwell's mind. He pulled up to his desk and extracted a folder from the top of the pile.

"I can't waste any more time on Greater Metropolitan. That case is done, and there's a whole lot more work for us to do, which brings me to Faith Temple and Pastor Renaldo Harris." His serious tone switched to a lighthearted one. With his thumb up, Maxwell extended his index finger and let his hand slowly rotate forward as he curled his other fingers inward, turning his hand into an imaginary gun. "The so-called mighty man is the next one in my crosshairs." He shut his right eye and drew his imaginary pistol hand closer. "*Pow, pow*, and that will be the end of him."

"I'm not so sure it's going to be that easy," Garrett replied. "I've been investigating this man and his ministry for seven months, and I haven't found a single shred of impropriety." Garrett scratched his head. "You're not going to want to hear this, but we might have found an honest pastor in the Philly area."

"Pu-lease! You can believe that he's hiding something. You're just not looking in the right places." Maxwell grimaced. "What's got you spooked?"

"I'm being careful, unlike you, who's turning this thing into something personal."

"Personal?" Maxwell responded in a slightly elevated voice. "This is business. Always has been, always will be," was the lie Maxwell uttered. Garrett grunted, but Maxwell wasn't dissuaded. He hurriedly shifted the conversation away from himself. "Usually, you're on top of your game, but looks like you're slipping, my man."

"One of us is slipping," Garrett said and got up to leave.

Before Garrett reached the door, Maxwell asked, "Aren't you forgetting something?"

The investigator froze, slid his hand into his pocket, and turned slowly.

"Well, do you have it?" Maxwell asked with slightly more force behind his words.

"Yeah, I have it."

"Then what are you waiting on?" he said, beckoning for Garrett to approach the desk.

Garrett pulled a business card from his pocket. "I'm not sure this guy is legitimate. I haven't gotten a chance to check him out yet. Give me a few days, and I'll run the background check."

He must be crazy, Maxwell thought as he kept beckoning for Garrett to come closer. Months of no credible leads, and Garrett expected him to wait around for a ridiculous background check. Maxwell was looking for a whistle-blower from Faith Temple Church, not a credible employee. He grabbed the card. "We'll check him out and see where this goes."

"There's always a clown out there seeking their fifteen minutes of fame. Don't get duped by a liar," Garrett commented.

"I'm not worried," Maxwell replied as he toyed with the card. "Besides, I can live with a liar, so long as they can hold up under intense cross-examination in the courtroom."

"So, basically, you don't care about the truth?"

"Truth . . . Now, I guess that depends on whose truth you're talking about." Maxwell grinned. He didn't fault Garrett for being naive. Maxwell had handled enough cases to know that sometimes the truth needed a nudge, and he was precisely the man to do the nudging. "I'll catch up with you later," he added, eager to end the meeting.

As soon as his office was empty, Maxwell called his administrative assistant. "I need you to drop everything and get a meeting set up with a potential client this afternoon." He stared at the business card before him. "Let me know when you're ready, and I'll give you Mr. Layne's number."

"Your schedule is pretty full this afternoon, all the way until seven thirty."

He pinched his lips and made his expectations clear. "This is top priority. Make it happen. Move my meetings around if you have to. Just get this guy into my office this afternoon."

"But—"

Maxwell cut her off and said, "Do you hear me? Get it done, no excuses. If he's alive, I want him in my office. Send a limo, a paycheck, whatever is required to get him here. Do you understand?" He said it in a way that must have enabled her to process the information accurately, because his assistant didn't offer any other resistance. Good for her, because Maxwell was growing weary of paying people who weren't getting the job done. Betrayals weren't to be tolerated in his world. He hadn't allowed it from his own parents during his childhood in Chester, Pennsylvania. Twenty-some years later and nothing had changed, which suited him just fine.

Chapter 2

Noon had come and gone. As 5:00 p.m. approached, Maxwell emerged from a conference room, with a young lady and an older woman on his heels, as his assistant stood nearby, poised to interrupt.

"Don't you worry one bit," Maxwell told the women as he shook the older one's hand. The younger woman was wiping her eyes with a tissue and sniffling. "I've seen this more times than I care to admit. Your granddaughter is not at fault, and I'll see to it that the church administrator pays handsomely. He won't do this to anyone else. I can promise you that," Maxwell said, with bravado oozing. "Dry your eyes, young lady. You did the right thing in coming forward. I'll take care of this."

His assistant came a few steps closer but didn't interrupt.

"We trust you, Mr. Montgomery," the grandmother said, grabbing Maxwell's hand. "At first we didn't want to say anything, because I don't feel quite right taking the church to court."

Maxwell was used to his clients being reluctant to expose failures in the religious community. Some had even stated that suing the church and clergymen was the same as suing God. Maxwell didn't agree, but it wouldn't make a difference if he did. He wasn't particularly interested in suing God, but Maxwell wasn't running away from the challenge, either. With his assistant anxiously waiting to give him an update about his next meeting, Maxwell had to cut his wrap-up short.

"Trust me, you're doing the right thing. Wrong is wrong, and your church leaders should know that better than anyone. I'll be in touch next week," he said, shaking their hands hastily and ushering them to the door.

Once they left, Maxwell's assistant rushed toward him. "Mr. Layne is in your office."

"What? How long has he been waiting?" Maxwell asked, briskly walking toward his private office.

"About twenty minutes," she answered, keeping stride with him.

"I told you this was top priority. You should have told me twenty minutes ago that he was here," Maxwell muttered, lowering his voice to barely a whisper before he got to his office.

"I didn't want to disturb your other meeting," she stated timidly.

About a foot from his door, Maxwell faced her directly. "When I tell you something is a top priority, that means everything else comes second. Do you understand?"

"Yes, sir," she said as her gaze dipped.

"Good, because if you want to keep your job here, you need to be clear on how I work and what I expect." He placed his hand on the doorknob. "Are we clear?"

"Crystal clear."

"Hold all my calls and cancel my remaining appointments." The assistant nodded in affirmation. "Oh, and, uh, unless the building is burning down, don't interrupt me, period."

"I understand."

As Maxwell turned the knob, he turned on his convincing appeal, determined to capitalize on the potential plaintiff sitting in his office. "Mr. Layne, thanks for taking time to meet with me," Maxwell said as he closed the door.

The guy rose for the greeting.

"Sit, sit," Maxwell said in a jovial fashion as he took a seat too. "I hope you didn't have to take too much time from work to meet with me."

"Oh no. I haven't worked in almost two years, not since I left Faith Temple."

"Really?"

"Yeah, and the lady who called me from your office said there was a hundred dollars in it for me if I could come in today. Is that true?"

Maxwell hadn't been made aware of the payment by his assistant but had no problem with her tactics. As a matter of fact, he'd applaud her tenacity later. "Uh, yes, of course," he stammered. "Cash or check?"

Mr. Layne squirmed. "Cash is king."

"Cash it is," Maxwell replied. "Now, let's get down to business. What do you know about Pastor Harris and Faith Temple?"

The man leaned back. "How much time do you have?"

"As much as you need." The possibility of getting incriminating evidence was too exhilarating for Maxwell, and he had trouble containing himself.

"I don't half know where to begin."

Maxwell wished there was a way to plop a memory stick in the man's head to extract the necessary information and then send him on his way with the hundred dollars. Dreaming was a waste of time, and he knew it. Truth was, Maxwell could already tell this was going to be a painful extraction. He braced himself for the man's long-winded recounting of the story, which seemed to be in the making.

"That Pastor Harris needs somebody to kick his behind."

"Would that be you?" Maxwell asked.

"Nah, not me. He kind of has a restraining order against me. I can't go near him."

Maxwell struggled not to show any reaction. He didn't know whether to burst out in laughter at Mr. Layne's predicament or kick him out for being stupid. He'd reserve judgment until after hearing more. "Do you mind telling me what happened between you and the pastor?"

"Long story short, Pastor Harris fired me because his wife had a soft spot for me."

"Say what?"

"You heard me right. I lost my forty-three-thousand-dollar-a-year job as director of music because that Pastor Renaldo Harris is the jealous type."

Maxwell still couldn't quite figure our Mr. Layne. Desperate to believe there was substance in his revelation, he was forced to block out the mounting red flags and kept listening.

"That man ruined my life. I've been unemployed for two years, while the pastor drives around in his fancy car. I thought the church would block my unemployment benefits, but they didn't. I'll admit that helped out for six months, but that ran out months ago. Since then I've been doing odd jobs here and there. Nothing permanent." The man finally paused, but his silence was brief. "I can't stand being broke like this. Pastor Harris probably eats steak and lobster every weekend, while my family gets by on cereal, beans, and hot dogs."

The story sounded eerily similar to Maxwell's past. He knew too well how it felt to be starving while the church leader lived lavishly on the sacrifices of a bunch of gullible followers. Maxwell's compassion kicked in. "You have a family?"

"A wife and three kids. I'm ashamed to say that my wife has been juggling two jobs to make ends meet while I've been out of work."

"You haven't been able to find any job in two years?" Maxwell asked.

Mr. Layne took offense. "None paying that kind of money. Pastor Harris robbed me of my blessing. That job was made for me, and he took it away, just because he could. This isn't right, and there ought to be something I can do to get my job back. I know you're that big-time attorney that helps people get paid. Think you can help me?"

Maxwell didn't respond rapidly. His internal struggle was raging. Although in his desperation, he had committed to overlooking the red flags, his instincts didn't allow him to be as accommodating. Something was off with Mr. Layne. Maxwell felt it, but he didn't have anyone else sitting in his office with a beef against Faith Temple or, better yet, Pastor Harris. Maxwell lowered his expectations and played along. "I've been known to settle a few hefty civil cases when circumstances warrant that level of action. To be honest, Mr. Layne, as ethically and morally wrong as it might have been to fire you, Pennsylvania is an at-will employment state."

Mr. Layne had a bewildered look, which Maxwell picked up on.

"Basically, that means an employer can fire you for no reason."

"But that doesn't make sense. How can you fire somebody when they have a family to take care of?"

Maxwell didn't care to give Mr. Layne a legal course. "Doesn't have to make sense. It's the law. And unless your civil rights were violated when you got fired, I doubt that you have a case."

"Seriously, you're going to let him get away with this?"

"I'm sorry, but I don't see how I can help you, unless your rights were violated."

Mr. Layne pondered this. "Can we get him on anything else?"

"Like what?"

"Anything . . . You know he's not perfect. What if I know about some other stuff?"

The comment garnered Maxwell's undivided attention. Now they were getting somewhere. "Are you talking about mismanagement of church funds, sexual harassment, fraud, or what?" Maxwell questioned. Then he mentioned a few more of the usual infractions.

There was a knock on the door. Maxwell ignored it.

Mr. Layne peered around the room, as if he were searching for notes on the wall, and then spoke. "Actually, I do know more, a lot more." He started cracking his knuckles. "I didn't want to put the pastor's business out there, but there's a whole lot more to tell if the money is right."

There was a second knock on the door.

"Hmm," Maxwell groaned. "Well, I'm definitely interested in hearing what you have to say."

The knocking persisted.

"Excuse me for a second." Maxwell was more than irritated. Unless the building was on fire, Mr. Layne wasn't the only one who'd be in the unemployment line. Maxwell yanked the door open and stepped out, then eased the door shut behind him. "It doesn't look like the building is on fire. So why are you interrupting me?"

His assistant struggled to speak up.

"I asked you a question. Why did you interrupt me after I gave you specific instructions not to bother me during this meeting?" He spewed his words like nails as his fury mounted.

"Your mother called and insisted that I let you know your father is back in the hospital."

Maxwell sighed.

"I didn't know what to do. She was very upset and begged me to get you on the phone. She was hoping you could come down to Delaware this evening."

Maxwell shut his eyelids and rested his forehead in the palm of his hand. When would he catch a break from those people called family? As angry as he should have been, it wasn't his assistant's fault that his mother had stirred a panic. "It's okay. Call her back and tell her I'll stop by in the morning," he said, sounding totally drained.

Just then Mr. Layne pulled the door open and pushed past Maxwell.

"Mr. Layne, we aren't finished. Where are you going?"

A bit cagey, he replied, "The wife is going to be home in an hour. She'll be wondering where I am if I'm not there. So I'm out of here."

Maxwell wanted to scream amid the rising chaos but stayed calm. "I understand."

"Yeah, you know how those wives can be," Mr. Layne said, chuckling.

Actually, Maxwell had no idea and considered it a gift. "Go on home, and we'll follow up with you. You'll get a call either from me or from a man named Garrett in the next couple of days."

"Cool. I'm glad to finally get some help. Money has been tight." Mr. Layne cleared his throat. "Speaking of money, can I get my hundred dollars?"

"Sure. Wait here." Maxwell went to get the money from the petty cash envelope in his desk drawer. When he returned, Mr. Layne snatched it out of his hand.

"Appreciate it," he said, folding the five twenty-dollar bills and sliding them into his pocket. There was an awkward pause, and then Mr. Layne continued talking. "Mr. Montgomery, there's no way I'm going to get home in time on the bus. You think I can get that limo to take me back home?"

"Why not?" Maxell turned to his assistant. "Can you arrange the ride for him?" he asked. "Tell them Mr. Layne is in a hurry, and I'll pay extra."

"I like the way you work," Mr. Layne commented.

"Thanks again for coming in. We'll be in touch," Maxwell smirked and then retreated inside his office. He leaned his head against the door, wanting to vanish. Between Pastor Harris and his father, peace was nowhere to be found. Time stood still as Maxwell rested in the moment. Eventually, he'd move away from the door, call Garrett, and put him in touch with Mr. Layne. But for now, he'd cling to his imaginary solitude, which was evaporating with each breath.

Chapter 3

Maxwell pressed the accelerator, anxious to get the last few miles behind him on his reluctant drive to Wilmington Hospital. It was nine thirty Tuesday morning. He would have already been planted at his desk for at least two hours had his mother not pleaded with him to come to Delaware.

Why was she insistent about him coming to the hospital? Didn't she know he had no interest in being there? He wasn't willing to come and play the caring son role each time his father had a heart episode. A stable bridge hadn't been built over the valley of distance between him and his father. He'd told his mother and sister to call him only in the case of a dire emergency. He doubted that this run fit the criteria. So why did he need to be at the hospital twice in the same month?

He looked into the distance, beyond the white dashed lines on the expressway. Far off in the haze, he could see the twenty-three years that had dawdled by since he'd run from the crowded two-bedroom apartment his parents called home. Back then he'd changed his name from Paul to Maxwell and cut his family out of his life.

The screaming siren and the flashing lights coming from an approaching ambulance rescued Maxwell from the memories lurking in his mind. He steered the car onto the shoulder and watched the ambulance whisk by. After a quick glance down at his watch, he pulled back onto the expressway and hit the accelerator, ignoring the speed limit. He had an urgent need to handle the hospital situation and get back to where he belonged.

Upon reaching the hospital, Maxwell parked his car, walked quickly inside, and headed straight for the information desk. Once he was equipped with the floor and room number for his father, he trudged to the elevator and got on when the doors slid open. When he stepped out of the elevator and onto the fifth floor, a nurse rushed past him. He hopped backward to keep her from slamming into him. There was some commotion at the end of the hallway. People were rushing around with their voices raised. He headed down the same hallway to room 524.

As he got closer to the room, he heard screaming and crying. A woman yelled out, "No, don't take him. Don't let him die." Maxwell felt his heartbeat speed up and a surge of nervous energy pass through his body. Could it be his father's room? Was his father dead? He took longer steps, refusing to allow his legs to break into a sprint. The screams got louder as he got closer. A doctor and two nurses pushing a defibrillator machine exited the room. Maxwell froze, sucked in a deep breath, and then his body was in motion again. When he reached the doorway, Maxwell was instantly relieved. The screams were coming from room 522. Maxwell swallowed hard as he brushed at the sleeve of his suit jacket.

He walked a few more steps and stopped outside room 524. The door was open. The room was empty, chilly, and quiet. Perplexed, Maxwell made an about-face and went directly to the nurses' station.

"Paul Montgomery is supposed to be in room 524, but I can't find him," he told the nurses seated behind a long counter.

The male nurse asked, "Are you a relative?"

Maxwell hesitated, then answered, "He's my father."

The nurse glanced over a chart. "Looks like your father went to radiology for some presurgery tests."

Surgery, Maxwell thought.

The nurse directed him to a waiting room around the corner. Maxwell's eyes shot up to the big white clock on the wall behind the nurses' station. The morning was advancing rapidly. Of course, no one else understood or cared that he had clients waiting for him back at the office. It was a reality he knew well. His priorities had never been considered when it came to his family.

Maxwell headed toward the waiting room. He stopped to collect himself before entering the room. As he stood in the doorway, Maxwell saw his sister, Christine, staring out the window. Her back was turned to him, but he knew it was Christine standing there, twisting her hair around her finger like she did when they were kids. He closed the door behind him, and she glanced over her shoulder.

A hard grin parted her lips. She rushed over to Maxwell and draped her arms around him. "I'm so glad you came. Mom and Dad need both of us."

Maxwell gave her a half hug with one arm and pushed her back gently to break her hold on him. "Apparently, Mom felt that I needed to be here. Where is she, anyway?"

"She's with Dad. He's having some test done," Christine offered, chewing on her bottom lip.

"Well, she kept asking me to come and wouldn't let up on the phone calls until I agreed." He sighed. "So I'm here. But I won't be for long."

Christine took a step backward. Her glance scaled his tall figure from head to toe. "Of course you won't. I'm so tired of this ridiculous ongoing battle that you keep fighting. Okay, so Mom and Dad made a mistake. They trusted Bishop Ellis Jones in what turned out to be a crooked real estate scheme. Haven't they paid for that mistake?"

"Do you think they have?" Maxwell retorted.

"Yes, a thousand times over," she answered. "You know they lost practically everything. They had to start over in a tiny apartment, but they made it. We made it."

"Speak for yourself. The transition wasn't easy for me," he said, consciously controlling his delivery. "I had to struggle and make my own way in college without a single dollar from them."

"All this because they lost your college fund? So what," she blurted, flailing her arms. "You got a full ride to college, anyway." Christine brushed her hand over the jacket of Maxwell's dark blue tailor-made suit. "Law school too."

"What's your point?"

"My point is that we survived. We're here. Isn't that a good enough reason to let this grudge go?"

Maxwell's left cheek quivered at the same time that his nostrils widened and then deflated. "You can't tell me how to feel. You don't even know the whole story." He jabbed his balled-up fist against his leg twice and darted to the window.

Christine followed him. "Okay, tell me what I don't know."

He thrust one hand into his pants pocket and braced the other against the large window frame. For a couple of minutes he was silent, until Christine touched his shoulder. He spun around to face her, and his feelings erupted. "You are right about my scholarship. It got me through college, no thanks to our parents."

"Good for you. So why are you upset?"

"Because the scholarship covered tuition, a room, and books, and that was it. Food was on me. I had to eat noodles practically every day," he ranted while pounding his fist into the palm of his other hand. "When I got tired of eating practically nothing, I had to tutor evenings and every weekend for food money. I didn't have any home-cooked meals or weekend trips home to do laundry. And

I darn sure didn't have my parents yelling my name on graduation day. Why was that, Christine?"

"That was your choice. You didn't want any of us there."

"So now you're going to blame me." Maxwell yanked his hand out of his pants pocket and clapped his hands together loudly inches from Christine's face. "When are you going to wake up and see that our father put the church before his own children? My father is—" He stopped abruptly. Maxwell's heart rate soared. His palms were sweating, and he realized he had been shouting. The people in the waiting room had stopped talking and were fixated on him and Christine. He was mortified. Refusing to be a spectacle, he adjusted his tone.

Christine leaned in closer to Maxwell with gritted teeth and a scowl. "You're right. I guess I didn't know how much you were hurt. How could I? You left home at seventeen, during your last year of high school. You changed your name and left us behind like you never knew us, remember?" She sighed and kept her eyes shut for a short while before speaking again. Her tone eased. "Dad is having open heart surgery and a replacement pacemaker today. We don't know how long he's going to be with us." She gently placed her hand on Maxwell's shoulder. "Let's worry about now and let the old stuff go. All that stuff happened over twenty years ago. Grow up and just let it go."

Maxwell and Christine stood toe-to-toe, with only stale air between them. Suddenly his phone blared from his jacket pocket, signaling the end of this round. Christine snatched up her purse from the chair behind her, and with every step, her heels stabbed the tile floor as she exited the waiting room. Maxwell silenced his ringing phone and put it on vibrate after seeing his assistant's number on the display. He loosened his tie, checked the wall clock and then his wristwatch. He needed to go, but it didn't seem fitting to walk out without at least acknowledging his mother. She hadn't come to the waiting room, so Maxwell walked swiftly back to room 524 hoping to find her there. When he got to the room, his mother was alone, talking on the phone. Her face blossomed as she stretched out her arm and extended an open palm to Maxwell. The moment he touched her hand, she folded him into her embrace. He stood there, stiff, staring at the empty bed. His mother wrapped up the call in seconds.

"I am so glad you came. I've missed you. The nurse is bringing your dad downstairs now. They just finished his tests. He will be going into surgery soon," she told him.

Maxwell felt antsy. Being close to his folks was too much of a reminder. He had clawed his way to the top and wasn't going to let them drag him back to the worst period in his life. "I can't stay long. I have to get back to Philly."

"You're going to stay for the surgery, right? Your dad is having a special pacemaker put in this morning. I forget what they call it. Anyway, the one he has isn't strong enough, because his heart has weakened since he had that massive heart attack last year." She gripped his hand. "You have to stay." She turned to check the doorway. "Did you see Christine?"

"I saw her. She's around here somewhere." Maxwell pulled his hand free and slid it into his pocket.

Shortly afterward, a nurse wheeled Paul Montgomery, Sr., into the room and helped him into bed. She advised them that he'd be going down for surgery in about twenty minutes, then left. Maxwell offered no greeting or acknowledgment of his father's presence.

His mother broke the loud silence. "Paul, your son drove down for the surgery. Christine is here too," she told her husband, rubbing his arm.

Paul Sr. responded, "Okay," without looking in his son's direction.

Maxwell dug his car keys out of his pocket. "I've got to get back to the office," he announced as he turned to leave the room.

His mother grabbed his forearm and led him over to his father's bedside. She squeezed Maxwell's arm and rested her hand on top of her husband's. "This has gone on too long. It's time for our family to be whole again. That starts with the two of you." Her gaze bounced between her husband and her son.

Maxwell didn't make eye contact with his father. Instead, he glanced out the window and let his thoughts drift back in time. His mom couldn't possibly think a hospital visit was going to turn into a family reunion. Memories, old hurts, disappointments, and anger pricked at Maxwell like needles underneath his skin. The heart monitor made a sharp beep and interrupted his time of reflection. He glanced at the squiggly lines that tracked his father's heartbeat.

The phone in his pocket vibrated. He reached for it and read a text message from Garrett: Call me.

Maxwell excused himself. "I have to make a phone call," he stated and then made a hasty dash to the waiting room. He pressed the number one on his speed dial. Garrett answered on the second ring.

"What's going on, man?" Maxwell's interest was apparent from the tone of his voice.

"Hey, how soon can we get together? I was able to check into Mr. Layne's claims. You'll be interested to hear what I've found out."

"Gosh, that was fast. We just spoke last night, and you've already made contact?"

"This was a quick one."

The news was encouraging. Finally, Maxwell had a ray of hope shining into his otherwise gloomy start to a day. He was energized and ready to wield a hefty dose of justice to the most deserving man in the area. Pastor

Harris, senior pastor and founder of Faith Temple, was arguably the most respected clergyman in the tristate area. In seven years the ministry had grown from twenty people meeting in the basement of a local beauty salon to a multimillion-dollar operation with a facility the size of a small community college.

Maxwell couldn't wait to do to Pastor Harris what he'd done successfully to many others, and that was to shove those greedy hypocrites out of their despicable pulpits and into bankruptcy or prison. Maxwell wasn't choosy. He'd gladly take either. His last case against Greater Metropolitan and the big-time bishop there had resulted in both. Maxwell was pleased. If his luck continued, the same fate awaited Faith Temple. Maxwell was intent on heaping as much disgrace onto Pastor Harris as he could. Garrett's call had him invigorated and ready to dash back for the update.

"I'm tied up with something at the moment, but I expect it to wrap up shortly. I'll call you as soon as I can break away, and we can meet at my office," Maxwell informed him. He ended the call, then dialed his assistant to get his messages before going back to his father's room.

Against his personal preference, he stayed at the hospital until his father's three-hour surgery was completed. The moment they found out Paul Sr. was in recovery, it was time for Maxwell to leave. His mother was unable to convince him to stay a minute longer. He had been out of his comfort zone far too long. He needed to put the hospital in his rearview mirror and reestablish the thirty-mile buffer separating him from his family. Once he was behind the wheel, Maxwell pressed down on the accelerator, intent on getting far away from the Montgomery family clutches. His restlessness dissipated as he crossed the state line. He was close to home and was relieved to be back on his own turf. His first love, work, was waiting.

Chapter 4

Maxwell got downtown in much less time than it should have taken. He didn't even mind the speeding ticket he'd gotten for driving twenty-five miles over the limit. Now he was where he should be, in his office, sitting in his Italian leather high-back chair, surrounded by law books and mounds of case files. His chair swiveled from side to side as his eyes explored each corner of the room. Why had he bothered to rebuild his four-bedroom house three years ago when this really was his home?

He kept checking his watch, expecting Garrett to roll in any minute. Maxwell had called him right after pulling out of the hospital's parking lot and had agreed to meet with him in an hour. That was fifty minutes ago, and Maxwell was anxious to get going with Faith Temple. He shut his eyelids and rubbed his hand across his brow.

"Looks like you're deep in thought," Garrett said, bopping into the office.

"Hey, just the guy I want to see," Maxwell said. "Have a seat." Before Garrett could sit, Maxwell was already talking business. "Please tell me that Mr. Layne has something we can use."

Garrett shifted his gaze away, which didn't give Maxwell a warm feeling. "Not a single thing. That man is a nut, and you'd be a fool to build a case around him."

"What about him getting fired? Anything we can get out of that?"

"Nope."

Intuitively, Maxwell agreed. He'd represented and sued a boatload of liars. He could practically smell them a mile away. Mr. Layne didn't have the full stench of deception, but there was definitely a foul element in his story. Yet Maxwell wasn't ready to concede. Even in the midst of a pile of garbage, there was bound to be valuable nuggets. It was Garrett's job to find the nuggets. Maxwell maintained a measure of hope.

"Trust me when I tell you that you want to stay clear of this guy," Garrett added. "He is not credible. Did he tell you about his family?"

"Yes. I think he mentioned a wife and three or four kids."

"How about a wife, two girlfriends, and two children outside the marriage?"

Maxwell's hope was eclipsed. "Are you kidding?"

"Wish I was. A real class act," Garrett joked. "I don't know what he told you, but apparently, Pastor Harris found out and tried to keep it quiet."

"I knew it. That's what those snakes do. Lie and hide."

"Maybe that's true for others we've investigated, but wait. I'm not finished. Pastor Harris was concerned about Layne's family being ridiculed. So the preacher required Layne to step down, confess to his wife, and go to counseling."

Maxwell didn't want to be impressed. He'd wait. There had to be more. "Then why did Mr. Layne end up fired?"

"Because he didn't want to confess to his wife, or at least that's the story." Garrett laughed. "If you ask me, he didn't want to give up the other women."

Maxwell normally laughed it up with Garrett. Not this time. He was too disappointed that nothing incriminating had materialized. "Forget about that lying Layne. What else do you have? There has to be something wrong with Faith Temple and Pastor Harris. Please, tell me you have something else . . . anything," Maxwell pleaded, shaking his fist in the air.

"I've scoured records, interviewed a ton of folks, and checked source after source. I can't even find an unpaid parking ticket for Pastor Harris . . . nothing."

"What do you mean?" Maxwell shouted. "Everybody has skeletons somewhere, everybody," he said, slurring. "You just have to know where to look."

"And I've looked. They're not there," Garrett said, rearing back in his seat.

"I can't believe this," Maxwell said, shoving papers to the side. "He's a preacher, for goodness sake. There's always dirt, shady dealings, and a trail of lies leading from their mouth to the pulpit." Maxwell stood and pressed his knuckles against the desk. "Don't tell me this Pastor Harris is the lone exception."

Garrett tilted his head slightly to the side and smirked. "Maybe."

"Oh, come on," Maxwell snarled. "I don't believe this crap."

"What do you want me to tell you? A bunch of manu-factured lies?"

"I want you to tell me that we're close to getting the evidence needed to bring down this pastor. That's what I want you to tell me." Maxwell's volume was elevated.

Garrett stood, frowning, but didn't approach the desk. Maxwell couldn't recall a time the two of them had felt such tension in a conversation, but this wasn't a normal case. Faith Temple was larger than Greater Metropolitan, with somewhere between four and five thousand members on any given Sunday, based on his research. Exposing the egregious behavior of a seemingly squeaky-clean community leader was better than toppling the empires of twenty small-time ministers. Going after the head of the snake was always best.

"In all the years that we've worked together, I never thought you'd be suckered in by a Bible-toting preacher," Maxwell declared.

"What are you talking about?" Garrett replied with a chuckle. "You're losing it, man."

Maxwell became overly outraged. "Me?" he said, coming from around the desk and stepping to Garrett. "I'm not the one who has lost perspective and has been drawn into Pastor Harris's web."

Garrett stepped back, and Maxwell did too.

"Maxwell, do you hear yourself? Seriously, you're talking crazy." Garrett took another step back. Maxwell returned to his seat. "If the dirt isn't there, it just isn't there, period."

"It's there, trust me. I just need you to dig deeper. Find something, anything, by whatever means you have to."

"What are you asking me to do?"

Maxwell stared at Garrett. "Whatever you have to do. I honestly don't care where you get the information or how you get it. Just get it."

"Seriously . . ." Garrett chuckled again. "What do you have against Pastor Harris? It has to be something personal that I don't know about, because you seem bent on going after him even when we don't have a case."

"This isn't personal," Maxwell replied with a tone of indignation. "I'm doing my job, and I need you to do yours. Money isn't an object. Pay whoever for whatever. I don't need to know the details of how you get my information. Just give me the bill, and I'll take care of it."

Garrett stood still for a brief moment before responding. "Maxwell, you're right. We've worked together for a long time, and you're all right with me. I'll even admit that we've done some borderline stuff when it comes to building cases, but not this time. I'm not crossing any lines. I had my fill with the last one."

"What are you talking about?"

"You know exactly what I'm talking about. Deacon Burton and Bishop Jones. I'm not going down the rabbit hole again and pulling out manufactured or coerced evidence, with the intent of railroading somebody." Garrett raised his index finger in the air.

"Are you accusing me of railroading the bishop and Deacon Burton?"

"What I'm saying is that you can count me out of this one. There's no amount of money worth my peace of mind." Garrett moved toward the door. "The next time I help to put someone in jail, you can best believe they'll belong there." Garrett reached the threshold and paused. "And it won't be because you have an out-of-control vendetta. This is on your head, my friend, not mine."

Maxwell knew Garrett wasn't sure if Deacon Burton or Bishop Jones was guilty of the crimes they'd been convicted of. Maxwell had his doubts about Burton too, but there were always going to be innocent casualties in war. That was what he had to accept if his conscience was ever going to get clear.

"Are you saying you're done with the investigation?" Maxwell asked.

"Maybe not done yet, but I'm getting close. I'm willing to do some more checking, but I won't make up stuff. It won't happen."

"Fair," Maxwell said, because he knew Garrett wasn't the only private investigator in town. There were plenty who'd clamor to produce the kind of results he was looking for, especially for the price he was willing to pay.

Garrett left, and Maxwell considered his next step. Nobody or nothing was going to block his path to Pastor Harris and Faith Temple, not Garrett, not his guilt regarding Deacon Burton, not even God.

Chapter 5

Maxwell lost count after he'd tossed his tenth wad of paper in the direction of his garbage can. The disagreement with Garrett shouldn't have bothered him to such an extent, but Maxwell found the discussion eating away at him an hour later. Business was business. He didn't expect to agree on every point for every case. His rational self understood this, but his emotions weren't in sync. Maxwell became increasingly irritated at himself. He had spent two decades distancing his goals from his feelings. He'd trained himself not to care about relationships. The only exception he'd made was with his nephew. Yet here he sat, sulking. He poked at folder after folder without making significant progress.

He wanted to shake Garrett off, but that guy was the closest Maxwell had come to having a friend. His investigator's loyalty had proven invaluable over the years. If there was anyone on the planet whom he remotely trusted, it would have to be Garrett. Having his trusty investigator and friend question his professionalism equated to betrayal. The throbbing vein on his temple pulsated faster. Finally, his frustration escalated to the point where Maxwell yelled out some unrecognizable phrase. The release didn't bring him instant clarity as he tackled his legal challenge, but he did feel eerily better.

His phone rang, and it was the line coming from his assistant. He rolled his neck before answering. After yelling so loudly, it wasn't difficult for him to wonder why she was calling. Maxwell was embarrassed. He was tempted to ignore the call and continue sulking in the privacy of his office, but that wasn't his style. Avoiding awkward conversations and situations had never been his way. No reason to change his winning formula now. Not for Garrett, not for his family, not for Deacon Burton, and certainly not for his assistant, who was still proving her worth. He snatched up the phone and commandeered the conversation. Setting the tone always worked best.

"What do you need?" Maxwell said in such a way that clearly demonstrated he didn't want to be bothered.

His assistant stammered, "I—I thought I heard a scream, and wanted to see if everything was okay."

Maxwell relaxed. He cleared his throat and altered his perspective. She wasn't his enemy. The church and all its associates were. He couldn't lose sight of what mattered again and burn precious energy on irrelevant sideshows. "I appreciate your concern, but I'm fine."

"You sure?"

"Absolutely. Now, let's get back to work." Maxwell had verbalized the message to his assistant, but he also processed it internally. He couldn't spend another second sitting around, licking his wounds, just because Garrett had painted a dim picture of the Pastor Renaldo Harris and Faith Temple case. There was more than one way to work a case. Some attorneys gave up at the first roadblock or sign of trouble. Maxwell wasn't one of them. People didn't rise to his level of success without stretching the limits. Perhaps if Garrett had the same perspective, he would know that it was impossible to keep one's hands clean when searching for dirt in a case.

Maxwell sighed and blew out a deep breath, feeling invigorated. This was his case, his mission to right the wrongs in the church, one minister at a time. A few hurt feelings and harsh words couldn't derail him so easily.

Maxwell opened his laptop and keyed in a search for private investigators whose licenses had been revoked. He wasn't surprised to see a long list of names pop up. Later he'd cross-check them against the criminal records database to find an investigator who might be bold enough and desperate enough to take on a special assignment. Glancing over the list, he was encouraged, almost optimistic.

Maxwell was on a roll. He had a list of investigators who didn't mind getting their hands dirty and pushing the limits. Bringing down Pastor Harris was real. It would happen, just like the pile of other tough cases he'd fought and won against the odds. Nobody expected a kid who had lived in a shelter would grow up to be a fearless attorney. Bishop Jones had broken Maxwell's spirit many years ago, when he was a helpless kid, but never again. The bishop had paid, and so would the pastor of Faith Temple. The only difference was that the charge against Pastor Harris wasn't personal. He merely happened to be the next in line.

Maxwell removed his cuff links and rolled up his sleeves. What was he thinking? He didn't have to depend on anyone. Maxwell remembered visiting Bishop Jones at Greater Metropolitan last year as he discreetly sought out information for the case he was building against the church. During their impromptu meeting, Maxwell discovered a stack of shady land deeds. That was the foundation of Maxwell's fraud and corruption case against the bishop. He'd found what everyone else had overlooked. His random visit with an unsuspecting culprit had paid huge dividends once, and Maxwell planned on using the same tactic again.

He was about to call his assistant and have her get Faith Temple on the line, then decided to make the call directly. He didn't have to search long for the number. It was prominently scribbled inside the thick folder on his desk.

"Good afternoon. This is Faith Temple, where the Lord reigns and the Spirit flows. How might I help you?" a female voice belted.

Maxwell wanted to gag at the rhetoric but stayed focused. "Yes, good afternoon. I'm Maxwell Montgomery."

"Oh yes, you're the young man who worked on the youth program with the mayor and Pastor Harris last year."

"That's right," Maxwell eagerly replied. He'd forgotten about working with Pastor Harris. He'd been so consumed with his case against the bishop last year that Maxwell had honestly forgotten about several projects. But the youth program was precisely the angle he needed. "I'd love to get on the pastor's calendar for a brief chat."

"About the youth program?"

"Of course," he stated. Maxwell wasn't pleased with his lie. The youth program was the one initiative that did matter to him. He'd donated over five hundred thousand dollars of his own money last year to rehab two community centers. His heart was in the right place when it came to helping at-risk youths in the neighborhoods. It helped him downplay his discomfort with lying.

"Okay, Mr. Montgomery. Give me a minute."

Maxwell anxiously waited. After the lady was gone for more than five minutes, he grew restless, wondering what was taking so long. As he was about to hang up and redial, the lady returned.

"The pastor can see you next Thursday, at two o'clock."

That was over a week away. He couldn't possibly wait that long. Maxwell wanted answers now. "Next week doesn't work for me." He laid on the charm, willing to try any method that would get him in sooner. "I wonder if it's at all possible to see him sooner. Is there any way you can help me?"

"I'll have to see. It took quite a bit to get you in next Thursday."

Maxwell wasn't ready to give in. This was too important. He continued pushing in an appealing tone. "I am so grateful for your help. If there is any way I can come in today or tomorrow, you will be my personal hero."

When Maxwell heard her giggling, he was relieved. "Let me see what I can do." For this round, she came back much quicker. "Can you come in this afternoon, at four thirty, or tomorrow—"

Maxwell cut her off before she could finish. "I'll be there at four thirty. Thank you. You're my hero."

"Oh, you're too kind."

They wrapped up the call, and Maxwell relaxed. His plan was coming together. *Forget about Garrett*, he thought. Maxwell would do his own investigation. One way or the other, Pastor Harris was going down. He just didn't know it yet. Maxwell reclined in his seat and delighted in this notion.

Chapter 6

Maxwell bolted from his office, a stack of files stuffed into his briefcase. He made a quick stop at his assistant's desk. "I'm going to a meeting and then going home afterward to work on a few cases. Call me if you need me."

"Will do."

Maxwell was about to dart out when he remembered his father. "I also need you to call the hospital and find out how much my father owes."

"The same one in Wilmington that you had me send money to three or four months ago?"

"You got it, except we won't be able to cover this next bill from the petty cash box."

"Then how should I pay?" she asked.

"Leave a note on my desk with the information, and I'll take care of it."

Maxwell dashed out of his office building, eager to get to his meeting with Pastor Harris in South Philly. With rush hour traffic gearing up, he was looking at a twenty-minute ride stretched to forty-five minutes or an hour. He wasn't panicked. In the worst-case scenario, he'd still arrive at least a half hour early. He hurried along. If luck was on his side, he might inadvertently uncover valuable evidence against the church. Nothing else seemed to be working. Wishful thinking was all he had at the moment.

Filtered light peeked through the partially drawn blinds in Pastor Harris's study, which was filled with books ranging from *The Grapes of Wrath* and *Native Son* to his two-thousand-page *Strong's Concordance*. He gently closed his Bible and stood up to stretch. Wednesdays were long. They began with 5:00 a.m. prayer at the church and wrapped up with the midweek service from 7:00 p.m. to 9:00 p.m., with counseling sessions taking up most of the hours in between. On a good day he took a break for lunch, but if an emergency crept in, like it had today, he forfeited the meal. He rubbed his stomach as it growled. He then poked his head outside the study.

"Martha, do I have time to grab a bite to eat before my next appointment?"

"Didn't Sister Harris send you with a lunch?" Martha said, laughing and peering over her reading glasses. "She doesn't let you leave home without a meal." Martha kept laughing.

"I know she doesn't." Pastor reflected on his doting wife. Fifteen years of marriage and not a single day of regret. God had been good to the Harris family, and the pastor knew it. "I gave her a break this morning. The kids were up sick last night. So I eased out this morning for prayer and made sure not to wake her."

Martha folded her arms. "You're a good husband, Pastor. God's going to smile on you."

"I'm a hungry husband, that's for sure," he said as his stomach growled again. "So do I have time to run down the street and grab a hoagie?"

"Let me see," Martha said as she rolled her chair closer to her desk. She slowly poked at several buttons on the computer while Pastor Harris patiently waited. She finally responded with her index finger pressed against the screen. "Not really, Pastor. You have an appointment at four, and it's already a quarter to four."

Pastor shrugged his shoulders. "All right."

"But I can get you some crackers or something ," she told him.

"No, don't worry about it," he said, waving her off. "I can wait until my meeting is over, and then I'll go home and eat with my family."

"Okay, but remember you have Mr. Montgomery coming in at four thirty."

"Oh boy, that's right. I'd forgotten about him." Actually, Pastor Harris wished he could have forgotten about Maxwell completely. After a long day at the church, he didn't want to end with an antagonistic attorney who was bent on destroying every church in town. Pastor Harris was known to possess an abundance of patience. Admittedly, when it came to Maxwell Montgomery, Pastor was experiencing a shortage. "I wonder if it's too late to reschedule."

Martha rolled her eyes at him. Her stare affirmed the answer.

"I know," he said, anticipating the meeting. "I won't cancel, but I might run out of energy before he gets here."

"Don't you worry, Pastor. I'll let both of your last appointments know that you have to cut the meeting short."

He wished that would be sufficient to bridle Maxwell's tongue. He'd seen the attorney in action several times during the youth project. He had also visited Maxwell's father in the hospital last year and had prayed with the family. Pastor Harris remembered how gracious Maxwell had been when his father was near death. However, as soon as Mr. Montgomery began recovering, the calculating man whom most ministers dreaded returned with a vengeance.

Pastor Harris recalled Maxwell's relentless attack on Greater Metropolitan and figured his church was on the same list. He should have been worried and would have been, had it not been for his faith. There was a simple truth that kept him grounded. Faith Temple was a church that belonged to the Lord. Pastor Harris was merely a steward entrusted to take care of God's house. So Maxwell Montgomery wasn't a threat to the pastor. The attorney's fight wasn't with him. It was with God. Maxwell didn't know it, but he'd find out in due time.

"Let me get ready for these last few meetings," he said, then retreated into the study.

Pastor preferred not to be bothered with Maxwell, but there was a tugging at his heart. All sinners, including an attorney who was bent on persecuting the church, deserved mercy before judgment. He was certain that there was a story behind Maxwell's plight that caused him to be so driven. Pastor Harris tapped into a deep source of compassion in his spirit. He'd need it.

Chapter 7

Maxwell cruised into the parking lot and took a few extra minutes to calm his anxiety. Going after the squeaky-clean Pastor Harris was turning out to be a larger job than he'd anticipated. But Maxwell wasn't concerned. There had been many squeaky-clean ministers whose reputations were shattered once their dirty secrets got exposed. Some had required more work than others, but if Maxwell shook the trees harboring secrets hard enough, eventually something fell out. Pastor Harris wasn't any different. Garrett just hadn't shaken the right tree sufficiently. That's why Maxwell was handling his own business.

He emerged from the Porsche, poised and ready. He made his way inside the monstrosity of a church. He wasn't sure how Faith Temple's square footage compared to that of Greater Metropolitan, but the church had to hold several thousand people. It was definitely big enough to hold Maxwell's attention. He could already envision the church being swarmed by the media when the case blew open. He savored the image. That was his platform, and no one in town managed the limelight better than he did.

Maxwell maneuvered through the front entrance and milled around the vestibule until he saw the receptionist. She beckoned for him to enter a room surrounded by glass a little ways down one of the hallways.

"Hello, sir. Can I help you?" an elderly lady asked as he entered the room.

"I'm Maxwell Montgomery. I'm here for a four thirty appointment with Pastor Harris."

"Oh yes. You're early. Please come in and have a seat. Pastor is in another meeting right now. He should be with you in about twenty minutes."

Maxwell took a seat and grabbed the outdated copy of *Gospel Today* and thumbed through the pages. Then he grabbed the *Reader's Digest,* which had only about 40 percent of its cover remaining.

"You're taking her side," Maxwell heard someone yell from behind the closed door.

"What was that?" he asked the elderly lady, who peered at Maxwell with a stunned look.

"I apologize, Mr. Montgomery. Pastor is in another meeting. Excuse me," she whispered and then went to the door labeled PASTOR'S STUDY. She knocked and turned the knob almost in a single motion. "Pastor, we can hear you out here. Did you want me to turn the music on out here in the waiting area?"

Maxwell couldn't hear the response, but his curiosity was soaring. Arriving early was routine for him, and it was situations like this that paid off. He wasn't sure what was happening, but whatever it was, Maxwell aimed to capitalize on the situation. He waited until the elderly lady closed the pastor's door.

"Is everything okay?" Maxwell asked with as much charm as he could muster for a woman old enough to be his mother.

"I'm so sorry you had to hear that, Mr. Montgomery. Everything is fine. Sometimes our church folks just don't want to be told what's right and what's wrong, but Pastor Harris tells them, anyway. He'll be finishing up soon and will be ready to meet with you."

Maxwell couldn't possibly be satisfied with her answer. She hadn't told him anything worthwhile. This was a golden opportunity. Judging by the yelling he'd heard, he knew there was at least one person who wasn't singing Pastor Harris's praises. Maxwell wouldn't rest until he had a name. The receptionist was his best option for finding out who was in that study.

Maxwell checked his watch. The most he had was ten minutes. He had to get busy and concoct a plan quickly. "Excuse me, Mrs. . . . ?" Maxwell said, searching for a name tag.

"Just call me Martha," she told him.

"Martha," Maxwell said, approaching her desk and letting his grin slowly materialize. "Can you do me a favor?"

"What is it?"

"I need to print off a copy of my presentation for Pastor Harris. Can you help me?"

"Oh yes," she said, seemingly eager to help. "Is it on one of those memory sticks?"

He placed both hands on the desk but didn't lean in toward her. There was a fine line between being charming and flirting. He was keen not to cross that line and alienate his only ally in the office. "It's actually stored in the cloud."

"What do you mean? Like the clouds outside?"

He chuckled. "Sort of, but it might be easier for me to pull the documents down from the cloud myself and print them, if you don't mind."

Martha still appeared confused. "Sure. Why don't you come on around here and print them for yourself?" She got up and let Maxwell commandeer her computer. "I'm an old lady. I don't know all this newfangled technology."

Maxwell accessed the Internet and pretended to do something productive.

"While you're using my computer, I'm going to get a cup of coffee down the hall. Can I get you a cup too?"

"Yes, please," he said, elated to have a few minutes alone.

"Cream and sugar?" she asked, walking away.

"Black."

Before the door closed behind her, Maxwell was clicking on her calendar in hopes of finding the name of whomever was in the office with Pastor Harris. It was 4:28 p.m. Adrenaline was racing through his veins. The yearning to get the information outweighed the fear of getting caught. He clicked quicker and read faster. Bingo. A few seconds later, he was staring at a name. Maxwell snatched a piece of paper and a pen from Martha's desk caddy, which was neatly and prominently displayed on top of her desk. Fireworks burst inside him as he jotted down the information. Not only was there a name, but he also had a phone number and a brief description of the nature of the visit. He was about to click on the description details when the door to Pastor Harris's study opened and a fairly tall guy stormed out and flew past Maxwell with a scowl.

Maxwell stood from the receptionist's seat and covertly jammed the piece of paper into his pocket as the pastor stared at him. Maxwell was conjuring up a lie when Martha whisked into the office.

"I'm sorry I couldn't help you. I hope you were able to print what you needed," Martha said.

"I couldn't find it in my online storage," Maxwell responded.

"Well, if you couldn't find it, there's no hope for me," she said, amused.

"No problem. I'll get it later."

"Mr. Montgomery, come on in," Pastor Harris told him.

Maxwell wasn't sure what the pastor was thinking. Hopefully, Maxwell hadn't raised his suspicion level too early in the investigation. He'd soon see. He followed the pastor into the study and shut the door behind them.

"Have a seat," Pastor Harris offered as he sat down on the sofa. "How's your father?"

The question caught Maxwell off guard. He wasn't prepared to address matters pertaining to his personal life. He was there strictly for business and opted to shift the conversation back to a topic within his comfort zone. "Looks like you had an angry customer before me."

"Oh, him? Nah. He's just a man saved by grace, like the rest of us sinners."

"Sinners, huh? I guess there are plenty of those around here." Maxwell finally took a seat

"How can I help you?"

Maxwell was disappointed that Pastor Harris hadn't taken the bait and dived into defending the church. He was confident there'd be another opportunity. "Figured we could reignite the youth initiative. I initially worked on the project with Bishop Jones, but, well, you know what happened to him."

"I do know. He was railroaded into prison."

Maxwell shifted his weight in the seat. "I wouldn't say he was railroaded."

"What would you call it, then, when an entire church is brought to its knees over the deeds of a few?"

"I call it justice," Maxwell snarled. "Bishop Jones wasn't an angel. He was prosecuted, convicted, and sentenced according to the law, or do you think the church is above the law?"

"Depends on whose law you're talking about."

"What other law is there?" Maxwell replied as his agitation rose.

"There's man's law and God's law."

"Please. You're not about to feed me a pack of mumbo jumbo to justify wrongdoing in the church, are you?"

"No, I'm not."

"Good, because I wouldn't want to lose respect for you that easily," Maxwell replied.

"Respect is freely given and freely received. It goes both ways."

Maxwell continued being surprised by Pastor Harris. He'd sized him up to be a timid fella. Turned out he might have underestimated the pastor's gutsiness.

"Greater Metropolitan had some problems," Pastor Harris commented.

"Selling prescription drugs in the church is more than a problem. It's a felony," Maxwell stated.

"And those responsible should be held accountable before the court and before the Lord. Their innocence and guilt would come forth in due season. But it's appalling for you to attack good people, like Deacon Steve Burton, to make a buck."

Maxwell ignored the comment about Burton, as he didn't think it was Pastor Harris's business. "Are you implying that I'm going after the church to make money?"

"Any other reason would represent pure evil," Pastor Harris said, leaning on the arm of his short sofa. He sat there, looking smug, spewing his self-righteousness. Maxwell was fuming.

"Turns out that I don't have to meet with you, after all."

"But I thought you wanted to talk about the youth initiative."

"Maybe another time," Maxwell replied, then stood and left the study, mad. He bolted past Martha and out the church doors.

"What is going on?" Martha asked the pastor when he appeared in the doorway to his study. "You had two rough meetings back-to-back."

"Looks like it. I guess people don't always want to hear the truth. As they say, you can run from your demons for a while, but eventually, they'll catch up with you, unless you take refuge in the Lord's protection. Both of those men need prayer and a lot of it."

Chapter 8

Sonya's heart raced as she returned to the pit of doom. Being back in Maxwell Montgomery's office was the last place on earth she wanted to be, but what choice did she have? With each step she took, her fury boiled. She drew in a deep breath, intent on containing her anger. She had to if there was any possibility of this man helping her. She drew strength, reached for the doorknob to his private office, and burst in before actions and rationale had time to collaborate.

She found Maxwell sitting at his desk, with a stack of folders and papers strewn around. Sonya wasn't surprised to see him alone and working on a Saturday morning. That was his regular schedule.

"Sonya," he called out, appearing uneasy. "What are you doing here?"

Standing in his presence ignited such rage that her head hurt. It was tough to stay calm as her hands began shaking. "Who the heck do you think you are? God?"

"I've been accused of being many things, but God hasn't been one of them. I take that as a compliment," he said, smirking, which irritated her more.

Sonya took several firm steps toward the desk, unafraid to close the distance between them. He had to hear her plea this time. He was indebted to her family, and she aimed to make him pay. "You can't just mess with people's lives, like some puppeteer pulling strings."

He grinned, and it set her off. She dashed forward and pressed her palms into the desk as her face came within inches of his. Maxwell immediately pushed back, creating space that she didn't want him to have. She wanted him to feel crowded, pressured, uncomfortable, and afraid, just like her uncle was feeling at this very second, thanks to the excuse for a man sitting before her. She was close enough to pluck out his eyes. Her adrenaline rose.

"Surely, the almighty Maxwell Montgomery, the hard-hitting Philly civil attorney, isn't afraid of a little woman like me. No, you're not afraid of anyone or anything, right?"

The ranting of his former paralegal rolled off his back, with nothing sticking. He could call security and have her thrown out, like she deserved, but he was willing to let her get this ridiculousness out of her system so they could both get on with their day. He could stomach another few minutes, but he wouldn't put up with it if she pressed him for too long. He had better things to do with his time.

"Sonya, say what you have to say and get out," he said, flipping his pen onto the desk and rearing back in his chair.

"You don't tell me to leave." Sonya walked around the side of his desk, getting even closer to Maxwell. For once he appeared very uncomfortable, and she didn't care. "I'll leave when I'm good and ready."

"Excuse me, but I'm trying to be nice, since you used to work for me, but don't make a mistake and take my kindness for weakness. I will call the police and have you thrown in jail."

"I'm sure you will," she said. "You're good at sending innocent people to jail. That's what you do best."

Maxwell sprang to his feet and walked around the opposite side of the desk from where Sonya was. "Now I get it. This is about Deacon Steve Burton." He rubbed the heel of his palm across his forehead.

"That's right. I'm here to make sure you help my uncle get out of prison, especially since you put him there."

Maxwell leaned onto his own desk, squaring off with Sonya. He smirked again. "Don't lay that on me. I didn't put him in prison. His trusted pastor did that, not me."

"What kind of a person are you? He has a wife and two little boys that need him, but you don't care." Her head continued pounding, but she wasn't going to let up. He had to do something. "He trusted you."

"He trusted his pastor, who's in jail too, right where he belongs. That's who you should be yelling at, not me. I followed the law."

"Ta-ha, yeah, right. My uncle came to you with good intentions. He was the one who helped you figure out what was going on at Greater Metropolitan. Uncle Steve did it, not you," she shouted. "After all of your investigating, searching, and trying to find something, you ended up with nothing, until my uncle came forward."

Maxwell looked away. She knew he didn't have anything to say.

"You know he wasn't involved with the fraud or the prescription drug sales. You know it," she said, pressing her palms into the desk again. "You promised to leave him out of this mess since he didn't do anything. You promised him!" she screamed. "And he trusted you. I trusted you." Her body tensed. "I was a fool for sending him to you. Shame on me."

There was a quiet pause as guilt circled the room.

"Sonya, I have work to do. So, if you've said everything you came to say, I'm going to ask you to please leave."

"I'm not leaving without your help. My uncle doesn't deserve to be in prison with a bunch of criminals, and you know it. I'm begging you to help him get out."

Maxwell hung his head. "He needs a criminal attorney to file an appeal on his behalf. I'm a civil attorney. I can't do anything for him."

"You can, and you know it. You have plenty of con-
nections. Clearly, you didn't have a problem turning a
boatload of crap over to the prosecutor's office. Without
pressure from you, they would have never pushed a case
against my uncle." She dashed around the desk to the
opposite side and stood directly in front of Maxwell, a finger pointed at him. "He can't handle ten years in prison."

Maxwell withdrew and went back to his seat. "Close the
door on your way out," he said, reaching for a folder.

Sonya stood there, totally confused. She could lunge at
him and scratch his eyes out. She'd gladly take that step
if it would help. But she knew it wouldn't. She could bark
out a series of profanity, but that wasn't going to help,
either. Threats were a waste too. Finally, she sighed and
accepted defeat. Her plea for compassion wasn't enough
to warm the heart of a cold-blooded person like Maxwell
Montgomery. She'd have to find another way.

"Trust me, this isn't over, not by a long shot." She
grimaced. "You better be careful how you treat people,
because you're going to get yours. That's a promise." She
bolted from the office, anxious to breathe fresh air.

Once he was certain Sonya was gone, Maxwell reared
back in his seat, with his hands interlocked behind his
head. He wanted to discount her ranting, but it wasn't
easy to do. Deacon Burton might not have been as
dirty as the rest of Greater Metropolitan's management
team, but he was guilty by association. When Maxwell's
father had been convicted for merely being the church's
treasurer, nobody had cared that he hadn't orchestrated
the real estate scheme. Ignorance wasn't a defense. At a
minimum, his father had been guilty of trusting a corrupt
pastor, and their entire family had paid dearly. Who had
been there to rescue Maxwell?

Admittedly, the deacon's sons had pricked at Maxwell's
resolve, but refused to fret. He had survived his shattered

childhood and had to believe those boys would survive their father's ordeal too. He was sure of it; otherwise guilt might rise up and create a distraction Maxwell wasn't prepared to handle. He shoved the disturbing thoughts from his mind and got to work. It was his best cure for a troubled heart.

Chapter 9

Deacon Burton lay on his bunk, closed his eyes, and gently massaged the tender spot on his side. His ribs were still sore from earlier in the week, but none of his woes mattered, not today. It was Sunday, and his wife would be visiting. Nothing could cast a cloud on the day for him. His joy rose, blotting out the darkness permeating the cell. He continued lying on the bunk, praying silently and dreaming about his family. Minutes tiptoed along as his anticipation soared.

An hour later, the prison came to life, and temporary freedom from his six-by-eight cell was granted. The prison doors on cell block D all slid open simultaneously. The deacon's cell mate pushed through the doorway first. Deacon Burton moved at a slower pace. He turned and gazed at the Bible on his bunk, then at the cement floor, and finally at the toilet. A cold chill whisked by his body, causing him to shiver and roll down his shirtsleeves. When he cleared the cell door, a warm gush of air swept by. Startled, Deacon Burton swung around briskly to check behind him. He hesitated briefly, but no one was there. So he trotted down the walkway, down the stairs, and to the dining hall.

He spent ten minutes at breakfast, consuming only a cup of milk and a slice of stale, dry toast. Excitement about seeing his wife was getting the best of him. He preferred to go back to his cell to calm his nerves, but inmates weren't allowed back on the cell block this soon.

Instead, he got up and headed toward the line for yard time. A few solitary minutes were needed to escape the prison walls, if only in his mind. Outside, the warm sunshine showered down on him. Near the fence was a rusty iron bench. There he claimed a seat away from the crowd of men playing basketball and lifting weights. He let the minutes tick by.

"Burton," a firm voice bellowed across the yard. "You've got a visitor."

Deacon Burton grabbed hold of the fence and stood. His sore ribs definitely impacted the pace at which he moved. The pain reminded him of the fierce blows he'd received just a few days ago. He didn't understand why that one inmate shoved him around every chance he got. He couldn't worry about that now, as his wife was waiting to see him. He followed the guard to the holding area, where he was searched and reminded of the visitation rules. One embrace at the start of the visit and one at the end. Hands on the table at all times.

There were twelve other inmates waiting their turn. Finally, the door opened, and Deacon Burton saw his wife sitting at a table across the room, in the corner. He was surprised to see his niece, Sonya, sitting with her. As he got closer, Burton could see the tears inching down his wife's face. When he reached the edge of the table, his wife stood and reached out for him. He gave a sharp glance over his left shoulder at the guard positioned at the desk near the door.

The deacon's wife stepped into his embrace and clung to him until the prison guard bellowed across the room, "Inmate Burton, step back."

The deacon broke free of his wife's hold. Sonya immediately wrapped her arms around his neck and kissed his cheek. After a quick embrace, he stepped back and sat down at the table. "I am so glad to see you both." He cleared his throat and swallowed down the emotion that dared to make his voice crack.

His wife leaned in closer to him. "Oh, my God, what happened to your eye?" she questioned, gently tracing her finger over her husband's right eyelid. Then she stroked the swollen pocket of skin underneath his eye. "Steve, what happened to your eye?"

Sonya chimed in. "Uncle, tell us."

"It's nothing. There was a scuffle in the food line. I'm fine."

"It looks like someone punched you in your eye. And you are so thin," his wife commented, brushing away her tears with the heels of her hands.

"I'm okay. Please don't cry. It's okay. Don't worry about me."

She snatched her glance away from Deacon Burton and then gave him a frozen stare. "How is it possibly okay when you're locked up in a prison? This is crazy. It all still seems like a bad dream, a yearlong nightmare, and I can't manage to wake up from it."

"My appeal is in the works. We have to hold on. I need you to be strong. You've got to be for the boys." Deacon Burton stroked the back of his wife's hand with his fingertips, then quickly placed his hands in front of him on the table. "You're bringing them soon, right?"

"Yes, and they can't wait. They miss you so much, but I don't want them to see you with a black eye," she blurted out. "That will absolutely freak them out. I can't believe you have a black eye. I still can't believe this is happening. I'm so afraid that something is going to happen to you here. What was the scuffle in the line all about? Tell me," she pleaded as worry consumed her conversation.

"Don't worry about it. I'm fine."

"You're *not* fine. What animal would punch you like that? You're not one of these tough guys." Her gaze slumped as she wrenched her hands. "You are not a young man. You can't be fighting with these people in here. I'm afraid for you."

Deacon Burton tried to change the subject. However, his wife wasn't going to have her concerns dismissed. The volume of her voice stepped up a notch as she leaned in close to him. "Stop telling me it's okay and you're fine. You're not fine, and your children and I are not fine. We don't have enough money to pay the mortgage. Our nine-year-old son cries himself to sleep every night. You shouldn't be here, and if it wasn't for Maxwell Montgomery, you wouldn't be in this hole."

Sonya couldn't be silent any longer. "I'm partially to blame for this mess." She stabbed her chest hard three times with her forefinger. "I said you could trust Maxwell Montgomery. I encouraged you to talk to that devil about your suspicions of illegal things going on in your church. I did that knowing he had it in for Bishop Jones and Greater Metropolitan. I just didn't know he had it in for you too, or I would have never . . . ," she uttered before becoming too emotional to continue. She shook her head from side to side.

"It's not your fault at all. You just—"

Sonya cut off Deacon Burton's words. "I'm so sorry, Uncle. I can't believe I ever worked for such a condescending, arrogant fraud. He's always talking about integrity and justice. Lies, all lies. We all know he could get you out of here, but he doesn't care. Maxwell promised he would protect you from prosecution if you helped him root out the wrongdoing in Greater Metropolitan." Her nostrils flared, while her heart pounded in her chest.

She continued. "I went to his office yesterday and tried convincing him to help you. He refused. He didn't even consider helping you, not for one second." Sonya's left cheek twitched as she pressed her fist against her lips.

"I got so mad that I had to get out of there before I lost it." Her eyes were swimming in tears, which clouded her vision. She slid her glasses off and swiped across her eyelids with the backs of her hands. "Please forgive me for getting you involved with that jerk, Maxwell Montgomery. But he won't get away with this. His day is coming."

Sonya shot up out of her chair so quickly, it fell over and hit the floor with a loud crash. Heads turned toward her. Coughing and sniffing hard, she managed to croak out, "I need some tissues." She needed a break, as her guilt was suffocating. Limited as to where she could go without leaving the prison, Sonya escaped to the one place allowed, the bathroom.

"See? I'm not the only one who blames that awful attorney. He's got Sonya so upset. She's right. He should do something to help you." Mrs. Burton's voice rose as she gritted her teeth.

"Honey, calm down. You know I hate that I can't be home with you and the boys. My appeal is our best chance. God will make a way. And don't worry about Maxwell Montgomery. He's fighting his own demons."

Disdain boiled over in her eyes as she twisted in her seat. "Are you serious? He's evil. Attorney Montgomery will be lucky if the demons he's fighting don't drag his soul to hell today. He is the single reason that you're here while your sons are at home without a father. Steve, the boys are being bullied at school," she exclaimed. "Kids are making fun of them, saying their dad is a crook and a dirty deacon." Her hand shot up into the air. "This whole thing is ruining us, and you're saying don't worry about him?"

Deacon Burton was silent for a few moments. He didn't want the conversation to escalate any further. He turned the focus of conversation to their sons and tried to catch up on what they'd been up to since he'd last seen them. There had to be a way for him to comfort his sons from a distance. He would write each of them a letter every day, instead of once a week. He had to do something to ease his family's pain.

"I'm sorry for the humiliation and the stress this situation is causing you and our sons. If I could change it, I would. You know that, right?"

"Of course," his wife responded amid grave feelings. "I love you. After all these years, I love you as much as I did the day we got married."

Deacon Burton slid his hand across the table and twisted the wedding band on her finger. "Sell the house if you have to. I don't want you worrying about money." Remorse shrouded in humility helped Deacon Burton mask his deep sorrow and keep it from his wife. He yearned to shoulder the burden of their predicament alone. Sonya rejoined them. She appeared calm and didn't mention Maxwell again. Grateful for that, the deacon stretched his legs out underneath the table and settled in for the rest of their visit.

Time whizzed by as the three of them talked about the boys, school, and other things, but nothing heavy. For a brief moment, the deacon and his wife were laughing and recounting family dinners at the kitchen table, yelling and cheering at their sons' basketball games, and going to church together on Sundays. The fairy tale didn't last, as every smile and echo of laughter was tainted with the bitter reality that their memories were frozen in the past and such events might not be possible for the next ten years.

Sorrow hovered over them.

"Visiting hours are over," a guard bellowed over the speaker.

Shortly afterward, Deacon Burton watched his wife and Sonya walk toward the exit. He moved to the guard's desk and waited for permission to leave the visiting room. Once he was allowed out, the deacon went down the corridor, with his head hanging and his shoulders slumped. The visit was over; his wife was gone. Though she had gotten upset with him, every second with her had fed his soul. He felt a heavy burden in his heart knowing that she was raising his sons without him. He told himself that God would provide for them financially. He had to belive God would not allow his sons to be tormented at school because of him.

Deacon Burton lifted his head as he reached the steel door leading to the yard. He had thirty minutes to spend outside before he had to report to work in the laundry room. He found his usual spot on the rusty bench, grateful to be alone. His mind raced uncontrollably as he clutched his chest. It was impossible to shake the realization that he'd been duped and his family was paying the ultimate price. Doubt and peace volleyed back and forth, with neither giving in. He was exhausted emotionally and wiped his brow, in desperate need of relief. He caressed his temples.

No matter how bad the circumstances appeared to be, he was determined to stay hopeful. He dug deep within and grasped a splinter of faith. He had to trust God. It was his only option. Attorney Maxwell Montgomery was a stark reminder that he couldn't trust the promises of a man. Saturated with grief, he prayed silently as dark clouds blanketed the sky and a deep sense of longing gripped his soul.

Chapter 10

Air in this wing of the prison was stale and muggy. Flies buzzed around, adding to the annoyances in the crowded space the deacon occupied. Voices on the TV inside the dayroom spilled into the hallway. Deacon Burton stood in a long line to use the phone. As his turn drew near, he repeatedly shifted his weight from one foot to the other, thinking about his sons. He licked his lips as he formed the list of questions in his mind. Were they helping their mom around the house? He wanted to know everything that he was missing out on.

Finally, after what seemed like an eternity, he snatched up the receiver, which was still warm to the touch, and punched in the number to his home. The collect call was accepted, and his wife's voice broke through the line.

"Steve, can you hear me?"

"Sure can," he said, leaning against the wall next to the phone.

"I know it's only been a few days since I saw you, but it seems much longer. Are you okay?" She asked.

Deacon Burton allowed his gaze to sail around the room. Inmates, young and old, were lined up on both sides, some dressed in orange jumpsuits and some wearing black khakis and white T-shirts. Despite their differences, they were all the same. Each one had a prison-issued inmate number and was confined to a place over which they had no control.

"I'm okay. Stop worrying about me," he answered as his gaze dropped to the floor. He could hear his sons' voices in the background.

"Mom, is that Dad? Let us talk to him." His youngest son's voice clutched the deacon's heart, and the boy's insistence prompted an uncontainable grin. They talked about school, basketball, his baseball cards, and his coin collection. The minutes melted by, and then his son had to go.

"Let me talk to your brother."

"All right. I love you. Come home soon, okay?"

The deacon attempted to respond with a strong "I love you too," but his voice trembled. He squeezed his eyelids tightly, choosing not to comment on the request for him to come home soon. What could he say to his son? He knew a child wouldn't understand. Shucks, he was a grown man, and *he* struggled with the situation. Prison bars and guards controlled his life. His oldest son was going to graduate from high school before he came home. The deacon overlooked his sobering reality to avoid ruining the brief time he had left to talk with his family.

"Hey, Dad, I almost forgot. We're coming to see you next weekend, right? We can't wait. I've been practicing this arm-wrestling trick that I learned. I'll show it to you when we come."

"Real good, son," the deacon said, swallowing his emotions. Showing any vulnerability in his current surroundings was asking for more trouble than he could handle. "Let me talk to your brother."

The deacon's oldest son jumped right in, leading the conversation and hardly giving his dad a chance to speak. So Deacon Burton listened. He was glad to hear some excitement in his son's voice. When it was finally the deacon's turn to talk, he wanted to be encouraging.

"You know you're the man of the house now. I need you guys to help your mother out. And it's your responsibility to watch out for your little brother. You hear me?"

"Yes, Dad."

"Okay. I'm counting on you."

They talked another couple of minutes before the emotional captivity that Deacon Burton had managed to escape momentarily reclaimed its grip.

"Hey, hurry up, old man. Don't you see there's a line waiting for that phone?"

Deacon Burton covered the receiver with his palm and turned his back to the inmate shouting at him. "I've got to go, son. I love you. Put your mom on the phone." The impatient voices rumbling behind him caused the deacon to tap his foot on the floor as he waited to hear his wife's voice. She'd said only a couple of words when the inmate urged him again to get off the phone.

"Didn't you hear me? Your time is up. Hang that phone up, or I'll hang it up for you," the inmate threatened, then shoved the deacon's right shoulder so hard that he spun halfway around and ended up facing the aggressor.

"I love you, honey. I'll call back soon." He heard his wife call his name as he hung the phone up and stepped away. The inmate glared at him with slanted eyelids and a wrinkled brow but didn't say anything else. The deacon checked the clock on the wall and headed toward the yard, rubbing his shoulder.

Deacon Burton wasn't in the yard long before his quiet corner near the fence was invaded. A crowd formed after the pushy inmate he'd encountered earlier started shoving and punching a kid, who appeared to be about eighteen or nineteen. The deacon wondered *why would an overgrown man be beating on a kid half his size.* The fear on the young man's face made Deacon Burton think of his two sons.

"Hey, leave him alone. He's only a kid." The deacon's strong voice leaped out of his throat before he could consider his actions.

The inmate who was assaulting the kid ignored the deacon. Instead of replying, he shoved the young man to the ground and began kicking him. The crowd was thick, and Deacon Burton hoped to hear the sound of guards approaching soon. The young man lay on the concrete, curled up in the fetal position, attempting to shield himself. Deacon Burton's focus ping-ponged from one face in the crowd to another. Maybe someone else would speak up too. The beating continued, and no one objected. He had no other choice. He had to be the one to intervene.

"Hey, stop it. Just stop. He's a kid. Leave him alone, please."

The aggressor, who had bulging muscles and was covered with tattoos, peered at those standing on both sides of him, roared with laughter, and said, "You don't want to get involved in this. Step off." He jabbed his finger forcefully into the deacon's chest as he was now standing directly in front of him. Still no guards arrived.

The young man's audible cries bolstered the deacon's courage. He wasn't concerned about his own safety. As a man, he was a protector. As a child of God, he was born to help others, even at his own peril. The strength of little David, the one in the Bible who fought a giant warrior with a slingshot and won, rose up in him. The deacon couldn't wait for help. He headed toward the boy, who was still lying on the ground, with blood dripping from his mouth.

"Oh, so, now you're going to disrespect me too?" the aggressor shouted.

The deacon kept walking as the aggressor barked out demands.

"Don't you touch him," he told the deacon and bent down to remove something from his shoe. Then with long, powerful strides, he overtook Deacon Burton and plunged a handmade shank repeatedly into his stomach.

Suddenly, the air was quiet. Then there was commotion everywhere. Yet Deacon Burton felt a surge of calm.

The aggressor got close to him and whispered, "Should have minded your own business."

Deacon Burton slumped to the ground, and blood oozed from his wounds, painting the cold concrete red—the color of both love and rage. Deacon Burton's emotions swirled, making it difficult to tell which was prevailing in his heart. As he peered into the sky, a faint smile appeared on his face. The few clouds moved away, and the sky was clear. The sun shone brighter, and he felt its warmth on his face. He sucked in a loud last breath. The air in his throat gurgled; then his heart stopped beating as he drifted away.

The kid crawled over to the deacon and shook his still body back and forth. "Somebody help him. He's bleeding to death." Both of the young man's hands were covered with blood as he lifted them in the air and flailed them around to get the guards' attention. "He needs help. Somebody help, please."

A breaking news flash on the television caught Garrett's attention when he saw the photo of Deacon Burton plastered on the screen.

He reached for the volume button on the remote. "Ow!" Garrett shouted after knocking his cup over and spilling hot coffee on his arm. He raised the sound rapidly, trying to catch the story.

"Dead at the age of fifty-three," the broadcaster said. "As many of you will recall, Deacon Steve Burton was convicted on drug distribution, fraud, and racketeering charges last year, along with Bishop Ellis Jones and others associated with Greater Metropolitan Church, based right here in Philadelphia. He'd served one year of a ten-year sentence. He leaves a wife and two sons."

"Tragic," the other broadcaster commented.

"Indeed. A sad story. Jim, back to you," the first broadcaster said, concluding the news report.

Garrett leaned on the counter. He was stunned and struggled to understand how this could have happened. It wasn't possible. Words escaped him. He fumbled with the half-empty cup for a while, wondering what else to do. Finally, he picked up the phone. There was one person he had to speak with, the one person who should be feeling as awkward as Garrett was, maybe even worse. Regardless of what happened next, Deacon Burton's picture and the word *dead* would forever reside in Garrett's mind. That he couldn't change. He punched Maxwell's number into his phone.

Maxwell answered his cell phone and found Garrett on the line. "What's going on?"

"We have to talk," Garrett said with a sharp edge to his voice, which caused Maxwell to take notice.

"You sound strange. What's going on?"

"Not over the phone. Where are you?"

"In my office."

"On my way," Garrett said and hung up before Maxwell had a chance to respond.

Curiosity immediately rose in Maxwell. He needed some type of answer, but none came. Maxwell guessed he'd get one shortly.

Chapter 11

Shuffling through the papers on his desk, Maxwell tried getting some work done before Garrett arrived. Suddenly, a heavy knock on the door sounded, and Garrett barged right in, with Maxwell's assistant hustling behind him.

"I'm sorry, Mr. Montgomery. He didn't wait for me to check with you."

Maxwell waved his hand in the air. "It's fine. Don't worry about it. Garrett is always welcome." He turned his attention back to the papers on his desk, hoping his comment would remain true given that their last meeting raised sufficient reason for doubt.

The assistant left and closed the door.

With quick, long strides, Garrett came to stand at the front edge of the desk and blurted out, "Burton is dead."

The papers in Maxwell's hand fell to the desk. Slowly, he stood up from his chair, with his stare fixed on Garrett's intense expression. His throat wouldn't release a sound. He covered his mouth with his hand and coughed twice to find his voice. "What?"

"Deacon Burton was stabbed to death," Garrett sputtered.

Still standing, Maxwell asked, "What? How did that happen?" Leaning forward, palms flat on the desk, he listened as Garrett recounted the details that one of his prison contacts had provided. The words hung in the air and paralyzed Maxwell momentarily. Suddenly, he heard the ticking of the crystal clock sitting on his desk. He retreated to the window. Big raindrops slammed into the glass. Earlier, it had been a clear, sunny day with no rain in the forecast.

Maxwell stood peering at the skyline then stared off into the distance. He couldn't escape the facts. He'd rightfully built the civil case against Bishop Ellis Jones and his corrupt ministerial pack. However, Deacon Burton was the whistle-blower, and his information had proven to be critical in the criminal prosecution of Greater Metropolitan's leadership team.

Maxwell refused to wrestle with his mounting guilt. Besides, why should he feel badly? He hadn't arrested Deacon Burton, and he hadn't sentenced him. If the deacon had got caught up in illegal dealings at his church, then that was on him alone. Every adult had to take full responsibility for his or her circumstances. Maxwell shifted the knot in his tie, tugged at the cuffs of his crisp starched shirt, and snapped the blinds shut to silence his thoughts.

He went back to his desk, reclaimed his seat, and continued searching among the papers on his desk. His glimmer of remorse was gone. "Nothing we can do about it now."

Garrett stepped back with his head tilted to the side and assessed Maxwell's steely demeanor. "That's it? It doesn't bother you that we might have caused an innocent man to get killed in prison?" Garrett scratched his head.

"Look, that case is done and over. Second-guessing won't change anything. We've got other cases to focus on, and Pastor Harris is at the top of the list, remember? Besides, I have a lead you need to check out. I met with Pastor Harris a few days ago. While I was waiting, there was a guy who was having it out with the pastor." Maxwell plucked a small piece of notepaper from the top drawer in his desk and handed it to Garrett. "This might be what we've been waiting for . . . a legitimate lead."

Garrett chuckled. "You're not going to get away with changing the subject that easily."

"Who wants to stand around, beating a dead horse?"

"You realize Deacon Burton has two young boys at home who are without a father, right? And now there's no chance of him ever going home. That doesn't bother you?" Garrett wanted to know.

Maxwell knew intimately the impact of a father not being in a boy's life, not being the source of strength and direction when he needed it. He'd pushed his way through his own challenges as a young boy when his father went off to prison. Even when Maxwell had left home and gone to college, his dad hadn't been a part of his life. He wasn't dead, but he might as well have been. Maxwell held Garrett's gaze and did not reply.

"You don't have anything to say?"

"Nothing."

Garrett rubbed the back of his neck intensely as he controlled his reaction. "Knowing that those boys lost their dad doesn't make you feel anything?" Garrett said and took a step closer to Maxwell.

If Maxwell was able to make it without his dad, the Burton boys would as well. Garrett wouldn't weaken his resolve by mentioning the boys. His moment of remorse had already passed. "Man, come off that soft mind-set. I can't let the dynamics of someone's life impact me because I built a case against them and they ended up in prison. Kids grow up without fathers in their lives every day. Whether the father is in prison or just not a part of the kid's life, it really doesn't matter. Everyone is in control of their own destiny. Those boys will be fine." Maxwell swiveled his chair slightly.

"Are you listening to yourself? You can't be serious." Garrett pulled his hand down his face and shook his head.

"Yep. Are you listening to me is the question?" Maxwell stated firmly.

Garrett stroked his neatly trimmed beard, turned, and slowly moved toward the door to leave. With only a couple of steps taken, he rubbed hard at the back of his neck again, then faced Maxwell. "I know you don't want to hear this, but I never believed Burton was guilty. He shouldn't have been in prison in the first place."

"Fine time to speak up now," Maxwell hurled back.

Garrett shook his finger in the air and chortled. "Oh no, no, no. I repeatedly told you that during my investigation. You wouldn't entertain even the possibility of him being innocent. When he figured out something illegal was going on at Greater Metropolitan, he came to you for help. That doesn't sound like the actions of a guilty man. Deacon Burton just got caught in the crossfire, and now he's dead." Garrett drew in and pushed out a noisy breath.

Maxwell leapt from his chair and briskly moved to the front of his desk, a couple of feet away from Garrett. "This is the second time you've accused me of railroading Deacon Burton. And I don't appreciate this coming from you." A vein on the side of Maxwell's neck was engorged.

Garrett responded with an equally strong tone. "Regardless of what you think about me, it doesn't feel good to believe we might have rushed an innocent man to his death. He's never walking out of prison, and there is nothing we can do to right that wrong."

Nothing else was said by the two men. Garrett left and shut the door behind him, leaving his words hanging over Maxwell like a dark cloud.

Maxwell withdrew to his desk and slumped down into the chair, spinning around. It wasn't easy for him to discount the accusations Garrett had made and simply return to his work. The death nagged at him and probably would for a while. He let his back face the door and tapped his foot rapidly. Five minutes flew by. Maxwell swung his chair around, hurled himself from it, and kicked the trash can. He stumbled into his private bathroom and slammed the door. Then he leaned over the sink and doused his face with cold water, ignoring the firm knock on his office door.

His assistant's voice announced her entrance as she opened his office door and stopped outside of his bathroom. "Mr. Montgomery, I heard a loud noise. Are you okay?"

"I'm fine," Maxwell replied through the half shut bathroom door.

"All right. Let me know when you're ready to review your calendar for tomorrow." She moved away from the bathroom door and left.

After allowing the cool water to run over his hands, Maxwell stood upright, dazed, and glared at his reflection in the mirror. He was determined not to be overcome by remorse, but the struggle became increasingly more difficult as Garrett's words continued pricking at him.

Chapter 12

Pastor Harris was sitting in his office, writing notes for his upcoming Bible class, when his wife appeared in the doorway. She offered no words and just stood there with a droopy face, fidgeting with her necklace as her purse hung from her other wrist. "Have you been listening to the news?"

"No, why?" Pastor Harris asked, detecting concern in his wife's voice.

"Deacon Burton from Greater Metropolitan is dead."

"What?" Pastor Harris asked, certain that he hadn't heard her correctly.

"I heard on the news that he died. I just can't believe it," she said in a saddened tone.

Pastor Harris got up from his chair and went over to his wife, towering over her at nearly six feet tall. He peered deeply into her gaze, trying to make sense of what she'd said.

His wife shivered, pulled at her sweater, and went over to the window. She cranked the handle and watched the window close. "I caught only a small piece of the breaking news, but I think he was stabbed. How awful. His wife and children must be devastated." She propped herself up against the window frame and swiped at her eyelids.

Pastor Harris was visibly shaken. "This is unbelievable. I can't make any sense of it. When I visited him about a month ago, his primary concern was his family and how much the scandal had hurt them and the church," he said, letting his gaze plummet to the floor. "I do believe he was innocent." The pastor shook his head from side to side. "What a loss, that's for sure."

"Honey, I'm going to call his wife right now," Mrs. Harris stated.

"That's a good idea." Pastor Harris sat down at his desk.

He didn't know what to think or how to feel. His initial reaction was to lash out at Maxwell Montgomery, the person who'd created this mess. But to give Maxwell that much credit was to minimize God's power to protect His people. Pastor Harris didn't know why God had allowed Deacon Burton to get killed, but he rested in the notion that God was sovereign. He was in control and had a plan bigger than Maxwell's misguided crusade. As much as the pastor wanted to shy away from Maxwell, he felt God's pull on him to continue reaching out. He wouldn't call them friends, but they weren't enemies, either, at least not in his mind.

After a brief shuffle through several business cards in his desk drawer, he opted to try Maxwell's office number. Someone answered and put him on hold. He waited, hoping the gatekeeper who had answered would put his call through to Maxwell. Three minutes later, a strong voice interrupted the hold music.

"Maxwell Montgomery speaking."

"Mr. Montgomery, Pastor Renaldo Harris. How are you?"

"I'm fine." Maxwell pinched at his bottom lip as he tapped his ink pen on the top of his desk.

"I'm calling about Deacon Steve Burton's death. Can you give me any information about what happened?"

Maxwell sat up in his chair, with his spine straight. "Why are you asking me?"

"Well, you're a pretty influential man in town. I know you and your investigator were involved with building the criminal case against Greater Metropolitan, and you led the civil case. I thought you might have more information than the rest of us."

Maxwell stood and paced the floor as he shared what he knew. "From what I was told, an altercation between him and another inmate started because he tried to help a much younger inmate who was being attacked."

"That sounds like him. He was a good man. What a horrible tragedy for his family. His boys will have to grow up without him."

"They'll be okay. I grew up without a father," Maxwell stated. "I made it. They will too." The words rose up out of his heart and found life in his voice before he knew it.

"At least your father was alive during your childhood," Pastor Harris said.

"I guess," Maxwell responded, not wanting to elaborate. "Burton is dead, and sometimes criminals get killed in prison."

"Interesting response. You see, I'm not so sure he was a criminal."

Maxwell shrugged his shoulders. "Believe what you'd like. I have to go."

Pastor detested Maxwell's cold indifference but wasn't ready to end the call. He just had to find a more suitable topic to engage Maxwell. "By the way, how is your father doing? Has he recovered fully? The last time I saw you was at the hospital in Wilmington after he'd suffered a massive heart attack."

Maxwell made a circular motion in the air with his hand, eager for the call to end. "He's hanging in there. I'm pretty busy, so if there's nothing else . . ."

"Of course. I understand. Thanks for taking my call, and I hope to see you soon at one of our services."

Maxwell planned on visiting Faith Temple, but it wouldn't be to get closer to God. Maxwell vowed that one day he'd make sure the clergyman ended up regretting the invitation.

As soon as the call ended, he reached for his phone again, eager to speak to someone he trusted. He dropped down into his chair and almost immediately placed the phone on the desk, realizing there wasn't anyone he could call. Just then the intercom on his desk buzzed, and his assistant's voice broke through his thoughts.

"Mr. Montgomery, there is a reporter on line one. He'd like a comment from you regarding Deacon Steve Burton's death. Shall I put the call through?"

"I have a comment for him, all right." Maxwell caught himself before he finished his statement. He swung his chair around, allowing his back to face his office door. "No comment is my comment." A reporter sure wasn't someone he trusted. "Just leave it at that for now."

"Sure. Sorry for the interruption."

The media was already working on sucking up all the community and human interest attention they could get out of this; anything to sell a newspaper or increase TV ratings. Well, those newshounds wouldn't get any help from him. His cell phone rang loudly. He plucked it from his belt and answered it.

No one responded.

"Hello. Hello?" Maxwell said into the phone.

Still no one answered. He heard only a whistling noise.

Maxwell pressed the END button hard with his thumb and tossed the phone onto his desk. He didn't have time to waste on someone playing games. For a few seconds, he thought of the deacon's sons. Had they been told about their dad's death by now? Did someone get to them before the news networks flashed it on the TV screen? His cell phone rang again. He scooped it up and recognized the incoming number as that of his mother. Why was she calling in the middle of the workday? He really didn't want to answer the call, but he needed a brief distraction from his thoughts.

"Yes, Mom, I'm a little busy. I can't talk long. What do you need?"

"I don't need anything. I was just checking on you. I called you a couple of days ago, and I never heard back from you."

Maxwell plopped his elbow on his desk, and his head fell into the palm of his hand. "Just busy, that's all."

"You work too much, son. There is more to life than work. I'll be glad when you realize that."

Work *was* life for him. It was work that consoled him, completed him, and it was the law that he was in love with. So she happened to be wrong. He wouldn't tell her that. But how could she understand his deepest feelings when they had been distant for so many years?

"There is someone at the door, dear. I better let you go. Come on down and see Tyree and the rest of us real soon. Okay?"

"I'll see what I can do. Goodbye." Making some kind of commitment to visit was the easiest way to get off the phone with her. However, he had no intention of heading that way anytime soon. Before he could put the phone down, it chimed, notifying him of a text message. He punched a few buttons and found an anonymous message in all capital letters staring at him.

SINNERS, ALL SINNERS, GET THEIR JUST REWARD. AND YOU ARE NOT WITHOUT SIN.

Chapter 13

Minutes later Sonya burst into Maxwell's office, with his assistant on her heels.

"Attorney Montgomery, I apologize," the assistant stated. "I couldn't stop her. Should I call security?"

Sonya darted over to Maxwell, leaving about a foot between them. The expression on her face caused Maxwell to react. He didn't want an irrational woman attacking him while he sat there idly. He got up and put another foot of separation between them. "It's okay. I'll handle this. You can close the door behind you," he told his assistant.

"Are you sure?"

"I'm sure," Maxwell assured her and slid his hands into his pockets. "I'm fine."

His assistant slowly retreated and closed the door.

"Back so soon?" Maxwell asked as soon as they were alone.

Sonya lit into Maxwell. "You killed my uncle! Yes, you, Mr. Hotshot. You used a good and honest man to get what you wanted from Greater Metropolitan, and then you threw him into the pit with a bunch of hardened criminals."

Maxwell stood still, with his hands fixed and his lips too. He'd let her finish the spiel, and then he'd get back to business. He suspected that she didn't have much more to say.

"I hope you rot in hell. And trust me when I say, you'll get yours."

"Is that a threat?"

"You take it any way you want."

She stepped closer, and Maxwell stood his ground, although Sonya was making him uncomfortable. Irrational people were unpredictable. Since she'd worked for him for several years, Maxwell would give her a break. But he wasn't going to wait the entire afternoon for her to finish the tirade. Time was running short, along with his patience.

"If it hadn't been for you lying to my uncle and allowing him to get swept up in some mess that he had nothing to do with, he'd be alive and at home with his family," she told him.

Maxwell maneuvered around Sonya and reclaimed his seat. He twirled his ink pen back and forth between his fingers and let her ranting and raving continue without interruption. Maybe Maxwell let her babble on because he was struggling with the way the case had played out. Not sure now if Deacon Burton was guilty or not, Maxwell tried unsuccessfully to block out the man's sons. They wouldn't go away. He kept thinking about how their lives were going to change without a steady income coming into the household. He couldn't wish his tattered childhood on any kid.

"Maxwell, I worked hard for you, admired you, and even left four churches because you were investigating them. I trusted you, and so did my uncle. Now we find out the hard way how sorely misplaced our trust was."

Maxwell could tell she was fighting back tears by the end of her emotional outburst. The storm appeared to be dying down, and then, without warning, it regained its fury. "I wish they'd put your butt in prison for one night and let those guys beat the heck out of you," she growled. "I wouldn't shed a tear if your body came up missing. Good riddance would be the closest I'd come to a condolence."

He'd finally heard enough. "Are you done?"

"No. You're not going to rush me out of here."

"That's precisely what I am going to do. In case you've forgotten, this is a place of business. As soon as you leave, I can get back to my business."

"You are a piece of work. You drove my uncle to his death, and then you don't have time to hear me out. What kind of a demon are you?"

"Good grief. Are you in denial, or does passing the buck run in your family when it comes to accepting responsibility?"

"You better keep my family out of this, Maxwell Montgomery," she told him.

He felt the sting in her words and opted to take a direct approach. "I understand that you're upset, and you have my condolences, but you can't keep running into my office, making threats and blowing off steam. Tell me what you want so we can finish this now."

She grunted and spewed her words at him. "I don't want anything from you."

"Like I said, I understand how you must feel. However, if you're sensible about this, you'll have to acknowledge that I'm not the guilty one. I didn't create the scandal at Greater Metropolitan. I simply helped lay out the evidence."

"Keep telling yourself that lie if it helps you sleep at night."

"I sleep just fine," he lied. Actually, he'd experienced many restless nights over the past year, since Deacon Burton was convicted. Something about the case had touched him in a way he hadn't experienced previously. Maxwell refused to call it guilt, because that would imply he'd possibly made a huge irrevocable mistake.

"Nobody as low down as you can sleep well. You're too afraid some of those knives you've shoved into the backs of people who trusted you are going to be hurled back at you. If you came up missing or dead, the police wouldn't have a clue where to start looking for a perpetrator. You have so many enemies that they'd have to interview most of the tristate area."

"I've heard enough, Sonya. If you're finished shooting your mouth off and blaming me for your uncle's predicament, I'd like for you to get out."

"When I'm good and ready," she said, reeling back on her heels, with her arms crossed and a piercing stare locked on Maxwell.

"Don't make me have you tossed out on your behind."

"You should be ashamed for using my uncle to further your career and for continuing this sick pursuit of the church."

Maxwell picked up the phone.

"Like I said, you'll get yours," she muttered. "I don't know how or when, but every dog has his day. Yours is labeled and waiting."

Maxwell chuckled as he held the phone receiver but did not dial. "Call the Better Business Bureau and wage a complaint."

"The bar association would be better."

He chuckled louder and threw Sonya's words back at her. "Whatever helps you sleep at night."

Sonya stomped out of his office and slammed the door.

His assistant rushed into his office. "Is there a problem?"

Maxwell continued to chuckle. "There's no need for concern. She's a disgruntled former employee and is upset about a case that didn't go her way."

"But she was very angry. I was worried when you had me close the door."

Maxwell let out a quick laugh to relieve his tension and dismissed Sonya's visit, as if her words hadn't affected him. "Let's get back to work. I have something you need to do right away. Grab your notepad." His assistant hustled out of his office. Maxwell sighed heavily.

Sonya had pricked a tender spot and, without realizing it, had stirred unrest in him. Sonya couldn't know about this, or he'd be seen as weak. Vultures preyed on the weak, like Bishop Jones had done to Maxwell's father so many years ago. Maxwell vowed never to be beholden to anyone. If he'd made a mistake with Deacon Burton, so be it. There wasn't anything he could do about it now. History had been written, and he was turning the page.

Chapter 14

Sonya was long gone, but her rant lingered. Maxwell shoved papers and emotions around, determined to carve out a work session filled with productivity. He hated that Sonya had gotten to him. *You killed my uncle* buzzed in his head, like an annoying fire alarm that couldn't be silenced. He hadn't literally killed the man. He wasn't confused about that, but Maxwell couldn't live with the idea of robbing two innocent young boys of a meaningful life filled with substance. Like it was yesterday, he recalled the agony of having his mother and father ripped from their home and sent to prison at the same time. He and Christine had been forced to stay with his mean and abusive aunt for what had seemed like an eternity until his mother got out. How many nights had he gone to bed hungry because there wasn't any money to buy food? Maxwell declared that no child would have to live like that if he could help it. He swiped his hand across his brow, remembering.

Maxwell had to clear his mind and get busy. Duty called, and he anxiously answered, thrilled to have the distraction. His work wasn't going to get done on its own. He opened a file sitting on the corner of his desk and flipped through several pages before slamming his pen on the desk. He reared back in his chair and growled. "What does it take to get a decent report around here?" he yelled out. No one was in the office with him, which meant he was yelling into the wind. It seemed useless, but the gesture helped Maxwell release his mounting frustration. It would be simple to say his angst was provoked purely by Sonya, a parasite determined to slowly bleed him dry. But that wasn't true. His torment was being fueled by a sense of caring. If there was a way to feel sorry for Sonya and Deacon Burton without appearing weak or wrong, he'd gladly do it. "Ugh!" he exclaimed.

Pining over a dead man and his erratic niece wasn't helping Maxwell's cause. He had to find a way to let the deacon go and move on. There was a ton of work that needed to be done in order to expose and ultimately bring down Pastor Harris and Faith Temple. Once he gathered some perspective, Maxwell settled in his seat and got busy. Over the course of twenty years he'd mastered the art of suppressing emotions. No one was better at it than him.

He dove into the documents on his desk, blindly pushing toward his goal. Apparently, Faith Temple had an uncanny ability to attract members from far and wide, generating over half a million dollars weekly in collections. Maxwell suspected the pastor was brainwashing naive members with false claims about miracles and faith. He was chomping at the bit to scour the details and find the dagger needed to bring down the unsuspecting young pastor. Maxwell dug deep while blocking out every distraction.

After an hour, he took a mental break to go through the stack of mail in front of him. In the middle of the stack was a plain envelope bearing his name and no return address. Maxwell opened it, pulled out the letter inside, and read the line of text in bold black print.

What goes around comes around. Your "just reward" is coming.

Maxwell's heartbeat increased dramatically, and his palms began sweating. He refused to read on. Who had time to waste on sending him pointless threats? He thought about all that he had endured. Maxwell even thought about the sacrifices he'd made in his personal life to improve the livelihood of many people who'd been ripped off by so-called religious leaders. To think this was the thanks he got made him angry.

Forget about the haters, Maxwell thought. He savored the satisfaction of hearing a gavel sound off in a crowded courtroom after the guilty party had received their penalty. The sound of victory symbolized the only peace he'd known for years. Maxwell crumpled up the letter and threw it into the wastepaper basket near his desk. He laughed aloud and picked up the phone to call Garrett.

"Guess what I got in the mail?" he said when Garrett picked up.

"Have no idea."

"A threatening letter from someone who has too much free time," he said, humored.

"Hey, you might want to take this serious," Garrett said after Maxwell read a section of the letter aloud. "Need I remind you that there may be some people out there who aren't very fond of you?"

"You sound scared," Maxwell said.

"I'm just saying that you need to be careful. You've brought down a long list of church leaders and bank-rupted countless ministries with lawsuit victories."

"And what's your point?" Maxwell wasn't humored anymore.

"I'm saying you might want to take a break and let the dust settle. Greater Metropolitan was a doozy. I believe we could both benefit from a rest."

"Come on, Garrett. You're not running scared again, are you?"

"Hold on. Nobody's running scared. I'm saying you need to take the emotion out of this, step back, and be rational. You're too caught up in this. If you're getting threats, which you haven't gotten before, that ought to tell you something."

"It tells me there are crazy folks out there who don't want to accept the failures of their church leaders. I'm not planting evidence on these people or trumping up charges. I'm only asking perpetrators to take responsibility for their actions."

"I'm just saying that we have to stay objective during the process of building a case." Garrett stated.

"Cool. Let's get to work. There are plenty of churches that still need to be exposed, and I won't be deterred by a ridiculous letter," Maxwell said, flinging the paper into the air.

Chapter 15

Maxwell drove for more than half an hour. It had been a typical long day, and he used the ride home to silence his raging mind. He was closing two cases before the weekend. And next week he would follow those up with a six-million-dollar civil suit against a prominent pastor in South Jersey who was accused of sexual indiscretions and embezzlement. Normally, he'd be excited to have so many cases wrapping up, but not this time.

Close to his home, which felt like an expensive hotel given how little time he spent there, Fairmount Park came into view. A black and white image of an eagle struggled to take flight in front of him. It was a kite attached to a string, and a little boy was flying it across the sky. As Maxwell drove along, his memories sailed across the sky, along with the kite.

He could see himself as a six-year-old, flying kites with his father in a huge park, much like the one in front of him. "Hold on to the string. Don't let go," his dad would tell him. The screaming horn from the car behind Maxwell silenced his past. He drove on, his gaze darting back and forth from the road to the rearview mirror. His car was moving, although he was doing a poor job of fleeing the childhood memories that pursued him.

After arriving home and parking, an exhausted Maxwell closed his garage door and turned the key that allowed him entrance into a dark house. It was empty and offered no one to welcome him home. He tossed his briefcase on the marble kitchen counter. Once he'd peeled off his suit jacket and his tie, he pressed the ON button on the TV remote, which ended the annoying, stifling silence. He flipped through the channels until he found the 76ers basketball game. His house phone rang, and he ignored it, not even glancing at the caller ID.

He opened the refrigerator door, and only carryout containers of half-eaten food and a case of water occupied the space. Forced to order from one of the many menus in his kitchen drawer, he settled in to wait for his pizza. His house phone rang again. Maxwell grabbed the cordless phone sitting on the island. The caller ID displayed RESTRICTED. It was eight o'clock at night. He was too tired to deal with telemarketers. He sat down at the counter and logged on to Faith Temple's web site. He clicked through pages of testimonies about healings and miracles that various church members claimed to have experienced. There were video clips of people bringing their sick children to the altar for prayer.

After ten minutes, he clicked on one of the Sunday morning services. Pastor Harris's voice was strong and held the audience captive as he preached about the devil's ability to deceive. The cell phone in Maxwell's pocket began to ring and startled him. He checked the number. That phone flashed RESTRICTED across the screen too. He gave a grunt and punched the IGNORE button, sending the call to voice mail. Someone purposely trying to conceal who they were would not get even a few seconds of his precious time.

Maxwell pushed up his shirtsleeve and gazed at the time on his Rolex. It wasn't too late for Garrett. He hit the speed dial button on his cell phone. As he expected, Garrett answered quickly.

"Hey, it's Maxwell. I've got a different angle I want you to check out with Pastor Harris and Faith Temple."

"Oh, yeah. What is it?"

"I need you to snoop around and find out what you can about his healing business."

"What do you mean?" Garrett asked.

"Looks like the pastor calls himself a healer of some kind. Who knows? Maybe he is paying folks to put on a show. That way he can perform a miraculous healing in the middle of Sunday morning service."

"That's an interesting angle."

"I thought so too. I was on his web site. One video clip showed crowds of people flooding the altar and waiting for him to heal them. A lot of them walked away with so-called healed limbs, restored sight, and even reports of cancer going into remission." Maxwell flicked a sheet of paper off the counter with his middle finger. "Do you believe he's for real?"

"Maybe," Garrett uttered.

"I don't, so let's see what's really going on at the church."

"I'll check it out." A phone rang in the background as Garrett was talking. "I need to take this other call."

"Oh, sure. I'll wait to hear from you."

Maxwell felt a surge of energy, and his dull headache had completely gone away. He snatched up an ink pen and started jotting down notes for case law and things his paralegal would need to check out. The ringing doorbell pulled him away from his data dump. It had to be his food delivery. The thought of pizza reminded him of his former companion, Nicole. She hadn't been much into cooking. She just hadn't had the time with her high-powered job. He remembered how much she had relied on ordering pizza during his visits to her house.

Thinking about her was a mixed bag of memories. Since they had never formally committed to a romantic relationship, he couldn't call her his girlfriend. Ironically,

that had become a problem near the end of their friendship. She had walked out of his life months ago and hadn't
contacted him since. Not even once, though reminders of
her nudged at him periodically.

Maxwell grabbed his wallet from his suit jacket and
yelled in the direction of the front door as the bell rang
again. "Coming. Hold on." He opened the door, paid the
driver, and secured his dinner.

Maxwell made his way to the kitchen, set down the
pizza box, and plucked out a slice of pepperoni, sausage,
and bacon pizza. Slowly, he chewed the single slice and
meditated on his surroundings. Then he slammed the
lid shut and forced the pizza box onto the bottom shelf
of the refrigerator, which was already crammed with a
myriad of leftovers that he'd cast aside. Once success was
achieved, he pressed the kitchen light switch. Darkness
partnered with silence and overpowered him. His stomach grumbled, but he marched up the stairs, disinterested
in eating another meal alone.

Chapter 16

Mrs. Burton peeked through a slit in the blinds. The collection of strangers outside her home added to the nausea that gripped her stomach. Another gulp of carbonated water probably wouldn't help, but she sucked down a big swig, anyway. Why wouldn't those nosy, heartless reporters leave her alone? Didn't they understand she was grieving the death of her husband? The widow dabbed a cold towel across her forehead and lifted the panel in the blinds a tiny bit.

Outside of her home, the street was silent, and cars lined the driveways. Neighbors watered their lawns and walked their dogs. Life went on for them. It didn't appear that sorrow had touched their lives. The reporters who held her captive came and went, staking out her house. They rotated in shifts, just sitting and waiting outside. They looked like heartless, hungry hounds, anxious to pounce on a carcass as soon as it was in sight. Mrs. Burton retreated from the window. She couldn't remain a hostage in her own home forever. So she would just have to face what was outside waiting for her.

The front door opened, and four people, huddled closely together, moved swiftly toward the driveway. Reporters with camera crews and microphones swarmed Mrs. Burton, her sons, and the woman with them. As they crowded them and demanded attention, each reporter hurled questions.

"Do you know the name of the inmate who killed your husband?"

"Can you forgive him?"

"Was your husband innocent?"

"Any details you'd like to share about the funeral arrangements?"

The questions persisted as the group crossed the lawn and reached a vehicle parked in the driveway. The word *funeral* had stabbed Mrs. Burton in the back like a cold six-inch blade. She hustled the boys into the car, slammed the door, and faced the reporters with her anger.

"Do you see these children?" Her voice was loud and strong, while her finger shook as she pointed at the car. With her hand flopping at the wrist, she pleaded with the woman who had accompanied her and the boys and was now in the car. "Go. Just take the boys. Get them out of here. I'll meet you there." Then she flung her body around to face the drooling pack of newshounds. "Get away from us. Get off my property. I don't have anything to say to any of you." Her eyes were swollen with emotion, and small beads of sweat covered the tip of her nose.

A woman reporter dared to step within inches of Mrs. Burton. Her tone was kinder than that of the others and laced with what sounded like compassion and sincerity. "What would you like to say to the community and the church members whom your husband loved?" The reporter slowly pushed the microphone close to Mrs. Burton's mouth.

With grief clawing at her throat, Mrs. Burton surveyed the faces of the reporters, who were silent and were staring at her. Tears slipped from her eyes and dripped down her cheeks onto her blouse. "He loved God, and he loved his church. He helped build Greater Metropolitan, and now the ministry is gone. The church has been abandoned, its doors are closed, and my husband is dead." She snatched a handkerchief from her skirt pocket and dabbed at her eyelids. "He was innocent and never should have been in a prison." She fell silent.

The woman reporter filled the silence quickly with another question. "Why do you think your husband was convicted on drug and fraud charges?"

Mrs. Burton flashed her bloodshot eyes at the nearest camera. "*Why?* I can tell you why. Maxwell Montgomery. He railroaded my husband into a guilty sentence that cost him his life." Her right cheek twitched a couple of times. She swiped at the tears on her face, sliding her hand over her quivering cheeks.

The other reporters sprang into action like a pack of hyenas chasing down a baby gazelle and barked out questions. Mrs. Burton ignored them and gave her attention only to the reporter she'd been talking with.

"Do you blame Maxwell Montgomery?" the reporter asked.

"One hundred percent. He's ruthless and doesn't care about who he hurts." She sucked in a big gulp of air and swallowed hard. "That crooked attorney knew my husband was innocent. He promised Steve wouldn't be involved in charges brought against the church leaders. He told my husband he didn't have to worry about going to prison. Obviously, that was a lie."

Sparks of light from flashing cameras caused Mrs. Burton's eyes to blink rapidly. Neighbors standing on their lawns or peeking through blinds watched the interview unfold.

The reporter inched the microphone closer to Mrs. Burton's mouth. "Are you saying Attorney Maxwell Montgomery built a case against someone he knew was innocent?"

"That's exactly what I'm saying." She looked away from the reporter and directly into one of the cameras aimed at her. "Maxwell Montgomery is shameless, irreverent, and willing to do anything to win." Her lips quivered as she spoke. "My husband paid the ultimate price, his life, for a crime he did not commit. Who knows who Maxwell Montgomery's next victim will be? What I do know is that my husband is dead. My children no longer have a father." She pushed the microphone away and tried to flee from the huddle of reporters. Her feet felt like they were sinking into quicksand with each step she took. Once inside the house, she slammed the front door hard, and the crashing sound was so loud that it set off the squealing house alarm.

The reporter wrapped up her interview, looking directly into her station's camera. "Mrs. Burton has accused the well-known civil attorney Maxwell Montgomery of indi-rectly contributing to her husband's death. You may recall that Steve Burton was the whistle-blower that uncovered corruption within one of the largest mega-ministries in Philadelphia, Greater Metropolitan. The ministry was reported to have close to three thousand members. After Bishop Jones, Deacon Burton, and other church leaders were found guilty of distributing prescription drugs, racketeering, sexual harassment, and fraud, there was no recovery. Sources close to the church say that the building was sold to the highest bidder, narrowly avoiding bankruptcy. With only a few hundred members left, maintaining the property wasn't feasible."

The reporter appeared distracted for a second, glanced down at her notecard, and then continued. She signaled for the cameraman to move in closer. "This is indeed a sad story, and it doesn't end here. Deacon Steve Burton's widow has cast more than a word or two of disparage-ment on Maxwell Montgomery. Is this attorney the ruthless, victory-seeking lawyer Mrs. Burton is accusing him of being? Was Steve Burton innocent? These are questions that may never be answered. But you've heard it all right here on Fox Twenty-Nine News, Philadelphia. I'm Monica Fowler, and we will continue to cover this community interest story, as Deacon Steve Burton will soon be laid to rest."

Standing in front of his desk, Maxwell pushed down on the power button. He'd heard enough. His TV screen disappeared into a mahogany cabinet, and the double doors closed to hide its existence. The interview had focused on the deacon's wife, but his thoughts always ended up with the two surviving sons. He knew the feeling of emptiness and loss would eventually slice into those boys' souls, with no relief to be found. Didn't those reporters and neighbors see the pain in those little boys' eyes as they were chased to the car? Why couldn't people leave it alone? Maxwell planted his palms on the top of his desk and hung his head. The familiar pain was so clearly visible.

A dull pain swept through Maxwell's chest. He released a noisy breath that felt like a heavy weight pushing the air out of his lungs. He closed his eyelids tightly and tugged at his tie. The pain in his chest wasn't real. Old issues and fragments of a life that he kept at a distance would not affect him. He wouldn't allow it. Maxwell stood up straight, loosened his tie, yanked it from the collar of his shirt, and tossed it onto his desk. He would remain in control, refusing to let burdens choke the life out of him.

He began stuffing several briefs and file folders into his briefcase. When he was done, his gaze fell on the bottom drawer of his desk. It had been a long time since he'd pulled the locked box from its hiding place. Why did it continue to taunt him? The years kept rolling by, and the skeletons of a previous life wouldn't disintegrate. His burning stare still fixed on the desk drawer. He reached for the keys in his pocket. The small key that fit the lock hung on his key ring, hidden from plain view. Bitter memories careened through him, then settled in his tight lips. He squeezed the keys until their ridges pinched his palm. The knock on his door jolted Maxwell from the haunting hold that his demons in the locked box had on him. He tossed the keys onto his desk, maybe another day. For now, he was glad to have the escape.

Chapter 17

Maxwell was mesmerized by the whisking sound of each car that zoomed past. He pressed down harder on the accelerator and punched the button that closed the sunroof and blocked out the hot, penetrating rays. His phone rang twice before he answered via the hands-free device on the steering wheel.

"Maxwell Montgomery speaking."

"The package you've been waiting for just arrived at the office. And I wanted to remind you about your three o'clock appointment with Garrett," his assistant announced.

"Thanks. I'll be back in time. I just need to make a quick stop."

"Oh, and you also got a collect call from a Bishop Ellis Jones. I didn't accept the charges. I thought you should know."

Maxwell gripped the steering wheel tighter. "Really?" He wondered why the bishop was calling him. Sonya had already worn on his nerves about the deacon. He didn't plan on giving the bishop a stage on which to read him the riot act too. Maxwell raked his teeth over his bottom lip. "Okay, I'll see you shortly." He ended the call and concentrated on the white dashed expressway lines.

Bishop Jones must have swallowed a lot of pride to have made a call to Maxwell's office. What did he want? Surely, he wasn't calling to apologize for the hurt and damage heaped on the Montgomery family. Maxwell's tires screeched as he made a sharp right turn after exiting the expressway.

Four blocks down the street and to the left, he whipped into the church parking lot. He let his car ease up next to the parking stall marked PASTOR RENALDO HARRIS. It was the middle of the day, and people were filing in and out of the tall stone church in front of him. What were they doing? Wasn't the church service on Sunday and the Bible class at night? He glanced at the parking sign that prevented anyone from parking in the pastor's spot. Then he took note of the church grounds which were adorned with a stone fountain that shot water high into the air. A perfectly manicured circular lawn surrounded it. Planted in the green grass was a marble sign that read FAITH TEMPLE CHURCH, WHERE ALL ARE WELCOME. GOD LOVES YOU, AND SO DO WE.

Maxwell perused the parking lot, with its many luxury vehicles, and noticed even more cars pulling in. Folks seemed to buy into the words on the sign and whatever religious rhetoric Pastor Harris was spewing from the pulpit. The ringing cell phone caused Maxwell to flinch as it snatched him from his thoughts. He answered.

"It's Garrett. I'm running a little behind, but I shouldn't be more than ten minutes late for our meeting."

"No problem. I am running a little behind myself. Guess what? I'm sitting here in the parking lot of Faith Temple Church, taking in the scenery. Our beloved Pastor Harris is sitting in his Christian tower for now," Maxwell proclaimed. "But we know his walls will come tumbling down soon enough." Maxwell glanced at the top of the church edifice and then let his gaze travel down until it reached the ground. Now the building was etched into his memory. "I'm done here for now, but I'll definitely be back," he told Garrett with a tone of certainty.

Garrett responded with, "We'll have a solid, confirmed case this time, right?"

Maxwell pulled the phone from his ear and stared at it, then shoved it back against his ear with a snarl. "What are you trying to say?"

"Just confirming our objective."

Maxwell tapped his chin three times with his knuckles. "The objective is to do what we've always done. Build an effective case against criminals." A few seconds of silence controlled the line. Maxwell loosened his tie. "I'll meet you at my office in an hour." He pressed down hard on the END button and held it. Finally, after tossing the phone onto the seat next to him, he cranked up the engine and yanked the gearshift into reverse. He pressed on the gas, with his eyes aimed at the church in front of him.

"Stop. Stop. Stop the car." A voice behind him yelled loudly and forcefully.

He slammed his foot on the brakes, and the car jerked as the tires screeched. In the rearview mirror, he saw a woman scooping a small child up into her arms. Maxwell was out of the car in seconds and standing in front of the woman. "I'm sorry. I didn't see him. Is he hurt?"

The woman examined the little boy, who was now crying. She nestled him to her and patted his back. "What's wrong with you? Why would you just blast into reverse like that? This is a parking lot, not an expressway."

With his hand on his chest, Maxwell pleaded, "I'm so sorry. It was a mistake. I was . . ."

The woman's words sliced into his apology like a sharp sword. "Yeah, well, your mistake could have killed my son. Pay attention to what you're doing."

He watched the woman walk away with her son still nestled in her arms. His cries were fading into whimpers. Maxwell stood there, kicking the pebbles on the ground. That could have been his nephew whom someone had almost backed over, the one he hadn't seen in many months. He reflected on how a mistake could change a person's whole life and someone else's as well. He watched the woman until she and the little boy got into a minivan and drove away. The confident attorney who was feared in the courtroom swallowed hard and released a sigh of relief.

Maxwell heard ringing coming from inside his car. He moved to the car door that was standing wide open and slid into the driver's seat. As he reached for the ringing phone, his body collapsed against the driver's seat. It was his mother, but he wasn't in the mood to argue. She'd have to wait for a better time. He glanced at his clock on the dash. He'd have to drive faster to make his meeting with Garrett.

He pulled the gearshift into reverse and cautiously backed out of the parking stall. Time and persistence had a way of unveiling the truth. Maxwell aimed to be front and center, leading the way.

Chapter 18

Between speeding and barreling through two yellow traffic lights that had turned red, Maxwell was sitting behind his desk in record time. Scribbling notes on a legal pad, listing questions, and plotting a timeline, he prepared for his meeting with Garrett. His phone rang, and it was his mother again. He wanted to ignore her, given that Garrett would be arriving shortly, but what if his nephew, Tyree, was in trouble? The mere possibility of such a situation compelled him to take the call.

"Maxwell speaking." Once he confirmed that it was his mother on the line, his concern was evident in his voice. "Is Tyree okay?"

"Perfectly fine."

Maxwell was relieved and equally motivated to get off the phone. "What do you need, Mom?"

"I've been trying to reach you, but I haven't been able to get through. Are you okay?"

"I'm fine. Just busy."

"You're always too busy for your family. Sometimes I feel like I have one child, when I gave birth to two."

"Mom, it's not that simple, but I can't get into that with you today," he said, glimpsing at the wall clock.

"I'm calling because your father is feeling a little stronger. The pacemaker is helping, but his health is still poor. None of us know how long we're going to be here." Her voice cracked.

Maxwell acknowledged her sentiments, and there was a part of him that actually wanted to comfort her, but it was way too risky. If he expressed too much concern, she'd mistake it for reconciliation, which couldn't be farther from the truth.

"Maybe you can come to Delaware for a visit. I'll whip up a bite to eat, and you can see your nephew. You know how much he loves you."

Her proposal was met with complete silence. His attention darted to the second drawer on the left side of his desk. He tugged at the drawer. *Good.* It was still locked.

"What do you think? Paul, are you still there?"

No sense correcting her. After all these years, she still refused to call him Maxwell. "I can't get away right now. I'm working on a case that requires most of my time." He sifted through the first few pages of the legal pad he'd been writing on. "Tell Tyree I said hello."

"Why not tell him in person yourself? He needs a strong male role model in his life. He needs someone to roughhouse with, you know, someone to play football and basketball with him, like your dad did with you. Poor child barely remembers his father. Tyree was just a baby when his father was killed in that car accident."

Maxwell listened and mostly agreed but couldn't afford to continue the conversation. "I'll give him a call."

"You can make a difference in his life."

He squeezed his eyelids shut tight and dropped back in his chair, bumping against the headrest. He would have been better off having not answered her call. The load she was heaping on him was not what he needed.

His assistant's voice burst through the intercom. "Mr. Montgomery, there are reporters here, asking to interview you."

He stretched the phone an arm's length away and covered the phone's mouthpiece. "Interview me? Interview me about what?"

"Deacon Steve Burton."

Maxwell spun his chair around and faced the wall behind his desk. With his teeth pressing on his lip, he shook his head.

"Paul, what's going on? Did you hear what I said?"

He put the phone to his ear again. "Mom, I've got to go. I've got stuff happening around me. I've got to hang up." He ended the call before his mother could say good-bye, and swung his chair around. His eyes shot from the intercom to the door of his office.

"What do you want me to do? Two more reporters just showed up," his assistant said over the intercom.

He picked up a pen and pressed the point of it into the legal pad sitting in front of him. Why was this death a leading story for the media? The man was dead. Why was he being resurrected? Maxwell slammed the heel of his hand into his forehead.

The intercom sounded. "Do you want me to have security escort the reporters out?"

As much as he detested the intrusion, Maxwell refused to run and hide from anyone, least of all bloodthirsty reporters. "No, don't do that. I'll be right out."

Prepared to handle whatever awaited him on the other side of the door, he rolled down his shirtsleeves and reinstated his cuff links. He slid on his suit jacket and buttoned it. Seconds later, he opened his office door and took four steps before several reporters armed with microphones had him sequestered. Instantly, Maxwell was under attack, with questions being hurled at him while the flashing lights of cameras blinded him. He caught a partial glimpse of Garrett leaning against the back wall in the reception area.

A female reporter stepped so close that Maxwell could smell the soft scent of her perfume. It was then that she launched a bomb that was heard above all the other reporters' questions. "Mr. Montgomery, do you feel guilty about Deacon Burton's murder?"

"Guilty? Why would I feel guilty? I didn't stab him." His focus briefly darted to Garrett and then returned to the reporter.

"Former members of Greater Metropolitan Church and the community believe Deacon Burton was innocent. What do you say?"

"I say that Deacon Burton had his day in court. Aren't you glad we're governed by laws, instead of public opinion?"

Maxwell turned his back to the reporter and answered questions from others. Just as he declared that there would be no more questions, the same female reporter taunted him. He faced her with narrowed eyes and brushed at the sweat forming on the palms of his hands.

"In the event that you did make a mistake, is there anything you would like to say to Deacon Burton's wife and sons?" she asked.

Maxwell tilted his head back and allowed a heavy grunt to scuttle from his throat. "You want to impact your ratings with this sensationalism and this antagonistic line of questioning. I get it." Maxwell paused to straighten his tie. "Deacon Burton's death is unfortunate and is a painful loss for his family and the community. However, the criminal case against him was built on credible evidence that led to a conviction." Maxwell zoomed in on the pesky reporter. "Didn't you hear that witch hunts are illegal?" Chatter and mild comments came from the crowd. "The prosecutor doesn't seek out innocent people to prosecute. This case was simple. The jury found him guilty, and the judge sentenced him. The judicial system works."

His gaze combed the room. He'd done a dance with the media for years. The end result was always better when he led. Maxwell's tone and the words he hurled made his position clear. He raised and pointed his index finger at the three reporters close to him. "You, you, and you, all of you should be ashamed. You're wasting time interviewing me instead of doing a human interest story on the Burton family. They've lost a provider because of a senseless crime committed in our prison system. Your outrage is misplaced. We should be outraged about a person not being able to pay their debt to society in the safe confines of our penal system. There's your story. There's your human interest piece. This interview is over." Maxwell felt invigorated and took charge. "Now I'm asking you to vacate my office, or I'll have to get security," he said.

The reporters tried pushing forward with more questions but eventually obliged. Maxwell peered past the reporters flooding out of his office and met Garrett's gaze. He beckoned Garrett into his office, then gracefully exited the reception area, frazzled but determined not to show an inkling of discontent. The media had always been his platform to showcase his talent. His involvement with Deacon Burton's case wouldn't unravel years of crafting his image, his brand. There would be a round two with the media. However, next time, it would be on his terms, and he would be ready.

Chapter 19

They retreated into Maxwell's office and shut the door. Maxwell stopped midway across the room and faced the desk.

"What a circus," he said.

"Are you sure you want to meet today? We can reschedule," Garrett told him.

Still wound up from the interview, Maxwell leaned against the front edge of his desk. "Forget about them. I'm more interested in what you've found out about Pastor Harris and Faith Temple." With his arms folded across his chest, he waited.

"I've done some digging, but you're not going to like the results. I haven't found one speck of dirt on Pastor Harris or his church."

Maxwell moved behind his desk, stared at Garrett, and fell into his chair. "This is not what I wanted to hear."

"Well, it is what it is," Garrett replied. "So far he's clean." Garrett took a chair in front of the desk.

"Impossible." Maxwell's arms flew from his chest, and then his palms smacked together hard. "He's a preacher, for goodness sake, and you're telling me you can't find anything? Come on."

"No, nothing yet. I have reviewed their taxes for the past twenty years. I checked his ministerial license to see if it was legit. His background check was spotless. The man doesn't even have a parking ticket."

"So that doesn't mean it's not there."

Maxwell rested his index finger against his temple. He imagined that many members of Faith Temple would be thrilled and relieved to hear that no improprieties had been discovered. Instead, this ignited a tougher fight in Maxwell. He was sickened, knowing that this pastor was preying on the weak without any accountability or scrutiny. Maxwell wasn't willing to let another church ruin families and not care. Pastors were like politicians and cops; they had a set of rules for others that they themselves didn't follow. Maxwell scratched his neck. Nobody was above the law, including Pastor Harris. If he could, Maxwell was going to save as many families as possible, even if his efforts were unappreciated.

He went on. "I'll give it to him. This pastor is slicker than the others and knows how to cover his tracks. But he's not going to play us for a fool. We just have to be smarter about this," Maxwell rose from his chair and leaned against the edge of his desk. "I need you to dig deeper." He waved his hand in the air, dismissing the possibility of Pastor Harris being genuine. "What about his past, before he became a pastor? Did he cheat on his wife? Are there any illegitimate children out there? He's bound to have dealt with some type of money problems. They always do. So double-check the finances. There are always nuggets of offenses there. We'll get the IRS involved, if necessary. Those hounds will sniff out an unreported dollar, and you know it." After removing his suit jacket and placing it on a felt hanger in the closet, he returned to his high-back chair. "What about his wife? What about the rest of his family?"

"You don't mean his children too, do you?"

"Of course not. They are the only ones off-limits," Maxwell replied.

"I'm way ahead of you." Garrett opened a binder and gave Maxwell a brief rundown of what he'd learned about both Pastor Harris's and his wife's background. "I can tell you where they went to school, how they met, and even their credit scores."

"Now you're talking."

"Don't get too excited, because neither of them has a criminal background. They've never been arrested for anything. His wife has a dental practice, and it seems to be pretty successful. They have credit scores of seven ninety-five and eight fifteen. From what I can tell, they're good people. The folks in their church support them. We'll have to find somebody on his staff to investigate, if we're going to find a legitimate angle." Garrett ran down a list of people on Pastor Harris's ministerial staff that he would be checking into as well. "I am just getting started with my investigation. It's too early yet to know what might or might not turn up. If there is something to be found, I will find it."

"I trust that you will find something that we can use to build a case. You say you checked his taxes for the past twenty years. Go back thirty years."

"He's too young for me to go back that far. He's only forty."

"Then find another way to put him under a microscope. You know what I expect." Maxwell unlocked the top drawer of his desk and pulled out a white envelope. He handed it to Garrett. "This should take care of your expenses and payment. If you need more, let me know."

Thirty minutes sailed by as Garrett proposed a few more areas for them to check out. "I can also visit a couple of church services, to get a feel for how the pastor works. You can learn a lot about a minister by sitting in his service." He patted his pants pocket, making the change in it jingle.

"Great idea," Maxwell said, getting excited. "If he pushes that donation basket around too much . . ."

"I'll know about it," Garrett interjected.

Maxwell leaned forward in his chair and snapped his fingers. "That's what I'm talking about. Let's get this dance started. We'll run into a few dead ends, but sooner or later we will come across some information that will lead us to the winner's circle with this guy." Maxwell felt rejuvenated having Garrett back on his team and eager to get the job done. Finally, there was hope. "Pastor Harris might have fooled some of the people some of the time, but he can't fool us any of the time." Maxwell chuckled. Garrett did too. "I can't wait for us to find out who this character really is."

Suddenly, hail began hitting the windows on both sides of the office. Maxwell's head swooped around, and he saw the small white pellets pinging against the glass.

Garrett closed his tablet and headed to one of the windows. The noise got louder. Pellet after pellet hit the window and slid down the glass. Garrett turned to Maxwell. "I'm willing to keep digging, but like I said before, we'll have to be absolutely certain, with no doubts at all, that Pastor Harris is guilty before we build a case. That is the only way I'll be involved."

Maxwell knew Garrett was serious by the inflection of his voice and had no choice but to agree. He needed Garrett's investigative skills. More importantly, Maxwell couldn't bear another Deacon Burton wearing on his conscience. "I've told you before, and I'll tell you again that I hear you." Maxwell let that close out the conversation.

Chapter 20

Maxwell's assistant belted over the intercom, "Mr. Montgomery, you have a call on line one from a Ms. Winston."

Startled, Maxwell immediately stopped paging through the law book on his desk and pressed the blinking button on the phone. After his long meeting with Garrett regarding Pastor Harris, he still hadn't made a dent in the mound of work in front of him. But Ms. Winston's call was a welcomed interruption.

"Maxwell Montgomery speaking."

"Mr. Montgomery. This is Jill, Jill Winston. Do you remember me?"

"Of course I do. How are you?"

"I'm doing much, much better than I was the last time we spoke."

Maxwell was pleased. "How about your sons?"

"Doing great. They're good boys. And thanks for the money. It has made life much better for us. I'm finally able to move to a nicer neighborhood, thanks to you."

"That's good to hear."

He picked up a small framed photo of his nephew that was situated on his desk. His sister had given him the photo last year, during one of his rare visits. His thoughts wanted to drift off to his disjointed family and what his mother had said about mentoring his nephew, but Jill's voice drew him back into the moment.

"I know you're busy, but I had to call. I want you to know that I've been clean for eleven months and twenty-three days, and it's been wonderful."

Maxwell was pleased. He shut his eyes tightly as his head nodded up and down.

"I'm a better mother thanks to you."

He harnessed his emotions and continued listening.

"Thank you for covering my bill at the rehabilitation center. I desperately needed the help, and there was no way I could afford anything like that."

"No thanks needed. I'm glad you accepted the help. That's what matters."

"At first it was hard leaving my kids. I worried about them every day. I didn't have any family I could leave them with, so I was forced to leave them with my trifling neighbor. Thankfully, it all worked out, and my kids and I are together again. That ninety-day inpatient program gave me my life back, and I had to call and thank you. I should have called sooner, but I was getting myself together."

Maxwell hadn't hesitated in writing the forty-five-thousand-dollar check for Jill's stay at the treatment center. Coming from the church, she was rare. Jill was honest and well worth the investment. "I'm glad it worked out. Your sons are the winners here. I'm glad you're doing better, really glad." He set Tyree's photo down and kicked out the horrific memory of the period in which he and Christine had stayed with their aunt. He was a grown man and could still feel the daily whippings.

Maxwell was bursting with questions. She clearly wasn't the same broken woman who'd sat in his office last spring and confessed to being involved with Minister Simmons at Greater Metropolitan, one of Bishop Jones's associate pastors. She wasn't the broken woman who had suffered with chronic back pain for several years. That frail woman had been used by the minister unashamedly. He'd supplied her with prescription drugs to ease her pain, and in return he'd taken various foul liberties with her. Maxwell's disgust simmered, but then it dissipated when he thought about the minister rotting in jail while Jill walked around free.

"Jill, I really want the best for you. Your sons need you to stay clean. Are you doing some type of follow-up meetings or support group?"

"Yes, definitely. I know that my back problem and the pain meds will always be a struggle for me, but the support group helps me. Don't worry, Mr. Montgomery. I'm going to stay clean. I have to for my kids."

Maxwell believed her.

"You have no idea how much emotional baggage I've been able to get rid of. I'm not living in fear anymore that they will be taken away from me because of my addiction."

"Jill, I'm glad to hear from you, and I'm pleased that you made the commitment to change your life. Do me a favor and keep in touch. Let me know how things are going for you and the boys."

"I will, and I also want to apologize for not helping you with the case against Greater Metropolitan. I'm sorry about not being able to testify against the minister, but my children are all I have. They are the ones that love me. They need me, and I couldn't take the chance of ending up in jail. The Department of Children and Family Services would have gotten involved, and I would have lost my boys. I'm sorry, but that's a chance I won't take for anybody."

Maxwell understood and harbored no ill will toward her. Actually, he admired Jill's devotion to her sons.

"It's over with, and you did the right thing. Don't worry about it. You did what you felt was best for your children. I can respect your decision. That's what parents are supposed to do."

If only his parents had felt the same way and had put their children before the church, maybe the Montgomery family would have a different ending . . . maybe.

Jill's voice went up an octave, and excitement laced her words. "Would you believe that after all that went down at Greater Metropolitan, I was able to find a new church that I really like? Imagine that. I never thought I'd want to trust God or anyone in a church ever again." She laughed softly.

Until this point, Jill had been speaking sensibly, and Maxwell couldn't believe what he was hearing now. "Well, how can you possibly trust one now, after everything you've been through because of the so-called righteous, 'let me help you' church folks?"

"There is something different about this pastor and his wife. They're down to earth and easy to talk to. When I opened my mouth to say that I didn't need help, the words wouldn't come out." She sniffed hard. "They took my hand and prayed for me. I feel like they really care."

"How did you meet this pastor?" Maxwell's hand flew up to the back of his neck. He squeezed hard to tame the knot of tension that challenged him.

"After Bishop Jones and the others were arrested, the pastor and his wife just showed up at my door a few days later. He said Bishop Jones and Deacon Burton had both mentioned my name. They asked him to check on me and be sure that I was okay."

Maxell closed the law book on the desk. He snagged a red ink pen, and his hand hovered over a legal pad, ready to write. "What's the name of the pastor and his church?" He would add them to his watch list.

"Pastor Harris at Faith Temple. He and his wife are so encouraging. They've never judged me. Not one time have they asked me why or how could I have gotten involved with drugs and risked losing my children. Not once did they condemn me." She giggled lightly. "I'm back in church, and I have you to thank."

Maxwell's joy deflated like air rapidly draining from a high-flying balloon. He didn't know whether to feel angry, annoyed, or inspired to go harder after Pastor Harris. This should have been his moment to bask in Jill's good news, but of course, the church had to find a way to ruin it.

Chapter 21

Maxwell was close to giving in to the nagging pang of doubt that demanded he consider the possibility that he'd made a mistake. He snapped the law book closed after wasting forty-five minutes staring at it without retaining a word. He strummed his fingers on the top of the book as he looked around the room, taking in the books that lined the shelves on each wall. Fed up, Maxwell sprang from his chair and hustled from the library. Passing the conference room and his assistant, he rushed into his office. He ignored the paralegal who'd called out to him, and closed the door hard behind him.

It wasn't long before Maxwell's desk was covered with papers. He'd pulled a box of files and photos from a locked cabinet, and the conference table was littered with its contents. A determined man dug through the information with a hungry vigor. There had to be something, some piece of paper, some document, some testimony that would shout to the rooftops that Deacon Burton was corrupt. There had to be if Maxwell was going to silence that rumbling uneasiness in his gut. He ignored the ringing phone, which attempted to summon him three different times. He sifted through mounds of paper until his eyes fell on a newspaper. The front page was filled with the faces of those arrested in the Greater Metropolitan case. Seeing the photo of Bishop Jones in handcuffs didn't hold Maxwell's attention. It was the picture of Deacon Burton walking into the courtroom with a Bible in his hand that captured his attention.

Maxwell had papers everywhere but still nothing solid that would quiet the nagging voice of his conscience, which continued asking, "Are you sure?" Maxwell flung the newspaper across the room. He considered the chaos of papers that was smothering him. What now? Would he just have to let it go? He did have other things to do, like being in court later that day and meeting with a new client for an initial consultation.

The intercom on his desk sliced through the quiet that owned his office. "Mr. Montgomery, you wanted me to remind you about the letters that need to go out today."

He shoved the cuff of his sleeve back and glanced down at his watch with a wrinkled brow. It was almost noon, and he'd accomplished nothing. "Sure. Let's get it done." He gathered the papers from his desk and tossed them onto the conference table with the others. "Come in," he called out when his assistant knocked on the door.

She stepped over the newspapers as she strode across the floor. The box, the files, and the stacks of papers sprawled across the conference table caused her to comment. "Would you like me to straighten up your office later?"

"No, I'll take care of it."

She sat down in the chair near his desk and opened her laptop. He dictated the letter quickly, as she seemed to keep up. Yet it wasn't long before his focus drifted from the task at hand.

"Scratch that. Start over." The methodical, "get it done" side of Maxwell hadn't shown up. Standing behind his desk, he attempted to finish the first letter, which he'd stopped and started twice. He dictated a few more lines, then stopped mid-sentence, snapping his fingers to summon the term he sought. With no success, he solicited the help of his assistant. "Read me what you have so far."

Maxwell struggled to clear his jumbled thoughts. The few lines she read back to him had no impact on his ability to stay on task. "Do you belong to one of the local churches?" he questioned.

"Excuse me?" Her eyes widened.

"It's a simple question. Do you go to church?"

"No, I don't. I'm an atheist. I don't believe in God. That's why it doesn't bother me to see you persecute churches."

Her statement grabbed him immediately. Maxwell faced her dead on. "I don't persecute churches. I prosecute those who are guilty of corruption, especially swindlers who take advantage of desperate people who are in need."

"I wouldn't want your job, Mr. Montgomery. Sometimes there is a thin line between right and wrong. I can only imagine how blurred that line might get for you."

He dropped down into the chair behind his desk. "We'll have to finish the letters later."

"But these letters need to go out today, and your afternoon is booked solid." She closed the lid of her laptop.

"So I guess we'll do a little overtime. You can handle that, right?" he tossed back at her in a frosty tone.

"Sure, Mr. Montgomery. Let me know when you're ready."

Maxwell was already on edge. Any slight hint of laziness on the part of his assistant or a lack of commitment to her job was sure to push his irritation too far in the wrong direction. With his elbows pressed into his desk, Maxwell tapped his fingertips rapidly as he grasped for composure. Didn't his assistant understand how serious his work was? He couldn't help but think about Sonya and how valuable she'd been to his practice. If she were there, he wouldn't have to dictate the letter. As a paralegal and an administrative assistant rolled into one, she would have written the letter on her own and shown him the final draft. When Sonya left, he was forced to hire both an assistant and a paralegal. The two put together weren't as efficient as Sonya. He longed to have her back, but with her uncle convicted of a crime and now dead, she was never working for Maxwell again.

Worse, the rage she'd unleashed on him a few days ago confirmed how much Sonya blamed him for her uncle's demise. His surge of emotions and his sense of helplessness rendered Maxwell speechless. The more he rehashed the situation, the more the mere presence of his assistant annoyed him. Settling for second best had never been his style. He stared long enough for his assistant to break the silence.

"Are you okay, Mr. Montgomery?"

That was a loaded question that he honestly could not answer. "Please excuse me, and hold my calls. I've got a lot of work to do." He shifted his attention to a document in front of him. The second she shut the door behind her, Maxwell headed for the conference table and dived into the stacks of paper he'd been searching through before his assistant interrupted. Two hours later, with no solid proof of Deacon Burton's undeniable guilt, he rubbed his eyelids with the heels of both hands. He glanced over at the newspaper articles still lying on the floor. Deacon Burton's image glared back.

A knock at his office door received a sharp response. "Yes? What is it?"

"I have a delivery for you, Mr. Montgomery," his assistant replied.

He responded through a closed door. "Just hold on to it. I'll get it later."

"The delivery person said I should give it to you right away."

He considered her comment for a couple of seconds. "Come on in."

His assistant quickly entered, strolled up to his desk, and pushed the envelope into his hand. "Here you are."

He turned the envelope over and tore into it with his fingers, ignoring the letter opener she held out for him. There was a thick red dot that looked like a bloodstain on a single white piece of paper. Only one sentence was on the page. *You will bleed.* He pushed himself up from his chair. "Who gave you this? Where is the delivery person?"

"He's probably in the elevator by now."

"Was it a man or a woman? What did they look like?" Maxwell had rattled off the questions so quickly that he figured she might not have understood him.

Without repeating his questions, Maxwell dashed past her, out of his office, and to the elevator. Punching the down button multiple times didn't make the elevator door open any faster. Down four flights of stairs, he hustled. When he got to the bottom floor, he pushed through the double doors of the entrance to the building. Standing on the sidewalk, he looked to his left, then to his right, and then left again. At the corner, he noticed a man standing beside a taxi with the door open. He aimed his finger at Maxwell and pulled an imaginary trigger before hopping into the taxi, which sped away.

Chapter 22

By 10:00 a.m. the next morning, Maxwell had run his regular five-mile morning route and had been at his firm for two hours already. Warm, bright sunlight seeped into his office through the vertical blinds, causing him to squint while reading the case file. He got up and snapped the blinds shut, denying sunlight the opportunity to interrupt him, then returned to his seat. Voices from the TV kept him company as he pored over a settlement agreement for one of his embezzlement cases. The cell phone on his desk buzzed. He recognized the untitled number that flashed. Why was Christine calling so early? What did she want? He poked the edge of the document he was working on with the point of his ink pen. The number continued to flash until the phone stopped ringing.

Fifteen minutes later the cell phone buzzed again. It was the same number. He might as well answer it. His sister would keep calling if he didn't. He grabbed the phone and tightened his grip on the ink pen in his other hand. "Maxwell speaking."

"Hey, Paul. How's it going?"

He hated when she called him that, but didn't bother correcting her. It would lengthen the call unnecessarily. "What do you want?"

"Why do you sound so dry?" she asked.

His tone might not have sounded inviting, but in general, Maxwell didn't have a problem with his sister, except when she pressured him about their parents.

"I haven't talked with you in a while. So it's not like I have been blowing up your phone. You can't be annoyed just because I'm calling you," she added.

"I'm just busy. I've got a lot going on."

"When aren't you busy? Anyway, I'm calling to see if you would at least consider coming to a small get-together for Auntie. She's turning seventy-four. And Mom wants to do something to celebrate her sister's birthday. Will you come?"

"Auntie. Are you kidding? I haven't seen that drunken child abuser since Mom got out of jail. I didn't like her then and care even less about her now. You can definitely count me out."

"She did the best she could to take care of us. Mom was only gone six months. We weren't with Auntie that long. And you know she is the only family Mom has. We were lucky she took us in and we didn't end up in foster care."

"Yeah, right. Foster care may not have been as bad." He swiveled his chair around and stole a quick peek at the TV while Christine made an attempt to convince him. He saw crowds of people trekking up the stone steps of Faith Temple as the commentator made mention of the funeral taking place there. A picture of Deacon Burton flashed on the screen. Maxwell's face scrunched up, his expression sour, like he'd just bitten into a lemon. He swung his chair back around, giving his back to the TV.

After a minute or two of fervent persuasion, she sealed her plea with, "Come on. You refuse every invite, no matter what it is. This means a lot to Mom. She wants you there. Please, Paul. Do it for her."

"Will you please stop calling me Paul? Why do I have to ask you that every time we speak?"

"Maybe it's because that's what our parents named you."

Slowly, he turned his chair around to face the TV again. The funeral for Deacon Burton was still the main story being covered by the local channel. The reporters went on and on about the man. An agitated Maxwell looked down at this watch and sliced into Christine's admonishment. "I don't have time for this. I've got to get back to work. I won't be there. I don't want to hang up on you, but I need to finish up here." He shuffled through the papers on his desk, making noise, and hoped it would persuade her into believing that he was really busy and had to go.

"All right, Maxwell. That is what you want to be called, right? I'll let our mother know that you refused to come to Auntie's party. You know, the one who took us in when we didn't have anywhere else to go."

"Whatever," he said, prepared to hang up cordially or not.

"You need to let go of the past and build a life in the here and now. Work on that."

Maxwell jerked his head and stared at the phone when a sharp click on the line announced that Christine had hung up on him.

He returned his attention to the TV and turned up the volume. It didn't take long before he'd heard too much. The irritating call was easier to shake off than the troubling thoughts about Deacon Burton. Maxwell got up from his chair, schlepped across the room to the bathroom, and turned on the faucet. The cold water ran down the drain until he shoved his hands underneath the fixture. He allowed the water to run over his hands and then his wrists, hoping his pulse would slow and his rapid breathing would calm. Finally, he bent over the sink and splashed the cold water on his face. He stood up and faced the man in the mirror, with water dripping from his chin.

He was tired of hearing how sad the community was to lay such a beloved man to rest. The TV news and the newspapers were making Deacon Burton out to be a saint. His thoughts chased one another. There were no saints, dead or alive. Maxwell was sick of dealing with charlatans. He shut off the water and snagged a hand towel from the cabinet under the sink. He wiped his face dry and shifted his tie into place.

Back at his desk, he shut off the TV, made a few phone calls, and answered some e-mails. He tried diligently to shift into that single gear that allowed him to concentrate diligently on a task until it was completed, regardless of the obstacles or interruptions. After several failed attempts, Maxwell realized he wasn't able to concentrate. A nagging feeling that he should be somewhere else would not release him. After a quick check of his watch, he put on his suit jacket. Maxwell stopped at his assistant's desk on his way out.

"I need to run out for a bit. I'll be back soon," he announced.

Minutes later he was in his car, zipping down the expressway and trying not to think of what he was about to do or why. Especially since it wasn't the wisest thing he'd ever done. Nobody could see him. There would be no way to explain why he'd shown up in the parking lot. He pressed a button on the steering wheel, and music filled the car. He raised the volume a couple of notches. Drowning out his doubts had to be possible somehow.

Maxwell exited the expressway and drove the short distance to a destination that beckoned him like water on a hot day. There stood the tall edifice, which he'd recently visited. A line of cars crept along, seemingly searching for a parking spot. A black limousine was quite a ways in front of him. He assumed the deacon's wife and sons were inside it, and probably Sonya too. Maxwell gripped the steering wheel tighter. He was almost at the entrance, where the parking lot attendants in orange jackets directed traffic. He grabbed his Ray-Ban sunglasses from the console and slid them on. He felt a bit less recognizable behind the dark lenses.

Driving slowly, he saw the limousine stop at the front steps of the church. Maxwell was forced to wait until the car in front of him eased up a few more inches. Maxwell tapped his fingers on top of the steering wheel. A couple of minutes later he was two car lengths away from the limousine when the driver got out, opened the back door, and extended his hand. The deacon's wife stepped from the car, dressed in black and wearing a netted veil. Her two young boys climbed out of the backseat behind her.

There was only one car in front of Maxwell now. He could see his targets clearly. The shorter boy, who looked to be the youngest, flung his body into his mother. She appeared thinner than he remembered her being in the courtroom last year. The boy seemed to be shaking as Maxwell inched his car closer. He pushed his sunglasses down toward the end of his nose and peered over the top of the rims. He watched Mrs. Burton lift the veil from her face and kiss the young boy's cheek as she dried his tears with a white handkerchief. The two boys positioned themselves on each side of her. She held their hands as they climbed the steps together.

Maxwell's gaze was fixated on the family, and then the piercing car horn behind him jolted his attention back to the line of traffic ahead of him. It had moved, and he had not. He inched along while watching the widow and the deacon's sons walk through the large polished wooden double doors until they were out of sight. Maxwell reflected on the feeling of loss and abandonment that awaited them inside the church and that would stay with them for days to come.

Peering ahead, he saw that news reporters were talking to some of the people as they approached the sidewalk near the entrance. Camera crews were snapping pictures. He couldn't risk being seen and having his picture end up on the front page of the paper, with some crazy caption. He had to scope out a quick escape. A man in an orange jacket frantically waved his hand for Maxwell to stop holding up traffic. After adjusting his shades to be certain his identity was concealed, he made the nearest exit his destination. He removed his foot from the brake pedal and pressed forward. He maneuvered his way out of the congestion and past the reporters. He was pleased to have made a clean getaway. No one would know he'd been there; no one except him.

Chapter 23

Early morning offered a whisper of humidity, which promised to turn into a cloak of sweltering heat by noonday. Maxwell left his home, the place where he slept, stored his valuable artwork, and showcased a piano that he hardly ever touched. Troubling images from yesterday rode along with Maxwell on his drive to the office. Glimpses of the televised funeral procession meshed with images of the deacon's sons climbing the steps into the church gnawed at him. After a fifteen-minute ride and a brief stop for coffee, he was at his firm downtown. He hustled to his suite on the fourth floor. The office was lifeless, and he was grateful for an hour of solitude. He opened the window blinds, plopped down into his chair, stretched out his legs, and planted his heels on the corner of the desk. With his eyes shut, he drank in the peace and quiet his sanctuary offered. Ten minutes later, he was ready to tackle the day.

He picked up the stack of mail sitting in the middle of his desk and sifted through it. The manila envelope with no return address stopped him. He turned it over and found nothing on the back side. He slid a pearl-handled letter opener under the flap and broke the seal. An obituary clipping fell out. Deacon Steve Burton's wide smile consumed the page. He flung the obituary onto his desk as if it were on fire and had scorched his fingertips. His coffee fell over when he snatched his feet down from the desktop.

"Shoot." Maxwell shouted as he brushed the coffee from his pant leg and reached for the tissues on his desk. Pacing the floor, he wondered who'd sent the envelope and why. He scratched his head. Could it be Bishop Jones? Although he was in prison, the bishop could have had someone mail it for him. Maybe it was that shifty Minister Simmons, who was locked up with Jones. Maxwell didn't know what to think.

The pacing came to an abrupt halt. He loosened his tie, got paper towels from the bathroom, and wiped up the spill. Then he stuffed the obituary back into the envelope and dropped it into the wastebasket. Within seconds, he retrieved the envelope. Somehow it just seemed disrespectful to toss it in the trash, but there needed to be distance between him and the deacon's haunting image. The box housing leftover Greater Metropolitan files was a good place to put it to rest. He tucked the paper away as a gnawing discomfort in his gut would not settle down. That was it . . . done. He had no control over that man's destiny, good or bad. Just then Maxwell's last meal climbed up his throat. The foul, bitter taste of a pending eruption sent Maxwell dashing to the bathroom.

An hour later, his firm was in full swing. His paralegal, his assistant, and a parade of clients spoke to the fast-paced environment that he loved. Preparing for an upcoming court appearance, Maxwell sat in the quaint law library and reviewed a brief that had been prepared by his paralegal. He marked it up with a red pen, made notes in the margins, and read it over twice. With his fingers tracing along the document and head shaking back and forth, he punched a button on the intercom.

"Would you come into the library please?" After he'd taken a long, cool drink from a water bottle, his paralegal joined him.

"Yes, Mr. Montgomery? Did you need my help?"

"Have a seat. Is this the final draft of the brief you prepared for the Graham case?" He pushed the brief across the table to her.

She flipped through the pages and responded, "Yes, it is."

Maxwell reached for the brief. "I mentioned some specific case law that I wanted you to include, which you did not. The summary is weak. The main problem is your lack of precedence. There were plenty of previous rulings that you could have cited and didn't." The unsatisfied attorney poked the brief with his index finger. "I need to be able to rely on you. I don't have time to redo your work. If that's what I have to do, then I don't need your services. Can you do this job or not?" Leaning back in his chair, he flung his right leg over his left knee, and his foot bounced up and down as he awaited her response.

She rested her hands, with threaded fingers, on top of the table and looked into his eyes. "I am twenty-seven years old, and this is my second job as a paralegal. My former employer gave me a great recommendation, which you said was impressive and was one of the reasons you hired me. I've tried to do a good job for you, although nothing I do seems to be good enough." She stared at the legal brief in front of him. "I know you had a great paralegal before me. You said that yourself, and I hear the same thing buzzing around the office whenever you are not pleased with my work. May I be candid?"

"Please do." Seeing that she'd already been candid, he couldn't imagine what else there was to say.

"I think it's because you expect me to step in and pick up where your other paralegal left off. The fact that you have no confidence in me isn't fair. You have me double- and triple-check everything, and then you still check it too." She pulled her hands down into her lap. "I hope I am not out of line, but you reprimand me at every turn." She cleared her throat and folded in her bottom lip.

The courage she exhibited in speaking her mind was unexpected. He stood, stepped quietly over to the window. Sunlight rushed into the room. Maxwell needed a paralegal he could count on now more than ever. He wouldn't admit it, but he had an escalating concern about making a mistake with each case. For that reason alone, he would not rip her apart. "There is never a reason for mediocrity. In this law firm, we go above and beyond." The sun cast a shadow on the conference table, making Maxwell appear taller than his five feet eleven inches. "Relax. I'm not the big bad wolf. I'm not trying to make you nervous. I do, however, expect you to be loyal, hardworking, and an expert in your field. So if there is something you need from me that will help you to be better prepared, let me know. Going forward, I expect you to deliver a quality product ten times out of ten, with no exceptions. Are we clear?" He held her gaze with a powerful silence.

"Totally." With her body turning slightly in the chair, the paralegal followed him with her eyes from the window back to the head of the table. "Thank you, Mr. Montgomery. I will digest the notes you've made and will provide you with a revised brief. You won't be disappointed again." She scooped up the brief from the table and made a hurried exit.

His day had begun with an obituary and the picture of a dead man thrown in his face. It was midday, and his employee had implied that he was intimidating, hard to please, and unsure of himself. What was next?

Chapter 24

The muggy air was interrupted by an occasional cool breeze that swept in to offer temporary relief. Maxwell placed his shades on the bridge of his nose while walking down the courthouse steps. His case was one court date away from a guilty verdict. Maxwell had already added it to the win column of his undefeated record. He strolled two blocks before reaching the city hall building. After filing the documents, he had enough time to make it back to his office for his afternoon meeting. It was shaping up to be a great day.

When Maxwell was a few steps away from the parking garage, he wiped the sweat from his brow. He couldn't wait to blast the air-conditioning in his vehicle. Perhaps the cool air would gently usher him toward the meeting he was headed off to. He took a quick swipe at his forehead, brushing away the beads of sweat resting there. If only wiping thoughts of the deacon from his mind were just as easy.

Maxwell was determined not to be late and stepped up his pace. He gripped the handle of his briefcase tighter as he rounded the corner. Maxwell's eyelids widened as he gasped and jumped back a couple of steps to avoid crashing into a man who was coming around the corner from the opposite direction. The man stopped mid-stride.

"Well, if it isn't Attorney Maxwell Montgomery. What a surprise running into you, literally," Pastor Harris said, humored. "How have you been?"

"I'm good. Just busy." Maxwell extended his hand.

Pastor Harris shook his hand without overthinking the encounter. He'd stopped trying to figure out why God kept putting Maxwell in his path. He wasted no time wondering. He would just follow God's lead when it came to Maxwell Montgomery.

"I'm in a hurry. Good to see you, but I better get going," Maxwell added.

"Okay. Then I'll catch you another time." The pastor began walking away but then turned back. "The doors to the church are open anytime you want to visit. We'd love to have you. In the meantime, I'm praying for you and your family," Pastor Harris told him. Then he turned and trotted down the sidewalk.

There was no response given. Maxwell didn't need his prayers. Didn't the good preacher have enough folks to pray for? According to Garrett, Faith Temple was taking in over a half a million dollars a week in collections. His prayers could be directed to the paying customers, and he could leave Maxwell out of it. Pastor Harris didn't know it yet, but his glory days were coming to an end. And when Maxwell was finished, the pastor would be concentrating his prayers on himself, with none to spare.

Ten minutes away from his office, Maxwell gave in to what he called curiosity, as he refused to label the emotion as anything else. He made a quick phone call first. "I need you to push my two o'clock meeting back a couple of hours. Something's come up. Give me a call back if you have a problem rescheduling."

"Sure, Mr. Montgomery. You've got several messages and a package that was delivered."

"It will have to wait until I get in." He ended the call and made a hard U-turn as his tires squealed loudly. Then he cranked the volume of the radio louder than usual. Perhaps the noise would drown out the loud voice telling him to go back and forget about what he was about to do. If Maxwell gave it too much thought, he might not do it.

What could he say when he got there? Would she listen to him? Would he even be able to get past the doorstep? For once, he had no plan of attack. He simply felt compelled to drive to the house on Stenton Avenue, and the closer he got to his destination, the stronger the pull became. He pressed down on the accelerator. The sooner he got there, the better.

He drove through the neighborhood. Nice homes, nothing fancy, but the homes and lawns were well kept. He turned the corner and reduced his speed. His car's navigational tool took him to the address he'd recalled seeing numerous times in the case files last year, before turning his evidence over to the prosecutor. As Maxwell approached a house in the middle of the block, he saw two boys playing basketball in the driveway. He wanted to get a closer look. The basketball rolled toward the end of the drive. The shorter boy of the two ran after the ball. Maxwell turned his head away and glanced across the street.

Why did he do that? He didn't typically avoid any challenge or uncomfortable situation. Surely, he could look a little boy in the eyes. He'd stared down plenty of crooks in his line of work. He parked the car at the curb, shut off the engine, then took the uneasy steps that placed him at the front door. Ironically, he was standing on a doormat that said WELCOME. He was sure that didn't apply to him. He heard the doorbell ring inside the house when he pushed the button.

"Hey, mister. Who are you looking for?"

The boys had stopped playing basketball. The taller, older-looking boy had spoken, forcing Maxwell to face him. "I'm looking for Mrs. Burton. Is she your mom?"

His gaze shifted to the other boy and then back to the boy who'd spoken to him.

"Yes. She's in the house."

"Is this your brother?" Before Maxwell could get the answer he wanted, the wooden front door flung open.

"Don't you talk to my boys. Don't you dare talk to my boys." Her hands flapped in the air. "Go in the house. Right now. Go," she told her sons.

Maxwell waited until the boys were out of sight. Then he said, "I'm Maxwell Montgomery, and I—"

"I know exactly who you are. You've got a lot of nerve coming here. Haven't you done enough? Did you come here to get my sons too?" She stepped from the doorway and onto the welcome mat, forcing Maxwell to stumble backward to get out of her way. Her head jerked from left to right. "Did you bring the police with you? I guess you came to arrest me next."

The unwelcome visitor wondered if the neighbors were watching. He didn't need anyone recognizing him. "Can we talk inside? I promise to be brief."

"Ha. Your promises aren't worth a rusty penny. You promised Steve you would help him stay out of prison. The world can see what that promise was worth." Mrs. Burton spread her arms wide in front of her, forcing him backward another step.

Maxwell sucked in a deep breath that stung his chest. His words were much softer than hers. "I know I could have handled things differently. I'm not saying that your husband was innocent. I'm simply acknowledging that I could have referred him to a defense attorney, discussed his options with him, or taken his call one of the several times he tried reaching me."

Maxwell's stare slumped, along with his body. He lifted his hands in front of him, making something akin to the gesture of surrender. He'd talk fast before she cut him off again and possibly slammed the door in his face. "It was my job to build a case with the evidence that I had. I honestly believed that evidence was used to prosecute the guilty parties. I had no control over that. I regret that your sons will grow up without their father. I truly do." His voice cracked. "I lived through something similar myself."

"I don't want to hear your sob story. You used my husband, and now you have the nerve to come here. Humph. Don't be fooled, Mr. Montgomery," she said, practically snarling at him. "I'm not mild-mannered, like he was. That same man you lied to would be praying for you by now."

She snatched her searing stare away from him, trying to force her lip to stop quivering. She looked back at him and hurled more of her anger. "But not me. To the devil's hell with you, as far as I'm concerned. Guilt brought you here, and you're going to leave with it. Remember that you have to live with the fact that you sent an innocent man to prison and he ended up getting killed. Whether it was a mistake or done purposely, you did it. You won't be able to clear your conscience by coming here. I have no mercy or forgiveness to give you. You get out of my face, out of my yard, and away from here."

Maxwell turned and retreated to his car. He offered her not another word. His mind was blank. He effortlessly drove his car to his office and parked in the stall with his name on it. The drive had been a blur. He wished the conversation with Mrs. Burton had been a simple blur, instead of a cold and brutally aggravating reality.

Chapter 25

Maxwell's day started with a five-mile jog before the sun rose. He showered, dressed, and had two cups of coffee before tackling the next stage of his morning. He reached for the soft Italian leather briefcase Nicole had given him. He didn't allow himself to think of her often. The briefcase's shiny solid gold letters *M.M.* brought back memories of a woman who had wanted more from him than he had to give. She'd wanted his heart. She'd wanted to be first on his priority list. Toward the end he'd realized that Nicole wanted him to need her and love her. How could he, when love and dependency were the two things Maxwell had intentionally left behind when he slammed the door on his family over twenty years ago? Vowing never to be clouded by a weak emotion like love or need had kept him strong and successful. There was no reason to change, or was there?

He stood captive by the briefcase and the woman it forced him to remember. Why hadn't she just left well enough alone? Things were comfortable between them. No real definition of who they were to one another, just an unspoken understanding. They were both career driven, they worked long hours, and they saw each other whenever they could. Admittedly, her desire for a committed relationship wasn't really random. It arose after a flight she was on nearly crashed. The incident caused Nicole to reevaluate her priorities. She wanted his to change too, but Maxwell couldn't do it. He couldn't abandon his self-appointed mission. Wind chimes hanging from the deck near his pool sang out, and the spell that had Maxwell drifting back in time was broken.

He picked up the briefcase and tossed his suit jacket across it, and out the front door he went. Maxwell was in the car before he realized he'd forgotten a file. Once he'd gone back inside and had the file in hand, the phone on his home office desk rang. He glanced at the wall clock and saw that it was 7:20 a.m. There was time. He decided to answer the call.

"Maxwell Montgomery."

No response.

He barked hello twice. Still, there was no response, so he hung up the phone. He was two steps away from the door to his home office when the phone rang again. He snatched it up. "Hello," he said with a strong voice.

He heard only the sound of heavy breathing. He pulled the phone from his ear, hit it against the palm of his hand a couple of times, and repeated, "Hello."

The heavy breathing grew louder. He punched the END button with his finger and tossed the cordless handset on the desk.

No time to waste on prank calls. He hustled down the hallway and out the front door to his car. He waved his key ring toward the front door, pressed a button, and engaged his house alarm.

The drive through his neighborhood showcased the usual early morning dog walkers and the sprinklers raining down on a host of lawns. Five miles into his drive on the expressway, Deacon Burton immediately flooded his thoughts. It had been a couple of days since he'd battled the deacon's voice in his head. Maybe that was progress; hopefully, a full night's sleep would soon follow. Maxwell pressed a button on the steering wheel and turned on the radio to drown out his internal chatter. Regret and second-guessing didn't pay the bills.

A need to regroup took over. He gave the command to dial to his hands-free device. He was about to disconnect the call when Garrett answered.

"Hey, man, I'm on my way to the office now. If you have time, I'd like to get together this morning to discuss your progress on our favorite project." Maxwell folded in his bottom lip and raked his teeth over it.

"Sure, but my morning is pretty tight. I can't get downtown until later this afternoon."

"This is important. I prefer to meet sooner," Maxwell stated.

"Uh, let me see."

"Oh, what the heck. I'm not too far away from your office," Maxwell said. "I can stop by now. Will that work?"

"Sure. I'll pull the file."

Maxwell ended the call, but his mind was stirred up. The investigation of Pastor Harris and his church had to be thorough. He didn't need any reporters or the community second-guessing his integrity or his intentions. Maxwell pressed hard on the accelerator, anxious to hear what Garrett had to say.

Thoughts bounced around in his head as he drove. Had Garrett found some dark secret that the perfect pastor thought he'd buried so deep that no one would find it? Maybe he'd changed his name too. Perhaps he had to because he was a child molester or a woman beater and wanted to bury his ugly past. Maybe he had an illegitimate child somewhere. Maxwell couldn't wrap his head around the wealth of possibilities. It could be anything. Whatever it was, he hoped it was juicy enough to be used as a cornerstone in building a case against Pastor Harris and his beloved Faith Temple.

Just then Maxwell's cell phone rang. He'd propped it up in the car's console, and when he looked down at it, he saw that the call was restricted. He wasn't about to allow any nonsense to alter his mood. He hit the SILENCE button, turned on the radio, and sailed down the expressway to his destination.

Chapter 26

The traffic was light, and only a few people strolled along the sidewalks. So Maxwell had his choice of parking spots along the street. He maneuvered into a space, hopped out of the car, and dropped enough coins into the meter to secure an hour of parking. Maxwell entered the building where Garrett's new office was, and checked the guide. Suite 238 was right down the hall. Just as Maxwell reached the door, Garrett appeared and unlocked it. Maxwell followed him into his office.

"Nice setup," Maxwell told Garrett, as he scanned the interior before sitting down on an expensive-looking sofa. "Looks like somebody is coming up." Maxwell grinned as he shook his head in approval.

"Business is good. Plus, I can't have you coming to a dump to meet with me—" The phone on Garrett's desk interrupted him. He went to the desk and pulled out a black folder and handed it to Maxwell. "Excuse me. I need to take this call." He headed into the next room.

Maxwell unbuttoned his suit jacket and settled back into a corner of the sofa with the folder. He opened it, and Pastor Harris's hazel-colored eyes seemed to jump off the page before Maxwell and glare at him as he stood behind a podium, pointing his finger. After sifting through a few more pictures of the pastor, his wife, and the ministerial staff, Maxwell paused. Then he flipped back to the photo of Pastor Harris at the podium before resuming his assessment of the folder's contents. It was packed with photos, background reports, job histories, and details about each person on the church's staff, including such tidbits as a spouse's maiden name and the names of children. The folder included information on several staff members whom the pastor had either removed entirely or given some type of disciplinary action and subsequent training. Maxwell wasn't pleased. Fifteen minutes elapsed, and every photo had been examined. Every report had been skimmed. Garrett entered the room just as Maxwell closed the folder.

Maxwell patted the bulky folder as he balanced it on his knee, then stood. "You have more, right?" he said with an undeniable note of frustration in his voice. Peeking inside the folder, he told Garrett, "This is nothing. Where's the meat?" He flailed his free arm in the air. "I could have gotten this from newspaper articles and a quick visit to the office of vital records." He shoved the folder at Garrett.

Garrett snatched the folder after giving Maxwell a hard stare. He went to his desk and dropped it there. Facing Maxwell and leaning on the front edge of his desk, he defended his work. "I'm still waiting for the personal tax returns, loans, bank balances, and the status of their faith-based grants." He hurled additional facts at his best paying client.

"This is not enough. What else do you know? There has to be something in his background." Maxwell shoved his hand down into his right pants pocket. "He's a preacher. Come on. We know there has to be dirt and corruption."

Garrett pushed himself off the edge of his desk and stood up straight. "Pastor Harris started preaching at nineteen. By the time he was twenty-five, he was an ordained minister. Over the last fifteen years he's built a ministry that's well established in Philadelphia and abroad. People come from all over to hear him preach and have him pray for them. They say he has a gift for healing. So far, no one has anything bad to say about him."

Maxwell burned with fury. "I don't want to hear this garbage. Everybody has an enemy. He's like all the rest, and I'm going to bring him down."

"Maybe not." Garrett brushed the imaginary dust from his hands as he maintained direct visual contact with Maxwell.

He shoved back the left sleeve of his shirt to check his watch. "Nobody is that clean." Maxwell whipped his body around and stepped toward the door. Quickly, he turned again to face Garrett. "You're missing something." He clenched both fists and shook them in the air in front of him. Maxwell wasn't accustomed to losing. He didn't plan on starting a new trend. "You have to dig up something."

The investigator stepped behind his desk, placed his palms on top of it, and issued a challenge. "And what if there isn't anything? Are you going to make it up?"

Maxwell didn't appreciate the insinuation. He stepped to the edge of Garrett's desk. "We've had this argument one too many times lately. I know what I'm doing. I've been doing this a long time. I'm telling you there is something about this man. I feel it under my skin. If you do a thorough enough investigation, you'll find it." He buttoned his suit jacket and glanced to the left and right of him, taking in the art on the walls, the furniture, and the designer tie Garrett wore. "We've both done well together. Let's not mess this up. Change your strategy if you have to."

Garrett tugged at his mustache and listened with his teeth buried in his bottom lip.

"Here's an idea. Let's put this character to the test. Maybe we can have an attractive woman come on to him, and see if he falls for her." Maxwell continued as the idea unfolded. "What if this woman pretends to have a lucrative business deal that appears to benefit Harris's church? Of course, the deal involves illegal activity. If the price is right, will Pastor Harris go for the deal and put the church in bed with a con artist?"

"That's pushing it," Garrett said. "I wouldn't know where to get someone to do that deed."

"I do. I know someone from out of town who could help make that happen. I'll get you his contact information."

"Are you for real?" Garrett had to ask.

"Absolutely, I am. If this Pastor is as clean as you say he is, that little test shouldn't shake him at all. Do your job. Make it happen." He pushed the black folder, which was near the edge of the desk, closer to Garrett. "I'll give it to Pastor Harris. He's a slick one, but we're going to get him," Maxwell bellowed. "From the looks of this office, I pay you enough to get it done."

Garrett almost let a few words fly but decided this wasn't the time.

"Get it done." Briskly, Maxwell turned his back to Garrett and marched out of his office, leaving the door standing open. His words hung in the air long after he was gone.

Garrett hadn't reprimanded his client, but there weren't going to be too many more opportunities when he'd allow Maxwell to speak so harshly to him without consequences. No one got away with bad behavior forever, not even the untouchable attorney Maxwell Montgomery.

Chapter 27

It was midday. Maxwell decided to ramble through the bundle of mail his assistant had presorted. As he shuffled through the stack, one letter in particular surprised him. The return address included an inmate number, K84600. He tossed the letter into the trash and continued looking through the rest of the mail. Curiosity about the letter he'd tossed consumed Maxwell. It wasn't long before he dug it out of the trash, opened it, and read the first page.

> *Mr. Montgomery,*
> *I imagine you are quite shocked to receive a letter from me. I wouldn't be surprised if you didn't read it.*

Maxwell flipped to the back page. He grunted out loud and leaned back in his chair after seeing the name Bishop Ellis Jones at the bottom. Most of him wanted to stomp on the paper with his foot, but the yearning to hear what his nemesis had to say was too intense. He read on.

> *I felt compelled to write this letter, whether you read it or not. I was bitter, angry, and unforgiving the first twelve months that I was locked away in this cage. I know you don't believe it, but I was innocent of the charges brought against me, all of them. I did not condone wrongdoing in my church.*

My testimony at the trial was true, every word of it. I didn't know that Minister Simmons continued to sell drugs after I ordered him to stop. I didn't know he had drugs and money stashed in the church. Well, you've heard all of this before. That guilty verdict crushed my family, ripped me from my home and out of the ministry.

With my long sentence, the biggest regret is not being able to protect my family. Since I've been in here, my grandson was shot during a robbery and almost died. I could have kept him on the right track had I been there.

Maxwell thumped the letter with his finger and nodded his head. He didn't want to hear the bishop's lies and excuses, but the pages piqued his interest. He continued reading.

I'm not bitter and angry anymore. God is in the middle of all this. No matter how bad this looks, He has a plan. So, for whatever reason, this is where I am. Initially, my goal in writing you was to ask that you not hinder my appeal. However, I've realized you are not in control of these prison doors opening for me. So I am not reaching out to you on my behalf.

However, I do want you to know that Deacon Burton was definitely innocent. He discovered corruption in the ministry and informed both of us. If there is anything you can do to restore his good name, it would be a blessing. I'm asking you to look at the facts more closely. Anything you can do to help his wife and two boys would be the right thing to do.

You may never believe anything that I've just said, but it still had to be said. Know that regardless of what you've done, I forgive you for taking me from my family. I forgive you for tearing down a ministry that took years to build. I pray one day, when your eyes are fully open and your vision is clear, that you will be able to forgive yourself.
Sincerely,
Bishop Ellis Jones

Maxwell flung the letter into the air and watched the two pages drift to the floor. "He forgives *me*?" he shouted aloud. Who did Jones think he was? Maxwell didn't need the forgiveness of a convicted felon. What the bishop should have done was ask Paul and Ethel Montgomery for forgiveness. They were the ones who had gone to prison and had lost everything back then, while Bishop Jones had lost nothing. Not even his reputation. When the dust had settled, he looked like the innocent party, while Maxwell's parents had been shamefully labeled the perpetrators.

Maxwell shot up from his chair and walked around his desk twice. He snatched the letter from the floor, walked over to the window in his office, and shoved it open. He tore the letter into shreds and tossed the tiny pieces out the window and watched them float to the sidewalk below. He turned and peered at the locked drawer of his desk. His heart was beating fast, and he could hear himself breathing harder and harder. Maxwell kicked the locked drawer, delivering a powerful blow, three times. The desk moved forward two feet. Maxwell grabbed the back of his chair and dug his nails deep into the leather. He was determined not to scream out and release the fury blazing within.

"Mr. Montgomery, everything okay?" his assistant called out to him from the other side of the door. She knocked on the door, almost demanding a response.

Maxwell controlled his rage long enough to respond. "I'm fine." He knew he had to respond, or out of concern for him, she might open the door. He was in no mood to have anyone challenge him about anything or invade his space. He needed to be alone. The word *forgive* had taken him to the very edge, and he struggled to pull himself back.

Chapter 28

The civil attorney who hadn't lost a case hustled down Market Street, toward the civil courthouse. The scent of hoagies and a freshly cooked Philly cheesesteak with fried onions from a food truck on one of the side streets hung in the air, but there wasn't time to stop. Eager to get inside, he climbed the steps and entered the cool building.

He got on the elevator, pressed a button, and the elevator doors opened on the fifth floor. Maxwell considered the key points he planned to make on behalf of his client. Over two million dollars in donations had been misappropriated by a local organization, Christian Education Coalition. The organization's president denied the infraction, but Maxwell was poised to prove otherwise and reclaim his client's 1.6-million-dollar donation.

As he made his way down the long, busy stretch of hallway, a familiar person came into view. With hair that swept across her shoulders, her tall body, curvy hips, and confident stride spoke her name as she walked toward him. As her full lips, smooth skin, and pearl-white smile came clearly into view, he saw what seemed to be a childlike excitement wash over her face. She was just a few feet away. He clutched the handle of his briefcase tighter and felt his pulse throb in his hand. Seconds later, he and Nicole were standing within arm's reach.

"Maxwell, it's good to see you. Where else would you be but in the courthouse? Still the busiest man in town, huh?"

Maxwell broke the awkward pause that followed by hugging Nicole loosely. She didn't hug him back very tightly, but he wasn't bothered. "It's good seeing you. You look wonderful."

She spun around, completing a full circle. She placed one hand on her hip, and the other she brushed gently down her side, accentuating her small waist and her slightly wider hip. "See what you missed out on." Her face blossomed. She nodded toward the briefcase and flashed a smirk at him. "Glad to see you got some use out of the briefcase I gave you. I guess you didn't destroy everything associated with our relationship."

Maxwell dropped his gaze down to the flap on the leather briefcase and stroked the solid gold initials *M.M.* "I get plenty of compliments on this briefcase."

Nicole stepped closer and tugged at his perfectly placed tie. "Since you're headed to court, we can't have your tie out of place." Only silence spoke for a few seconds. Nicole retreated backward a couple of steps and lifted her wrist to check the time on her Cartier watch.

The ring on her left hand sparkled with prisms of color as it taunted Maxwell. The question leaped from his mouth. "You're married?"

"Engaged." Nicole lifted her hand and spread her wiggling fingers. The sparkling four-carat diamond, with sapphire baguettes raining down on both sides of the band, confirmed her statement. She shifted the ring on her finger, making sure it was positioned just right, as a wide, closed-mouth smile deepened the dimples in her cheeks.

His gaze bounced from her eyes to the large screaming diamond and then back again. He cleared his throat, initially not sure how to react. "Are you happy?" was the only complete sentence Maxwell could manage.

"Yes. Very."

"Then I guess congratulations are in order," Maxwell uttered, not sure if he meant the words or if he was jealous or simply shocked.

"Thanks. How about you? Are you seeing anyone?"

"No, no. I'm pretty busy. I have several cases in progress, and I don't have time for much else."

Her smile faded away. "Nothing has changed for you," she said. "I hate to hear that."

Again, silence attempted to take control. Maxwell stepped back into character. He was smooth, in control, and he kept his first love as his top priority. "I better get going. I can't be late to court."

"Of course not." Nicole leaned in close and embraced him.

With only one arm, he hugged her, stealing a hint of her perfume. Quickly, his arm fell away from her and was back at his side, where it belonged.

"Take care of yourself."

"Goodbye, Maxwell."

He stepped away first. No need to linger. His footsteps came to an abrupt halt as the urge to turn around and watch her walk away became too great. She was gorgeous, successful, and intelligent. If she hadn't become so needy last year and hadn't demanded more of a commitment than he could give, then maybe they would still be together. Nicole turned the corner and was out of sight, but Maxwell couldn't shake her scent. He felt a tinge of loss.

Dang. Why did she have to mess everything up? They'd had a good thing going for several years, with both of them placing their careers first. Then, all of a sudden, their casual, "no ties" relationship wasn't enough for her. She wanted love, kids, and a life together. That was crazy, Maxwell figured. What would he have done with a wife, kids, and a dog? Why would she think he could take time away from his top priority and feel good about himself? He turned and walked in the opposite direction from the one in which she'd gone. Twenty more steps gave him time to force feelings about Nicole out of his head. He pulled at one of the double doors and walked into the courtroom, a domain that always welcomed him.

A little over an hour later Maxwell emerged from the courthouse and became increasingly agitated. He hustled to his car in the parking garage, unable to force Nicole out of his mind. The drive back to his office took much longer than usual due to unexpected traffic. He tried playing music and listening to the news. Neither distracted him from Nicole.

Twenty minutes later, he parked his car, and made his way through the lobby of his building and got on the elevator. *Engaged!* He shut his eyes and shook his head, but only briefly. Maxwell refused to relinquish his power to a failed past. He had become an expert at doing that very thing and began regaining confidence in the way he handled his personal life.

Once he was securely behind the closed doors of his office, he booted images of Nicole out of his head, planted himself in the chair behind his desk, and got busy. He reached into the top drawer of his desk and pulled out a file. His gaze fell on the second drawer of his desk. He removed his keys from his pants pocket and stared at the drawer for a few seconds. *No sense looking backward.* He tossed the keys on top of the desk and revived his mission.

After he plotted the path for his case and made a phone call to the state's attorney, his concentration deserted him again. Nicole's words sang out in his mind. *Nothing has changed.* It wasn't long before he surrendered to the magnetic pull of the locked drawer in his desk. Before he could change his mind, his key was in the lock. The drawer inched open, and there it was. A lonely box covered with dust occupied the dark, cryptic space. Maxwell placed the box on top of his desk and brushed the dust from it with his hand. He lifted the lid, opening a tomb of wounds that he'd kept nearby for years. He emptied the contents of the box. Pictures, letters, unopened envelopes, greeting cards, and papers were sprawled across his desk.

A frayed picture that was over thirty years old and had begun to fade dared to face him. The four people in the picture wore smiles and held hands as they stood close to each other. They were a family then, and now they were strangers. He didn't know Paul Montgomery, Jr., anymore. He'd left that kid behind years ago, after running away from home his senior year of high school.

He sifted through the other items, which represented his past. There were unopened birthday and Christmas cards, along with letters that had been mailed to his office over the years. Why would anyone keep mailing things to someone who never replied? That just didn't make a lot of sense to him. He picked up several items and examined the postmarks. Then he raked up the bitter past and began shoving it back into the silent hiding place. The last item he held was a picture of Nicole. The picture spoke to him. He could hear the sadness in her voice and the words she'd said to him when she walked out of his life. *We're not traveling the same path. We don't want the same things.* A knock at the door freed him from the grip of dead feelings and a life that no longer existed.

"Just a minute," he called out. Maxwell dropped the picture into the box, slammed the lid on, buried the box back in the desk drawer, and then locked it. Now he was ready. "Come in."

His assistant opened the door and entered the room, talking. "You have an offsite meeting with Garrett in an hour and a half. Here's today's mail. The stack on the left needs your immediate attention," she announced, placing two stacks on his desk. "Would you like me to order you some lunch?"

His gaze shot down to the locked drawer in his desk and then dashed back to her. "No. I don't have an appetite. I have too much to do." He paused and then continued. "Can you call Faith Temple and see if Pastor Harris is available this afternoon."

"If he is do you want me to schedule a meeting?"

He stared up at the ceiling for a moment. "No, don't set up a meeting. Just let me know if he's free. Thanks."

Chapter 29

The fire burning within began consuming Maxwell to the point of desperation. He couldn't think clearly when it came to Faith Temple and his desire to destroy the church. He was willing to try just about anything. Maxwell sat in his car, behind his dark shades, ready and waiting for the opportunity to have a few minutes alone with the receptionist in Pastor Harris's office. It had been relatively easy to get a peek at her computer before, when he was waiting to meet with the pastor. Maxwell was disappointed to have gotten only one name during his initial visit. If he could get the woman away from her computer again, there was no telling what information he might uncover.

He looked down at his watch and tapped his finger on its crystal face. Wasn't Pastor Harris ever going to leave the church? When Maxwell's assistant had called earlier, she'd been told that Pastor Harris had appointments outside the church the entire afternoon. Maxwell didn't want to sit there all day, waiting for Pastor Harris to leave. Since it appeared that the pastor was going to be late caring for the blind and the lame, maybe Maxwell needed to do something drastic to get his behind moving. Maxwell could have someone call and say the pastor's house was being broken into to get him to leave. He was willing to try anything to get the pastor away from that church long enough for him to work his charm again.

Maxwell removed his shades for a clear view of the man walking toward the car parked in the stall close to the church's entrance. Yep, that was him. It was about time. The attorney posing temporarily as a spy was parked on a hill across the street. It was unlikely that the pastor would see him as he drove off. Still, Maxwell hid behind his shades again and slumped down in his seat.

He peered over the steering wheel and watched the tail end of Pastor Harris's Volvo exit the parking lot. He waited five minutes, then drove over to the church parking lot, reviewed his plan in his head, and stepped lively to the front door. He followed the once traveled path to the main office. If the same woman was there, he'd have a decent chance. Hopefully, the pastor didn't have more than one woman working in his office. Maxwell cleared his throat, shifted the knot in his tie, and stepped into character just as he walked through the office doorway.

His bright greeting, which showcased his expensive dental work, was his first smooth step in dazzling her with his charm. "Good afternoon," Maxwell said, discreetly reading the nameplate on her desk. "It's Martha, right?"

"Yes, Mr. Montgomery. How are you today?" She stood to greet him.

"Any chance I could speak with Pastor Harris?"

"No, sorry. He had an outside appointment."

Maxwell snapped his fingers in disappointment. "Oh, that's too bad. I had hoped to maybe bribe him with some lunch so we could finish our conversation from the other day. I should have guessed that he was out. I guess that means no shouting voices today." Maxwell pointed at Pastor Harris's study door and released a lighthearted chuckle.

Martha chuckled with him. "Would you like for me to check his calendar and try to fit you in this week?"

"Yes. Thank you."

She sat down at her desk, and with a couple of key strokes, Pastor Harris's calendar was in sight.

Maxwell stood in front of her desk, with his hand poking the side of his leg and his eyes scrutinizing the papers on her desk.

A young man's voice blasted into the room from the hallway. "Miss Martha, can you please unlock the gym? I need to get the floor cleaned."

"Yes. Give me a couple of minutes. Let me take care of Mr. Montgomery first."

"Oh, no problem. I can wait. We wouldn't want to hinder anyone who is anxious to get to work." Maxwell nodded his head at the young man.

"All right. Have a seat, Mr. Montgomery," Martha replied.

The patient attorney unbuttoned his suit jacket and sat down in the armchair behind him.

Martha pulled a large ring of jingling keys from her desk drawer. "I'll be right back," she assured him.

The clicking of Martha's heels was music to Maxwell's ears. Those noisy shoes would serve as an alarm to alert him when she was on her way back. He rubbed his palms together and shot out of the chair like a rocket and landed at her desk. He was relieved she hadn't locked her computer. She probably didn't know how. He searched through the pastor's calendar since it was already open. He froze for a couple of seconds, as if a snake had crossed his path, when he saw several dates marked with appointments with Deacon Burton's wife. Maybe Pastor Harris was providing more than grief counseling. Maxwell wasn't sure if there was something to probe there. He couldn't find any details about the reason for Pastor Harris's appointments with the widow. He could easily speculate but opted to search for substantial evidence. So, he ignored the visits made to Mrs. Burton and scanned through the various folder titles.

Bingo. This could be something. He clicked on the folder labeled "budget." He craned his neck to the right and looked toward the open door. No clicking heels sounded in the hallway. He'd better be quick, though. The folder opened, and there was a string of files for him to choose. Scanning the list, he stopped at *benevolence fund* and *pastor's salary.* Both options made him lick his lips. Maxwell chose the file marked *pastor's salary.* Before he could bite into the information and the numbers in front of him, someone gave him a harsh reprimand.

"Hey, just what do you think you're doing? Get away from that computer right now." Pastor Harris's voice rumbled with his fury. His eyeballs bulged out like bright headlights as he stormed toward the intruder.

Maxwell stumbled back and dropped into the chair as he scurried to get out of Pastor Harris's path. Pastor Harris pivoted the computer monitor so that it faced him. Dollars signs, his last year's salary details, and tithing records jumped off the monitor at him. Maxwell managed to get out of the chair and slide to the end of the desk. Pastor Harris shifted the monitor so that it faced Maxwell, and pointed at the numbers on the screen.

"I guess this is the information you were searching for up in the cloud somewhere, right? I suppose your next statement is that you were just helping to download it."

Maxwell straightened his tie and met the pastor's gaze straight on. "Actually, I was just—"

"I don't want to hear your lies. You were snooping into private, confidential records." The pastor pressed the power button, forcing darkness to overtake the monitor. "Aren't you sworn to uphold the law, or does your license give you special privileges to break the law? What's the word you like to use so much? *Hypocrite*?" Pastor Harris leaned across the desk, getting in Maxwell's face, and shouted, "Get your nickel-slick, con-artist behind out of this office. You were probably up to no good when you were here the other day, and I found you behind Martha's desk. Get out of here right now, before I call the police," he shouted.

"Police." Maxwell gave a hearty laugh. "You'll be calling an attorney when I'm done with you." He slid up closer to the edge of the desk and leaned in to face Pastor Harris. Maxwell lifted his head in the air and sniffed. "I smell federal warrants demanding that all church financial records be surrendered coming your way." The bold attorney licked his finger and shoved it in the air, pointing south. "I'm pretty sure you can expect an audit of your personal taxes as well. This big, towering mon-strosity of a building"—Maxwell waved his hand in front of the pastor's face, making a full circle—"will not protect you from the strong winds of justice blowing this way." The heated attorney's voice rose two notches in volume. "Make no mistake about it. I'm going to bring you down."

The pastor's volume matched Maxwell's as he struck back quickly. "With what? Lies, conjured-up evidence, and witnesses who you'll probably pay to spit out any venomous script you write for them? You may have other folks intimidated and scared, but I'm not. I've got two things on my side that I'm pretty sure you don't."

"And what would those be?"

"The truth and God."

Maxwell buttoned his suit jacket. "God can't protect you from me. Maybe when you get to those pearly gates in the sky." His gaze darted upward as he pointed toward the ceiling. "But while you're here on earth, your butt is mine."

The pastor slammed his fist down on the desk and sent a jar of mints crashing to the floor. "Get out of this church. Right now, get out. Do you hear me? Now."

"What in the world is all the yelling about?" Martha inquired, stepping only halfway into the office.

Maxwell tugged at both sleeves of his shirt. Slowly, he moved past Pastor Harris. He noticed the rise and fall of Pastor Harris's chest, and he could hear his heavy breathing. "Don't have a heart attack. I'm leaving. But you can believe I'll be back, and I won't be alone next time." Maxwell pressed his wrists together, then struggled to pull them apart as if handcuffs restrained them. He strolled from the office, right past two people huddled in the corner, and out the big wooden double doors of Faith Temple. Now Pastor Harris had been formally notified that his head was on the chopping block.

Chapter 30

"Martha, how in the world did Maxwell Montgomery get access to your computer and confidential financial records?" Pastor Harris's arms flew up in the air and then fell back down, his hands crashing against his body.

"What? What are you talking about?" Martha shook her head and scrunched up her lips.

The pastor stomped to her desk and swiveled the computer monitor around so that it faced Martha. He punched the power button hard. "*This* confidential information." He lifted up the monitor and held it in front of her. "Information like this has to be guarded. You know that. Obviously, you did not lock your computer. I've asked you more than once to lock it. This is not acceptable," Pastor Harris scolded.

Martha turned her back, and with her shoulders slumped and her head hung, she began to weep. She slipped a handkerchief from her skirt pocket and blew her nose.

Pastor Harris quickly put down the monitor to console her. He wrapped his arm around her shoulder and guided her to the chair at her desk.

"I'm so sorry. I would never do anything to intentionally hurt the church." Her words dripped with regret. Martha coughed and began gagging.

Pastor Harris got a small cup of water from the cooler in the corner and placed it in Martha's shaky hand. Martha gulped down the water and gasped.

"Please forgive me," Pastor Harris said. "I didn't mean to upset you. It's not all your fault. That Montgomery character is just a sneaky snake purposely using whoever he can to get what he wants." The remorseful pastor folded Martha's hand in his. "I need your help. So I'm going to need you to pull yourself together, okay?"

She sniffed hard, dried the tears from her cheeks, and picked up a pen from her desk. "Yes, sir. What can I do?"

"Call a meeting for this evening. I need the finance team and the senior ministerial staff. Everyone here, no exceptions. Tell them to skip dinner if they have to. I'll order something for everyone. This is a mandatory emergency meeting." Pastor Harris poked his finger into the palm of his hand. "Six o'clock sharp. Call our outside accountant. I need her here as well. We've got to cover all our bases. Tell each of them to be prepared to give a financial update on every department associated with this ministry. I'll be in my office. Let me know when everything is set."

Martha's pen zipped across her tablet as he spoke. "I'll get the calls started, and I'll order in some dinner."

Pastor Harris retreated to his private study, closing the door behind him. He paced the floor from the door to the window several times. He pondered what Maxwell Montgomery was looking for, wondering if it was something specific or any old tidbit he could blow up into a case. He plucked his glasses from his face and tossed them onto his desk. He plopped both flat palms against the wall and allowed his head to fall between his arms. His gaze landed on an ant crawling along the carpet. That was probably how Maxwell saw him and Faith Temple. Like a small ant, weak, insignificant, and something that he would crush under his foot on his way to the next church.

The pastor pushed his body away from the wall and stood tall. Maxwell Montgomery had better be ready to do battle with him and God if he expected to take down Faith Temple. Pastor Harris was secure in his role as a soldier in God's army. With God on his side, the pastor was confident that he couldn't lose.

Martha rapped on the office door and entered without waiting for a response. "I've gotten through half the calls. So far, everyone will be in attendance. I have ordered dinner and will set it out in the large conference room. Do you need anything else?"

"No, that should do it. Just let me know when you finish making the calls."

She floated out of his office, seemingly much calmer than before.

The remainder of the afternoon sputtered by for the pastor. Six o'clock couldn't come fast enough. He needed to get everyone in one room and prepare them for what was headed their way. More importantly, he needed to be sure Maxwell Montgomery wasn't going to find any whiff of impropriety when it came to the church's finances and investments. He sat down at his desk, scratched a few questions on a list for the emergency meeting, then popped up from his chair. Finally, the clock struck 5:40 p.m. The pastor darted to the conference room. By 6:00 p.m., the last person had arrived.

"Thanks, Martha, for setting out the food. Go on home now," Pastor Harris said once everyone was present.

"I'll see you in the morning," she replied, then left the conference room, pulling the door closed behind her.

Pastor Harris surveyed the faces around the large, oval conference room table. Every seat was occupied, and everyone peered toward the head of the table, seemingly waiting for him to speak. The pastor led the group in a brief prayer and took his seat. "I appreciate each of you coming out. I realize the meeting was called with very short notice. I need you all to know that our ministry is under attack."

"Attack? What?" one man said, glancing toward the window, while the others present whispered to one another, obviously concerned.

The pastor's voice rose over the others. "Is there anyone here who hasn't heard of Maxwell Montgomery?"

Rumbling voices were heard around the table.

"Who hasn't?" one person said. "He's the one who shut down Greater Metropolitan, and you know how big they were."

"Maxwell Montgomery . . . he's the attorney who goes around completely destroying churches. I've heard he's never lost a case," responded a silver-haired man sitting close to Pastor Harris.

Another person joined in. "Oh, Lord, please don't tell me he's coming after our church."

The man sitting on the left side of Pastor Harris gave a hoarse cough, and the piece of meat he was chewing flew right out of his mouth and onto the floor.

The last straw was the middle-aged man who tossed his ink pen into the center of the table, fell back into his chair, and said, "If he's coming after us, we don't have a chance. That guy goes in like a wrecking ball, and he doesn't leave a pulpit standing."

Pastor Harris slammed both palms of his hands into the table. "Stop it. We will absolutely not think that way. I need everyone at this table to grow a spine, and let's face this attack head on. Yes, Attorney Montgomery has launched an investigation of me and Faith Temple, but he's a man wrapped in flesh. He is not more powerful than God. So stop panicking," he demanded. "We're here tonight to make sure Faith Temple is on solid ground when it comes to church business. It is critical that there is nothing out of order with any of our finances, offerings, investments, anything."

A hush claimed the room, and all eyes around the table landed on Pastor Harris.

"Now, we know Montgomery is a hard hitter. He is going to turn over every possible stone during his investigation. We have to be sure there is nothing for him to find. Martha told each of you to bring the necessary detailed records for your areas. Let's start with the treasury report, followed by department budgets and spending," Pastor Harris directed.

The finance director was the last one to give a report. "Every penny is accounted for, and the financial reporting guidelines were followed with all the faith-based initiative federal and local grants. We are in good shape." The plump man, with a thick, bushy mustache that curled up at both ends, flashed a hard look at the accountant and back to the pastor.

"So everyone is saying our finances are squeaky clean in every area. Great." Pastor Harris thrust his palms together in a loud clap, then pushed both palms up into the air. "Awesome. Now, let that Maxwell Montgomery bring it on."

The female accountant turned to the plump man with the handlebar mustache. "You didn't tell him?" she said.

Joy drained from the pastor's face. His gaze fled from the accountant and rested on the plump man. "Tell me what?"

The finance director didn't respond.

"You tell him, or I will," the accountant insisted firmly after snapping shut her folder of documents.

"Somebody tell me something. What is it?" Pastor Harris rose slowly and planted his hands on the back of his chair and squeezed.

The finance director began rattling off details. "Remember the investment broker I told you I was working with last year, the one who I'd decided the church should discontinue using?"

"Get to the point," the pastor instructed.

"Well, he was found guilty of insider trading, and some of the church's portfolio consisted of investments he had made using that insider information. It's a—"

The pastor shouted, "What? Are you kidding me? This—"

The plump finance director cut the pastor off. "Wait, wait. It's all taken care of. We agreed to sell the portfolio under the margin of profit and relinquished all ties with the broker. He informed the trade commission that the church was completely uninvolved in the selection of investment items in our portfolio. The broker had full control of that. Of course, the more money his clients made based on his investments, the more commission he earned. So that was his incentive in padding the church's investment portfolio. But everything is okay now."

Pastor Harris whipped around to face the window, giving his back to the group. He folded in his lips, determined to think before speaking. This couldn't be happening. He trusted the educated and highly success-ful finance director to oversee the church's investments, and he'd allowed a fraud to sneak in the back door. Pastor turned slowly to face the silent group.

"How was this discovered?" he asked.

The accountant spoke up. "I found some reporting discrepancies when I performed an unscheduled audit of the church's investments." She held on to the plump man's stare until he snatched his gaze away from her.

"And nobody thought it important to tell me?" Pastor Harris slammed his fist on the table. "So we are just going to give Montgomery ammunition against us? I can't believe this has happened. There is no reason for us to be in this precarious situation. Each of you know exactly what I expect. We have an outside accountant as part of our team that manages our finances." The pastor waved his hand toward the female accountant. "The whole purpose of having one is to avoid any suggestion of impropriety and to provide an extra layer of checks and balances." He stepped away from the table and paced to the door and back to the table. "It's simple, people. Don't you know how critical it is that we safeguard the church's integrity? If our accountant found it, you better believe that bloodhound Maxwell Montgomery will find it."

Pastor Harris swiped his hand down the front of his face, stared at the floor, lifted his head, and allowed his stern gaze to pass over each face in front of him. "We will meet again tomorrow, same time, to devise a plan to offset the fallout if news of the investment fiasco bites us in the butt. This meeting is over. I will, however, be scheduling a one-on-one meeting with each of you. Martha will call you to schedule it. You can all leave."

People wasted no time backing away from the table, gathering up their belongings, and dashing for the exit.

"Not you. We need to talk." Pastor Harris stretched out his arm and pointed his finger at the finance director. As the head of the finance committee, he couldn't think the pastor was letting him off that easy. He had put the ministry at risk, then had covered it up, further jeopardizing Faith Temple's good name. The eager pastor watched the last person file out of the conference room. The man he'd asked to stay behind stood a few feet away from him.

Pastor Harris shook his head, his gaze burned into the man's face. He was accountable, and there would be consequences. That was Pastor Harris's way. He wasn't inclined to change.

Chapter 31

Memories of Nicole had haunted him every day since he'd run into her a week ago at the courthouse. Was it because she still looked great, or was it the engagement? He wasn't sure. Either way, he couldn't shake her off. Married? That was hard to digest. Who was this guy? Maxwell's curiosity pushed him to action. After arriving at his destination, he decided to see if her number was the same. He scrolled through his contact list and stopped at her name. He pressed down on the phone icon. Three rings and she was on the line.

"Maxwell, this is a surprise."

"I see you still have the same phone number."

"Yep. So.what's going on?" she asked.

"Nothing really. Just thought we might get together for lunch whenever you have time." He wrapped his palm around the wood-grain gearshift.

"Ah, really? Why?"

"You're getting married. Figured we could celebrate, if you're not too busy."

"Sure. Why not? When and where?"

"How about this afternoon?"

"I think I can squeeze you in," she replied.

"How about twelve thirty at the restaurant downtown? The one that serves the cherry pie you love so much."

"You remember that?"

"I remember more than you think."

"What is that supposed to mean?"

"Nothing, really."

"Okay, Maxwell. Then I'll see you soon."

Maxwell ended the call, climbed out of his car, and went into the bank across the street.

"Mr. Montgomery, good to see you again. How may I help you?" The short man in a suit welcomed him with a firm handshake.

"I need to set up a trust fund anonymously. Actually, two trust funds. The money is to be specifically used for college. Can you help me with that?"

"Absolutely, Mr. Montgomery. Right this way."

Thirty minutes later Maxwell reviewed the details of the trust funds. The bank had also drafted a letter confirming that the two interest-bearing accounts, each with a balance of one hundred thousand dollars, had been established for Mrs. Burton's sons. No information regarding the source of the funds was provided; the letter said only that the accounts were an anonymous gift. The letter was to be hand delivered to Mrs. Burton.

At least she wouldn't have to worry about how to educate her children. Maxwell's parents had been swindled out of his college fund. As a result, his road to college had been a rocky one. Maxwell's cloak of guilt felt a little lighter, until he considered the boy's current well-being. What good was a college fund down the road if Mrs. Burton couldn't put food on the table today? Maxwell found his personal banker, who hadn't gotten far away.

"I need two thousand dollars a month sent indefinitely and anonymously to Mrs. Burton. Call it a survivor's stipend or whatever."

"But Mr. Montgomery, there will be tax implications if she receives a regular payment."

With as much money as Maxwell kept in the bank with his business account alone, he expected his request to be handled without resistance. "Do what has to be done so that she gets the money. The taxes are on me."

As he walked out of the bank, his eyes darted up to the clock on the wall. He had just enough time to get downtown after he made a quick call. He dialed his assistant and strolled across the parking lot with his phone to his ear. "I'll be back in the office around two thirty. I have a lunch meeting this afternoon."

"Oh, I don't have that meeting on your calendar."

"I know. I scheduled it myself. I'll be in later." With his assistant informed of his plans, he ended the call, hopped in his car, and drove straight downtown. He was anxious to see Nicole.

The valet parked his car. Maxwell entered the restaurant and was seated right away. When the waiter came to his table, he quickly ordered for both himself and Nicole. Ten minutes later, he was typing a short note on his tablet. His attention darted toward the front door when Nicole entered the building. She took confident strides, her six-inch heels sounding against the marble floor. Her hair bounced around her shoulders, and the tan linen skirt suit she wore accentuated her flat stomach and trim waistline. When she reached the table, her vibrant eyes engaged him immediately.

"You're here before me?" She tapped the crystal on her watch with her finger. "That never happened when we were together."

"You're hilarious," he tossed back as she sat down.

"I was surprised by your lunch invite."

"Why? I know you enjoy a good meal," he replied.

"What are you trying to say?"

"Not a thing," he said, grinning. "You look amazing. I can tell you've been working out."

Nicole lifted her arm and flexed her right bicep muscle and poked it with her fingertip. "I've got to look good in my wedding dress."

Just the topic of conversation he was interested in. "So, how are the plans coming along?"

"Pretty good."

The waiter appeared with two tall glasses of sparkling water, chilled salad plates with colorful garden salads, and warm freshly baked bread. "Enjoy. I will check on you shortly."

"Well, aren't you efficient, Mr. Montgomery. Thanks for ordering my favorite." She smiled, and they continued chatting as they ate.

"Who is the lucky guy?"

Her ring drew his attention for a few seconds. "His name is James Washington. He's a psychiatrist from D.C., never been married, and has no children. He's a really nice guy."

In Maxwell's profession, he'd learned to read people well. Where was the sparkle in her eyes when she said his name? He didn't detect any enthusiasm when she talked about this James fella, or was Maxwell seeing what he wanted to see? He wanted to poke around the subject a bit more. "What is it about him that makes him 'the one'?"

"He knows how to make me a priority. I can tell you that," she snapped.

The questioning attorney's brow wrinkled. He lifted both palms so that they faced her. "Sorry. I didn't mean to upset you."

A weak closed-mouth smile claimed her lips. "No, *I'm* sorry. I don't know where that came from. Let's talk about something else."

He obliged. For the remainder of their lunch, Maxwell masked his curiosity with questions about her firm, where she'd traveled lately, and what piece of art she'd added to her collection. When lunch was over, he escorted Nicole to her car and found a surprise.

"I thought you didn't like sports cars." He tipped the valet and held the car door open for her.

"Well, people change," she responded.

"Yes, I guess they do."

She slid behind the steering wheel, thanked him for lunch, and left him standing at the curb, watching her burgundy BMW turn the corner.

Lunch had gone fairly well. Maxwell shifted gears in his mind as he revved up his engine and drove off in the opposite direction, quite intrigued. He'd go for dinner next.

Chapter 32

Pastor Harris picked up his Bible and rubbed his fingers across the raised letters that spelled out his name. He was a man of God, and God would have to take care of the situation he'd prayed about. All he could do was be obedient and just keep preaching. God would have to do the rest.

He grabbed a seat in his study at the church and read the article about Maxwell Montgomery's investigation of Faith Temple. Of all the churches in the area, Pastor Harris couldn't figure out what was motivating Maxwell to come after his ministry. The headline read WILL FAITH TEMPLE WITHSTAND THE MONTGOMERY MACHINE? Pastor Harris answered that question for himself. Nothing had been confirmed: there were no improprieties, there was no issue with the church's 501c3, and the board of trustees was beyond reproach. His salary was managed and paid by the board of trustees. He never touched a dime from any of the offerings that were collected. The treasurer and finance director were bonded and handled the church's money and investments meticulously. He was certain they could account for every penny, even those that fell onto the floor and rolled into a corner.

Maxwell had messed around and picked a fight too big for him to handle. Pastor Harris aimed to let him know. He scrolled through his directory. When he found Maxwell's number, he dialed and waited patiently for someone to answer.

"Attorney Maxwell Montgomery speaking."

"This is Pastor Harris. I appreciate you taking my call. I know you're busy working on the case against me."

"Nothing personal. I'm only doing my job."

"Well, I want you to know I don't have anything to hide. My ministry is an open book."

"Are you sure about that? Everyone has something to hide."

Pastor Harris sat up straight in his chair. "Does that include you?"

"Humph. I'm not the one on a stage every Sunday morning, putting on a show to take people's hard-earned money."

"Then why bother digging for information when you can ask me whatever it is that you want to know?" Pastor Harris retorted.

"You expect me to blindly believe whatever you tell me? That's called faith, right? Well, the law isn't founded on faith. It's founded on proof. You know, a little something called evidence. So I'll stick with the investigation process. It's proven to be most effective in the past."

"Well, Mr. Montgomery, complete your investigation. When you come up empty-handed, and you will, the doors of the church will still be open to you. Until then, I want you to know that I forgive you and will be praying for you. Have a good day, Attorney Montgomery."

The line went dead. Maxwell was the only one still holding the phone. *He forgives me*? He slammed his hand down on the desk, thinking about the pastor's arrogance. His breathing got heavy. A vein in his right temple became engorged and began to pulsate at the same rapid tempo as his heartbeat. His anger thrust him from his chair and drove him to pace his office floor. Why did *he* need forgiveness? For doing his job? For daring to be the one who challenged organized religion? Did he need forgiveness for being the one to hold the church accountable?

Maxwell marched back to his desk and yanked open the top left drawer. He rummaged through it with determination and fury, shoving things out of his way. The furious attorney latched onto the stress ball as if it were a lifeline. He squeezed it and counted under his breath, "One thousand one, one thousand two, one thousand three . . ." He stopped when his palm was tired and cramping. His breathing had slowed, and the vein in his temple was no longer swollen.

He plopped into his high-back chair, planted his arms against the armrests, and tapped his left foot. The intercom on his desk buzzed. Before it could buzz a second time, he reached over and hit the DO NOT DISTURB button. With his head pressed against the headrest, Maxwell slowly swiveled his chair around. His back faced the office door. He closed his eyes and allowed the quiet to wash over him.

Pastor Harris sat there, silently considering his conversation with the attorney. He was driven by a mission that seemed right. Something the attorney had said echoed in the pastor's mind. *Everyone has something to hide.* The pastor considered the implications of those words. Perhaps there was another phone call that he now needed to make—one that Pastor Harris had hoped to avoid, but Maxwell wasn't giving him much choice. He had to find a top notch defense attorney just in case this battle went the distance. He didn't know where to begin looking and would have to rely on God for direction.

Chapter 33

Sitting on the sofa in her living room, Nicole reached for the glass of wine her fiancé was handing to her. He sat down next to her and placed his glass on the sofa table behind him.

Nicole fidgeted, like she couldn't find a comfortable position next to him.

"Relax so we can talk about our plans."

"Not now. I'm tired. I just want to unwind," she said, sipping the wine.

"I get that, but every time I bring up the wedding plans, you want to change the subject."

"That's not true," she replied.

"Okay, so when are you selling this condo and moving into my house?"

Nicole was ready for marriage, at least she thought she was. It was refreshing to have a man who knew what he wanted and wasn't afraid to commit, but she didn't want to get lost in his world. She'd worked hard to be her own woman. She was a senior executive who could make her own decisions. Selling her place meant surrendering a piece of her independence. Once she moved into James's house, he'd be able to call the shots. That didn't sit well with her.

"I have not decided whether to sell my condo or keep it as a rental property. We're still discussing that one, remember?" There were several other issues that had to be resolved, but she didn't want to deal with it right now.

She'd rather change the subject. "I need your help." She grinned and stroked his forearm.

"Sure, babe. What do you need?" he said, gazing at her.

"Well, I sort of committed us to babysitting this weekend."

"Who are we babysitting?"

She snuggled closer to him and offered a soft answer. "My friend's two-year-old daughter."

He leaned back, putting a slight bit of distance between them. "Now, you know I don't do the kid thing."

"Come on. Help me out. We'll spend a few hours watching a cute little girl play with her toys. It'll be fun." She squeezed his shoulder. "Besides, this will give you a good taste of what it will be like as a parent."

"Nicole, stop it. I don't want to debate this. You can't manipulate me into changing my mind about having kids. I do not want children. I've told you that repeatedly, and I mean it."

Nicole sat up straighter and faced him. "But you'd be a wonderful father. I know it."

"Maybe, but it's not for me. You know I grew up in a lousy family. My parents argued from sunup until sundown. I have a dysfunctional relationship with my parents and my siblings. It's a shock that I made it out of there with any type of emotional stability. I'm not doing that to any kid. That's final."

She popped up from the sofa and pushed up both sleeves of her blouse. "You don't have to help me babysit, but this discussion isn't over if we plan on getting married. The bottom line is that I want children," she muttered. "And that's that," she stated and headed toward the kitchen, deserting him completely. Her words were heavy with annoyance and hung in the air.

***

In his office downtown, Maxwell struggled to focus. He had too much to do to allow his concentration to be derailed. He shoved Nicole from his thoughts. It had been over a week since they had had lunch. He needed to harness his thoughts. He had no time to spare, and there was no room in his mind for anything but exposing the senior pastor of Faith Temple. Maxwell was determined to unmask Pastor Harris in a very public manner. After calling a couple of contacts in the state capitol and the local media outlets, he jotted down another angle to pursue in his investigation. Maxwell wasn't one hundred percent comfortable with Layne's story about Pastor Harris and Faith Temple, but there wasn't any other story that he could leak to the media. A moment later there was a knock on his door. He couldn't be disturbed. The knocking persisted. He went to the door and snatched it open. His assistant was standing there.

"I'm pretty tied up. What do you need?"

"Sorry to disturb you, but there's a woman on the phone who will give only her first name, Nicole. She said you'd want to speak with her."

Maxwell became chipper. "Yes, uh, please forward her call, and thanks," he said, closing the door before his assistant could respond.

The line had barely rung before he grabbed it. "What a surprise hearing from you," he told Nicole in a light-hearted voice. "You must need an attorney." He considered the files and papers scattered across his desk, which dared him to stop working. He took the challenge and turned his chair away from the desk and stretched out his legs. Maxwell loosened his tie and gave her his attention, something he would not have done a year ago.

"Don't need a lawyer. Just a friend."

"Are you okay?" He tightened his grip on the phone. His faint smile dissolved.

"I guess I'm okay."

"You don't sound okay. What's up?"

"Nothing really. I'm just a little frustrated."

"I can stop by your place when I finish here if you want to talk. I'll bring some of that hand-packed butter pecan ice cream you like."

"No, that would be disrespectful to James, having you come over. I appreciate the offer, but I'll have to pass. I'll be fine."

"I understand." But Maxwell wasn't giving up so easily. "But didn't you tell me you need a friend? If so, I'm your man."

She laughed.

They engaged in small talk briefly.

"So what is it that has you all frazzled?" he asked.

"I guess I'm still a little upset. James and I had a disagreement."

"Couples do have those occasionally."

"I guess, but you and I didn't have disagreements, until I wanted to take our relationship to the next level and you didn't."

"And now you're getting married."

"Yes, I am."

He searched for excitement in her voice, but it was yet to be realized. He hadn't heard it in her voice when they met for lunch, and it wasn't there now. "Are you happy?"

Nicole was slow to answer. Seconds later she replied, "I'm getting married. Why wouldn't I be happy?"

His ability to extract information from an unwilling party kicked in. "Something is wrong. That's clear to me as your friend and as someone who knows you. I heard it in your voice when you called. You can talk to me."

Nicole cleared her throat but did not respond.

"Listen, Nicole." His voice softened. "What's wrong? I care about you. Whatever you tell me, it stays between us. Let me be your friend."

To her, he seemed genuinely concerned. That was unexpected coming from Maxwell. She allowed a quiet breath to slip across her lips. Afterward, words spilled out of her heart like water bubbling up from a fountain. "I don't know what's wrong. I'm happy. At least I have a measure of happiness. Don't get me wrong. I have no doubt that James loves me. He's very attentive, makes me a priority, and I enjoy spending time with him. We have a lot in common—"

Maxwell interrupted her. "You can have a lot in common with an enemy. There has to be more there, right? What is it?"

"He's a great guy. He reminds me of you in some ways. He's very driven and definitely knows what he wants and doesn't want." Her voice dipped. "Unfortunately, what he doesn't want is a child." She sighed.

"And you do?"

"Definitely. As a matter of fact, I don't think that I can be happy without children in the marriage. I want that special bond with my husband. I want to share the experience of having a child together. The pregnancy, the swollen feet, and especially the midnight cravings, I want it all." She pressed her palm against her flat stomach to soothe the ache inside.

Maxwell had nothing snappy or witty to say. For once, words escaped him. Being a friend was more difficult than he'd realized.

Chapter 34

Maxwell eased out of the parking lot and into traffic. He took a quick sip from his Starbucks cup and turned off his windshield wipers. The brief summer shower had only antagonized the humidity. He clicked the down arrow on the temperature control unit. As he stopped at a red light, he shifted his cell phone back and forth in his hand. Should he make the phone call he'd been considering for the past couple of days? It wasn't his business. Would Nicole be angry if he told her what was going to do? The green light gave him the go-ahead, but only in traffic. Still not sure he should do it, he drove another ten minutes toward city hall. In an instant, he whipped his car across a lane of traffic, with a screeching car horn loudly admonishing him. The NO PARKING sign at the curb did nothing to deter Maxwell.

No sense in calling Garrett for help. Maxwell remembered there was an old business acquaintance he could call. He'd used his services before meeting Garrett. Maxwell punched the CALL button the moment he located the name. The gatekeeper put his call right through.

"Hello, Mr. Montgomery. It's been several years since we've spoken. How may I help you?"

"I need a background check on someone." He tapped his fingertips against the steering wheel.

"We'd be glad to take care of that for you. You're not using Hughes Investigation any longer? We would be glad to get your business back."

"It's nothing like that. Garrett's pretty swamped with a project right now. I simply need the background check. Are you able to do it or not?"

"Of course we'd be glad to take care of it. I will get one of my investigators on it right away. What information do you have on the person?"

"The name is James Washington. He's from the Washington, D.C., area. Probably in his thirties. I think he's a psychiatrist in private practice. That's about all I have."

"That's a good start. I will get the information to you by the end of the week."

"Friday at the latest, right?"

"Absolutely, Mr. Montgomery. Not a problem."

"Okay. I can wait until then." Maxwell ended the call and pressed down hard on the accelerator. He was as eager to get to his destination as he was for the calendar to say Friday.

Quiet filled the house. No barking dog pleading to be taken outside. No wife and children to hustle out of the bathroom. No dirty pots left from the prior evening's home-cooked meal messing up his kitchen. Maxwell didn't have to be bothered with any of those inconveniences. He plopped down on the sofa in the living room with a glass of ice-cold ginger ale, a ham and cheese hoagie, and the remote control. The Philadelphia Eagles football game would fill his Sunday afternoon.

Sitting idly, he tried faithfully to push her from his mind; he had yet to be successful.

"Mr. Montgomery, I'm almost finished. As soon as I fold the last load of laundry, I'll be leaving," his cleaning lady called out.

"I forgot you were here. You're always so quiet."

"Well, you don't pay me to talk," the elderly lady said. "Half the time I don't believe you should be paying me to clean twice a week, when your house doesn't need it."

"We aren't going to have this discussion again, are we?" he said, very humored.

Maxwell enjoyed having her come regularly. She was the closest he had locally to a mother figure. She'd endured a hard life as a single mother who'd put her children through college, only to have her son die of cancer and her daughter in a car accident. She was a trooper with pride who wasn't looking for a handout. Maybe that was why he was so eager to help, without compromising her dignity. Paying her three hundred dollars twice a week for basically doing nothing was fine with him. The fact that she didn't go to church and was willing to work on Sundays ensured her employment with Maxwell indefinitely.

"By the way, I didn't cash my last week's paycheck. You made a mistake and paid me five hundred dollars too much. I have the check in my purse. I will get it, and you can write me another one."

"It wasn't a mistake. Your birthday was last week. The check is right. Cash it. Do something nice for yourself."

"Oh my," she said, choking up. "Every year you remember my birthday. I appreciate it." She dropped her head. "After my two children died, I didn't expect anybody else to do anything for me on my birthday, not having any other family and all." She slipped a handkerchief from her dress pocket. "It means so much to me that you remember my birthday. Not a year goes by that you forget. You're like a son to me." She dabbed at the corners of her eyes.

Maxwell was genuinely touched. "You deserve every dollar I pay you. I don't have time to even toss a load of towels into the washer. You take good care of this place."

"I try, and by the way, I just finished the kitchen floor. Be careful and don't you scuff it up now." She snickered at her own comment. "Oh, by the way, I think it was nice of you to attend that deacon's funeral." She untied her apron and folded it over her arm and turned to leave.

"What? What are you talking about?"

The cleaning lady faced her employer. "That deacon who was killed in prison. I figured you'd gone to his funeral. I just think that was nice of you."

His arm stretched out toward the TV, and he muted the volume. "I didn't go to the funeral."

She took a couple of steps closer to him. "Oh no? Huh. That's strange, because my neighbor was a close friend of the deacon and his wife. She told me she saw you there."

With his head tilted to the left and with a wrinkled brow, he was adamant. "I was absolutely not in that church, attending anybody's funeral."

"But my friend saw your car there when she walked up the sidewalk. Your plates say JUSTICE. She remembered seeing your car in the driveway a few times when she dropped me off here to work. That's how she knew your license plates. She said the funeral was so sad. The wife was just torn up, and those poor boys cried and cried."

"Would you mind getting me some potato chips to go with my sandwich?" he asked totally out of sorts.

"Sure thing, Mr. Montgomery. You wait right there." Off to the kitchen, she trotted.

Maxwell shot up from the sofa and fled to his office and shut the door. With his back pressed against it and his hand still holding the doorknob, the less than calm attorney gasped. He needed an escape. He had been certain no one saw him in the church parking lot the day of the funeral. His tinted car windows and dark shades hadn't provided the anonymity he'd hoped to maintain.

"Your chips are on the table, next to your sandwich. I'll see you next week," the cleaning lady called out to him.

He did not respond. The house phone rang. Glad for the distraction, he hustled over to the desk and snagged the handset quickly. It didn't even matter who was on the other end of the line.

"Son, it's your mom."

"Uh-huh." He peered through the blinds and watched his cleaning lady get into the passenger seat of an early model Impala, which then drove away.

"Paul, are you there?"

"Yes. I'm just busy."

"It's Sunday. Don't you ever rest?" his mother asked.

"Crime and hypocrisy don't rest. Why should I?"

"Well, I won't keep you long. I wanted to know if you will at least consider coming to a barbecue here at the house. Think about it before you say no. I really want you to come. Your father is feeling a little stronger. He has some good and bad days, but he's been feeling pretty good lately. A family barbecue would be nice. Your dad needs his family around him."

"Don't beg him. If he doesn't want to come, that's fine. Just leave him alone, Ethel," Maxwell heard his father's stern voice say in the background.

"Beg me. He should be begging me for my forgiveness. Mom, I've got to go. I won't be there. Tell Tyree I'll see him soon." He dropped the handset down onto the cradle, glad his father had given him a reason to decline the invitation.

He hurried up the stairs, taking them two steps at a time. With a fierce determination, he peeled off his clothes, tossed them to the floor, and pulled on a pair of swim trunks. Down the stairs and straight to the swimming pool he went. Maxwell dived in and sliced into the water with his muscled, heavy arms. He swam twenty laps in the regulation size pool, hoping to shed the family problems that nagged him.

After the last lap, he emerged from the cool water like a drowning man desperate for air. He propped his arms on the side of the pool and sucked air into his lungs while water dripped down his face. If he weren't the hard-core, "I don't need anybody" type, the water dripping from his face could have been mistaken for tears.

Chapter 35

Almost finished, Pastor Harris headed out of the social hall and up two flights of stairs. His long legs took some steps two at a time. He checked out the computer learning center, the conference room, all four bathrooms, and the youth recreation room. His weekly assessment of the entire church was complete. The new tile in the social hall had been installed. The church was spotless and ready for Sunday service. When he was on the way to his office, that nagging thought popped into his head again. Maybe having Maxwell Montgomery checked out wasn't a bad idea. What could it hurt? As he entered his study, his receptionist was preparing to leave.

"I'm heading out to lunch. Can I pick something up for you?" Martha asked.

"No, but thanks for asking." He stopped at her desk.

"Okay, but you know I'll have to tell the first lady. She gave me strict instructions to be sure you ate lunch."

"I'll grab something later, and I'll tell my wife you're on top of your assignment." Pastor Harris rapped his knuckles on her desk with a grin before he went on his way.

Maxwell's words followed him inside his study and wouldn't go away. *Everyone has something to hide.* What could Maxwell Montgomery be hiding? There had to be a deep-seated wound that was causing him to lash out so viciously against the church. Perhaps if the pastor understood the underlying source of Maxwell's anger, he could help him. It might be a long shot, but Pastor Harris was willing to proceed with finding an investigator. He sat down at his desk and swiveled his chair around to face the computer monitor. What criteria should he use to choose an investigator? His wife or someone on his staff usually did research for him, but this was something he had better take care of himself. Pecking with both index fingers, Pastor Harris punched *private investigator* into the search engine. Pages of results popped up on his screen. Then it hit him. Perhaps he should hire an investigator from another state. Maxwell Montgomery was very well known in Pennsylvania. With that in mind, he searched for investigators in Chicago. After reading through a few advertisements, he clicked on the ad that read, *No one or their secrets can hide from us.* That sounded like a good place to start. He grabbed the phone and dialed the number in the ad. If there was no answer by the fourth ring, he would hang up. One, two, three rings . . .

"Remington Investigation, how may I help you?"

Doubt crept in the moment someone answered the phone. Should he do it? Maybe he was completely off base.

"Hello? Is anyone there?"

The pastor's voice burst forth. "Yes, I'm here. I need some background information on someone. Can you help me?" His heel tapped against the floor rapidly.

"Sure we can. What's your name, sir?"

"Pas—" He stopped. Maybe it was better not to use his title. "Renaldo Harris," he stated.

"Who is the person you would like to have investigated?"

"Attorney Maxwell Montgomery. Have you heard of him?"

"No, but that won't hinder us. What kind of information are you looking for?"

"Basic background information, I guess. Who is he? Where did he come from? Does he have an arrest record? I don't know. You tell me. I just need to know as much about this man as possible."

"Not a problem. Anything worth knowing about him, we'll find it."

The investigator took some information from Pastor Harris, asked him several questions, and explained how the investigation would work. They talked another few minutes, and the pastor rattled off his credit card number before ending the call. He picked up an ink pen from the desk and tapped it against his lips. This investigation idea would probably turn out to be a waste of time and money. Certainly an attorney as smart and as hard-hitting as Maxwell Montgomery would have a squeaky clean background, with no surprises.

The inquisitive pastor wrote the name *Maxwell Montgomery* on a blank sheet of paper and circled it. He traced the circle several times, making it darker and darker. What if the investigation actually turned up something? Wouldn't it be interesting if he got a glimpse of the man behind the attorney's title? He dropped the pen on the paper. A heavy knock at the door stole his attention.

"Come in," he spat out while simultaneously sliding the paper with Maxwell's name on it underneath his Bible.

A short man dressed in a suit and carrying a package entered the office. "Hey, Pastor. Your receptionist wasn't at her desk. So I signed for your package."

"Thanks, Minister Townsend." He took the package and placed it next to his computer monitor.

"Pastor, do you have a few minutes to talk?"

"Sure. Have a seat. What's on your mind?"

The young minister unbuttoned his suit jacket and plopped down in the plush chair in front of Pastor

Harris's desk. He removed his glasses and rubbed at his eyes, fidgeting. The man placed his glasses back on his face and made visual contact with the pastor. "I hope you don't take this the wrong way, but all this stuff in the news about you and the church being investigated by that attorney, Maxwell Montgomery, is a real mess." He rubbed his palms together fast and felt the heat between them.

"What are you trying to say?" the pastor inquired.

"I know I've only been here a couple of years. I'd hoped to become one of your senior ministers eventually." He took his glasses off again and, staring at the floor, stammered, "I'm n-not sure being here right now is the best thing for me." Minister Townsend slipped his hand inside his suit jacket and pulled out a long white envelope. He stood and placed it in the center of the desk.

Pastor Harris scooped up the blank envelope. "What is this?" he inquired after turning it over and noticing it was sealed.

"It's my resignation. I really hate to do this, but I don't see any other option. Every church that Montgomery guy goes after gets shut down. The leadership ends up paying stiff fines and going to prison. I just don't want to risk that happening to me."

The stunned pastor slowly rose from his chair, still holding the envelope. "Do you think that I've done something illegal that would cause that to happen to our church or to our leaders?"

"No, Pastor Harris, I don't, not at all. You're a good man, and you've been a good leader for this church."

"Then why would you resign?" He dropped the envelope on top of his Bible and moved to the front of the desk and sat on the edge. "Sit down, please. If you don't believe I've done anything wrong, why would you leave the church?"

The minister took a seat. His attention darted from the pastor, to the certificates on the wall—the pastor's ministerial license, his Ph.D. in theology, and his master's degree in psychology—and then back to the pastor. "You've done so much with your life, and you've helped so many people. That's the kind of minister I want to be. I'm just not sure that being innocent is enough to keep that attorney from bringing this ministry down and me right along with it." His gaze fell away, and he hung his head.

Pastor Harris went to him and rested his hand on his left shoulder. "Listen to me, son."

Minister Townsend darted from his seat. "Please, Pastor. This is hard for me, but I have to leave. I found out two weeks ago that my wife and I are expecting our first baby. She's worried about me going to prison. I can't have her upset and stressed out about this. We've talked about it, and I believe leaving is the best thing for me and my family. I'm sorry."

A quiet swept over the room and lingered briefly. Pastor Harris inhaled a silent breath and gave words to his heart. "I understand," he said, fuming inside. "Congratulations to you and your wife. Your first child is a very special gift from God." He offered the minster a firm handshake and a pat on his shoulder. "You are a good man yourself, Minister Townsend. I will keep you and your family in my prayers. I know you'll be fine wherever you end up."

The minister grabbed Pastor Harris, hugged him, and hurried from the study without another word. Pastor Harris's gaze was glued to the door after it shut. He stood motionless for several moments. Then he stared at the section of the wall that showcased his degrees. He briefly considered each one. Afterward, he retreated to his desk and dropped down into his chair with a thump. Pastor Harris slammed his fist against the desk as he glanced back up at the closed door. This thing with Maxwell Montgomery was out of control.

The pastor had done nothing wrong, and neither had anyone on his staff. Yet Maxwell's vicious pursuit of him and Faith Temple had begun to result in casualties. His head whipped to the left side of his desk, where his Bible rested. He lifted it and snatched from underneath it the sheet of paper with Maxwell's name on it. He'd made the right decision in launching an investigation. That brought a brief sense of satisfaction, but it wasn't enough. He was delusional or misguided in thinking Maxwell was going to give him a fair fight. If Pastor Harris was going to stand firm against the attack, there was only one path he could take to ensure victory.

He clutched the Bible and dropped to his knees. "My Lord," he cried out. "Not my will, but yours, be done."

Chapter 36

Pleased to put the solitude of Sunday behind him, Maxwell welcomed Monday and the bustle it had to offer. His morning had been occupied with court appearances for two clients. On the elevator ride up to his office, he thought again about Nicole's fiancé. He'd better call the investigator. Friday had come and gone, and he hadn't received the background report. He stopped at his assistant's desk to collect his messages.

"The phones have been ringing nonstop today. Here are your messages. The first five need your attention right away. This was hand delivered for you." She handed her boss the stack of messages and the large sealed package. "The man was very specific that I should give it to no one but you, which is ridiculous. Who else did he think I would give it to?" She snickered.

"Thanks, and please hold my calls for the next half an hour," he told her.

"No problem." As soon as the words were out of her mouth, the phone rang.

Maxwell hustled into his office and plopped down onto the corner of his desk. He ripped into the adhesive seal on the package to find a smaller sealed manila envelope labeled JAMES WASHINGTON.

The eager attorney tore into it, careful not to rip the contents. He began to devour the several-page document intently. When he turned the third page, Maxwell sprang from his desk and hungrily digested the last page. He stared at it for a few seconds and then flung the document behind him and onto the floor. With the heel of his right hand, he pressed against his knuckles. His bones popped loudly. He did the same with his left hand. His laser-like gaze burned into the phone on his desk. How could Nicole not know all about the man she was about to marry? The information wasn't hard to come by. Why hadn't Nicole learned all that she could before committing to having children with this guy? Maxwell clenched both his fists so hard, he felt his pulse throbbing in his fingers. What was next? He had to calm himself in order to think clearly.

He eased the cell phone from his belt clip. No way around it. He had to make the call to Nicole. The ugly truth would have to be told. Three rings and she was there.

"Hey, I know it's the middle of your workday, but I need to talk with you. It's pretty important. Can you get away for about an hour?" he said.

"What's going on? Are you sick?"

"It's nothing like that. We just need to talk. Can you meet me in Love Park? I can be there in fifteen minutes."

"Make it thirty, and I'll see you there."

The short drive didn't make the necessary conversation any easier to have. Maxwell parked and climbed out of his car. Time was up. Nicole walked toward him, and he still didn't have the words to break her heart.

"Okay, Mr. Montgomery, what is so important that you summoned me from my air-conditioned office on this blisteringly hot day?" She tilted her head down and looked over the top of her sunglasses at him and smiled. "So, spill the beans. What's going on?" She sat down next to Maxwell on a bench.

"You know me. I don't like to beat around the bush. There is something I think you need to know about your fiancé."

"You've never met my fiancé. What could you possibly know about him that I don't already know?"

"When you want to know something, you just have to ask the right questions." Maxwell removed his shades and placed them in his shirt pocket.

"What is it? What are you trying to say?" She crossed her legs and swung her arm over the back of the bench.

"You told me that your fiancé doesn't want to have children. Did he ever tell you why?"

"We talked about it briefly. Something about the way he grew up and he just wants to enjoy being married without the responsibility of raising a child. Why?"

"That's not quite the truth."

"Really, for someone who doesn't like beating around the bush, you are wearing the bush down. Spit out whatever it is you're trying to say."

He placed his palm on her hand gently. "He was married, and he has an eight-year-old daughter. He divorced his wife after five years of marriage. He filed under irreconcilable differences. Apparently, marriage and children weren't for him, and he refused to be trapped."

She snatched her hand away from his touch and pushed her shades onto the top of her head. "What? That's ridiculous. You don't know James. Who told you those lies?"

"There's more. He was arrested a couple of times for domestic violence. He broke his wife's arm."

"Are you serious? That can't be right. I know him. He's not that kind of man. You must have him mixed up with someone else." She tapped her foot rapidly and chewed at her bottom lip.

"Nicole, I had him investigated. I don't have him mixed up. He lied to you."

"And you couldn't wait to tell me."

"You need to know who he really is. He's not the kind of guy you want to marry."

She shot up from her seat and knocked her purse off the bench. "Why would you have him investigated? I didn't ask you to do that." Her voice trembled. "If I thought it needed to be done, I could have hired an investigator myself." She spoke louder and waved her hand frantically in Maxwell's face. "I don't believe you. I don't believe anything you just said. You're lying, and I don't know why."

He shifted his eyes from left to right, hoping people weren't paying attention to them. "It's true, every word of it. I wouldn't have told you if it weren't true. I had him investigated because I care about you. I don't want to see you hurt."

"Care about me? Don't want to see me hurt? Seriously, you mean like you hurt me?" Nicole's voice got louder.

Maxwell knew people could hear them by now.

"So, what is it? You didn't want me, but you don't want to see me happy with anyone else? What is wrong with you, Maxwell? You have your ways, but I never thought you'd go this far."

He stood and stepped closer to her. "You know—"

She stepped back and jerked her purse up from the ground. "I don't want to hear it, Maxwell. Mind your own business. You have enough issues of your own. Handle your life and let me handle mine. Go back to doing what you do best— which is working around the clock. And while you're at it, I suggest you get a better investigator."

He stood there, frozen, and watched her dash away. What had just happened? He hadn't intended to make her angry, but he'd done the right thing, so long as it didn't cost him their friendship. Watching her flee a second time bothered him. Maybe their friendship wasn't the only thing he wanted to preserve.

Chapter 37

Nicole drove through traffic as tears blurred her vision. She had called James's office before taking off and had found out that he'd gone home for lunch. Pedestrians and downtown traffic didn't allow her BMW to go as fast as Nicole wanted. She wiped at her eyelids with the backs of her hands. The things Maxwell had told her couldn't be true. She just had to get to her fiancé and have him reassure her that it was all a lie, a mistake, something, anything. There was a reason for this error, and they would figure it out together. But the gnawing ache in her gut was stirring up a fear inside her that hung on to every word that had been spoken by the man who wouldn't commit to her.

She zoomed into the driveway so fast, the car stopped only two inches from the garage door. Nicole marched up the cobblestone steps to James's front door, the key still in the car's ignition and her purse on the passenger seat. She pressed the doorbell repeatedly. Less than thirty seconds later, her knuckles pounded on the door.

"James. James. I know you're in there. Open this door."

Just as she lifted her hand to pound the door again, it flung open. "What's wrong?" He peered around the doorway. "What's going on?"

Nicole stomped past him. "We need to talk."

"How did you know I came home for lunch?" He followed her inside.

"I called your office, of course." Nicole stood in the middle of the living room with her hands on her hips and her piercing stare shooting darts at him.

"You have me worried. What's wrong?"

She gasped and then slowly exhaled. "I need to ask you a question. Please, please tell me the truth."

"Ask your question, babe. I don't have anything to hide." He closed the distance between them and slipped his hands into hers, forcing her hands to fall from her hips.

"Have you been married before?"

A couple of silent seconds spoke first. Then he answered, "You know that I haven't. Why would you ask me that question?" He allowed her hands to slip out of his grip.

"I don't want you to lie to me. I need to know that I can trust you. Tell me the truth. I can find out if I have to. So, don't make me go chasing a lie." Her bottom lip quivered slightly.

The psychiatrist, who was usually on the other end of the hard questions, squeezed his eyelids tightly. He hung his head and walked a few feet away from her. He randomly unleashed a fierce right punch into the air. Finally, he faced her, with the truth on his lips. "Yes, I was married, and I have an eight-year-old daughter."

"Oh, my God. It's true." Her hand flew to her chest. "You have a child?"

"Wait. Give me a chance to explain before you go off. Let's sit down and talk about this." He waved his hand toward the love seat.

Nicole clenched her fist and pounded it against her leg. "I don't want to discuss it. Just tell me the truth. You were married? You are married? What?"

"We're just going to stand here in the middle of the floor? Please sit down." He stepped toward her. His eyelids were wide, and his voice was softer.

Instantly, Nicole moved away from him, closer to the fireplace. "Why did you lie to me?" The corners of her mouth twitched.

James plopped down onto the arm of the love seat. "What was I supposed to do? You made it very clear that when you got married, it would be to someone who had never been married. You didn't want to deal with the drama of an ex-wife and past issues that would prevent you from holding that special place in your man's heart. Do you remember?"

"And *that's* your excuse for lying to me?"

He lifted his right hand and placed it on his chest. "I'm not making an excuse. I'm telling you the truth."

"Huh?"

"What do you want me to say? I was interested in you. I couldn't tell you that I'd been married. I thought for sure you wouldn't want to see me again."

"Exactly when did you plan on telling me? After we got married? When your daughter dropped in for a visit?"

He stood slowly and dragged his hand down his face and pulled at the ends of his mustache. "Why did you have to dig this up? Why does it matter that I was married or have a child? I told you I don't want kids."

"What do you mean? You already have one," Nicole cried out.

"Yes, I have a daughter, but her mother keeps her from me. Regrettably, she's not a part of my life. The woman I married knew I didn't want children. I believe she got pregnant on purpose. Neither of them has anything to do with us."

"The woman you married? You mean your ex-wife? I guess she's your ex."

"Yes, she is."

"Don't make it seem like the assumption is automatic."

"Come on, Nicole. My past has nothing to do with us. We have a good thing going. Why ruin it?"

"Are you kidding? Your past has everything to do with us. I want to marry a man I can trust, one who shares his whole life with me, the good and the bad. I want a man who will protect me and respect my feelings, not hurt me. I don't have time for a lying fiancé." She turned her back to him quickly, determined not to shed a tear. She massaged her forehead with the heel of her hand to soothe the headache that had formed above her right eyebrow.

James went to her. He gently planted his hands on her shoulders. "Babe, please . . ."

Her rage immediately erupted. She jerked her shoulders from his touch and spun around to challenge him. "Don't you touch me. I don't even know you. From the day we met, you've been dishonest. How can you have a child and not be a part of her life? What kind of a man does that?" She waved her hand in front of him. "Wow. What a sorry excuse for a man."

"I'm still the same man you agreed to marry."

She gave a hearty laugh. "No, you're not. I thought you were honest, genuine, someone I could trust, a man I could raise a family with. I can't believe I wasted my time dating a stranger that I almost married."

"Stranger? Come on, Nicole. I'm the same man you met at Heathrow Airport in London eight months ago. I'm the same man that makes you laugh." His voice was inviting, and he dared to take a step closer to her.

"Stop." Her hand flew up in front of his face. "I don't want to hear any more of your lies. You obviously don't know how to be honest," she yelled as her nostrils flared.

"Hey, why are you yelling? Calm down. I've got neighbors."

"And I bet they would love to know that you abuse women."

"Are you crazy? I've never laid a hand on you." His cheeks blossomed red as fury claimed him.

"But you broke your wife's arm, right?"

Three wide steps and he was standing in front of her. With almost no distance between them, James growled, "Who told you that? Where did you get that from?" He grabbed her arm hard, demanding answers.

Nicole screamed, "Let go. You're hurting me." Terror gripped her body.

James recoiled. "I'm s-sorry," he stuttered. "I'm not that guy."

She quivered, though her arms were crossed and her hands were tightly gripping her shoulders. "I don't know *what* guy you are."

Nicole could feel his breath on her face. His next words sounded like the roar of an angry lion. He was too close. Nicole stumbled backward, almost falling to the floor to escape his towering physique.

"Get away from me. I'm done with you, whoever you are." She slid the sparkling, bold diamond engagement ring from her finger and threw it at him. It hit James in the chest. His eyes followed the ring as it landed on the floor and bounced close to a table situated in the expansive room not too far from the front door.

"Nicole, don't do this. We can work it out." He stooped to scoop up the ring.

The wounded fiancée had already begun to make her exit. She stepped briskly to the front door, passing the marble table with the eight-by-ten framed photo of her and James on the beach in Aruba.

"Nicole, just hear me out," he pleaded when she reached the front door.

She didn't respond. Instead, she planted her feet on the other side of his doorway, making it to freedom. Nicole ran across the yard to her car as James continued calling out to her. She backed out the driveway, her tires squealing, and left tread marks behind on the street.

James made it to the driveway as she sped away. He ran to the sidewalk, calling after her. "Nicole, Nicole, stop. Don't do this."

Two neighbors stood in their yard and looked on, and another one stopped mowing his lawn to watch the action unfold publicly. James took notice and retreated inside. Secrets had a way of being revealed at the most inopportune time. This was his time.

Chapter 38

Maxwell sat in a chair, flipping the pages of a magazine too fast to get a good gander at the images or to read one word. He scanned the lobby while his right foot tapped rapidly against the floor. A man approached him with his hand extended.

"Mr. Montgomery, good to see you. Follow me. I will assist you in accessing your safety deposit box."

He followed the man to the secure area. Maxwell signed his name on the required signature page and then placed his key in one of the many locks. The man inserted his key into the lock just above Maxwell's. The locked door opened, and the man slid a long steel box out of its dark tunnel. The man excused himself and left his bank patron in the private room with the door closed.

Maxwell opened the lid on the box, then removed a thick envelope from the inside pocket of his suit jacket. He opened it and ran his thumb across the stack of hundred-dollar bills inside. Then he placed the envelope in the box and started to close the lid. He paused for a few moments. On second thought, he'd just take a quick peek in the box and make sure everything was in order.

The inquisitive attorney removed the items individually. He started with the new envelope. His last will and testament lay prominently on top. The deed to his house was underneath. He opened the folded document and slid his fingers over the name Tyree Washington. His nephew would own the house free and clear if something were to happen to Maxwell. Tyree's father was gone, but Uncle Maxwell would always make sure Tyree was taken care of. Next out of the box was a trust fund document, which was also in Tyree's name. Maintaining a home took money. It wouldn't make sense to give the young fella a beautiful home if he couldn't afford the upkeep. A five-hundred-thousand-dollar life insurance policy with only one beneficiary, his cleaning lady, lay before him. Her two children were dead, and there was no one else to take care of her. Maxwell would gladly do it. There were four other documents in the box, and he checked only to be certain they were there. He did not examine them like he did the others. Next, he fished four envelopes of money from the back of the box; they were labeled CHRISTINE, ETHEL, and PAUL SR. After a quick glance into each envelope, he tossed them back into the box, along with the new envelope. He was tempted to scribble the words *Deacon Burton's Family* across the new envelope but didn't. He wouldn't earmark the cash for anything, in case another situation popped up that required quick, untraceable cash. He hoped there wouldn't be too many more of those to deal with, but hard-fought wars had casualties. Maxwell gripped the back of his neck with his hand and squeezed hard, forcing the knot of tension to settle down.

He replaced the other items. With everything back in the safety deposit box, he slid the box back in its dark tunnel. Maxwell shut the little metal door and turned the key, securing the future of those he cared about. His phone chimed with a text message. He slipped his phone from his belt clip. It was Garrett.

Need to talk. Do you have any time this afternoon?

Maxwell composed his reply. I'll call you. Then he sent the text and checked the time on his phone.

Chapter 39

Maxwell thought of Nicole and patted his hand against his pant leg. She was probably still angry, but he couldn't allow that to stop him from checking on her. Hopefully, she would answer his call. He breezed through the bank lobby, paying no attention to the caramel-skinned woman with a model's looks who slid her shades down the bridge of her nose as he walked past. He didn't have time for distractions.

In the bank's parking lot, he pointed his key fob at his Porsche. He climbed behind the wheel, and with the engine purring and cool air pouring out of the vents, he pushed the call button on his cell phone, hoping to get an answer this time.

"Nicole King, please."

"I'm sorry, sir. Ms. King is not in the office today. May I take a message?"

He jerked the phone from his ear and peered at it through squinted eyelids.

"Sir, are you there?"

"Sorry. Yes I am. She's not in the office now, or she hasn't been in the office at all today?"

"She won't be in the office today or tomorrow. I would be happy to take a message."

"No. No thanks." He ended the call.

Nicole wasn't in the office. That was definitely out of character for her. She lived in her office, just like he did, or at least Nicole used to when they were together.

Maxell backed out of the parking stall slowly after looking to his left and his right multiple times. He didn't want any more near collisions, like he'd had in the parking lot at Faith Temple several weeks ago. He gave a command to dial to the hands-free system in his car, expecting his call to go to Nicole's voice mail. To his surprise, a live voice answered.

"What do you want, Maxwell?"

He spun the steering wheel hard to the right and pulled his car to the curb and out of traffic. "Hey. I called your office and found out you're not going in to work today."

"No, I'm not working today. I'm okay, though, or at least I will be."

"Nicole, I'm sorry—"

"I really don't want to talk about it," she snapped. "My personal life is no longer your business."

"I'm not trying to upset you. I just wanted to check on you."

The sincerity in his voice softened her reaction. "I'm sorry about biting your head off. I do believe your concern for me is genuine, unexpected but genuine."

"Definitely genuine. I know you're hurting. If you—"

"I can't deal with this right now. I've got to go."

Dead air on the phone line screamed back at Maxwell. She'd answered the phone, yet there was a heavy cloak of emotion blocking their friendship. He couldn't let the call end that way. "Dial Nicole King." Before the voice command was executed, he changed his mind and hit the CANCEL button on the steering wheel. He'd give her some time. A self-sufficient woman like Nicole would be fine. However, the sadness she'd exhibited when they broke up made him a little less sure.

Maxwell couldn't sit there forever and lament the past. He had a meeting back at the office with Garrett. On second thought, he wanted a change of scenery. Maxwell made a call to Garrett as he drove toward the office. "Can you meet me at the coffee shop in the lobby of my office building?"

"Sure. I'll see you in twenty minutes."

The minutes and blocks flew by as Maxwell struggled with Nicole's situation. He really didn't have the right to tell her anything about the man she was engaged to marry, or did he? Was she right? Maybe he should have stayed out of her business. Worse yet, what if she passed on this guy too quickly and ended up never getting married? His mind raced to a few decades down the road. What if Nicole blamed him? His initial inclination was to feel badly, but he abandoned the notion. There was already a hefty portion of guilt on his plate. He didn't need another serving.

Maxwell parked his car in the stall labeled with his name and went directly inside. He hadn't eaten lunch, but coffee was what he craved. Sitting in his usual spot, a booth with a window, he faced the door. People walked up and down the sidewalk. Some holding hands, some kissing, and others exhibiting that look that said they knew happiness. His mind fluttered with the past and questions about the future. Suddenly Garrett appeared at the table. Maxwell hadn't noticed him enter the coffee shop and hadn't even heard his footsteps.

"I hope you haven't been waiting too long. Traffic was thicker than I expected," Garrett said, still standing.

Maxwell jerked his head away from the window and gazed up at his investigator. "I've only been here a few minutes."

Garrett sat down across from him in the booth, eager to jump right into why he wanted to meet. A waitress interrupted before either man could speak. Both of them ordered coffee and nothing else. The waitress returned promptly with their coffee.

Garrett kicked off the meeting once they were alone. "I've got feelers out, and I am hearing crazy noise that might not make you too happy."

"What are you talking about?" Maxwell took a sip of his coffee and then dumped in another spoonful of sugar.

"There's an article coming out that could be damaging."

"Damaging to whom?" Maxwell asked. "Reporters are already breathing down my neck, trying to stir up doubt about Burton's guilt."

"This is worse." Garrett gulped his coffee. "There's a reporter who is paying close attention to our investigation of Pastor Harris. He's coming after you."

"Let him. Won't be the first person."

"I'm not so sure that's the position you want to take. My source tells me the reporter is working on an angle that could tie Greater Metropolitan and Faith Temple together. He believes there is more driving you than just your interest in bringing down corrupt church leaders. He thinks it's personal, and he's determined to find out what it is." Garrett strummed his fingers on the table.

"So what. I know a bunch of reporters, and they were quite interested in what I had to tell them about Pastor Harris and Faith Temple a few weeks ago."

"Ah, you're the reason I've seen more coverage on the news lately."

Maxwell swished his cup around. "Whatever it takes to crack this case, I'm going to do. That's the bottom line."

Garrett slapped the table. "Seriously, what is it with you? Is there something you're not telling me?"

"Look, you know me, and you know my agenda. My mission hasn't changed from my first case fifteen years ago to the ones in play today. These powerful, corrupt church leaders need to be held accountable." He balled up his fist and slammed it into the table. "So some reporter has it in for me and is trying to discredit my investigation. This isn't personal. It's just real."

"There's a microscope of scrutiny on this thing. Pastor Harris is well liked. He's highly regarded in the community. People won't believe he's guilty of any wrongdoing. If you keep going after him, your integrity and your reputation will take a beating." Garrett delivered the news with a firm expression and direct eye contact.

The amused attorney shifted in his seat and glanced down at his sleeve, adjusted his cuff link, and snickered. "Is that supposed to make me do something different, like stop the investigation, or what? I'm confused."

He pushed his coffee cup to the side. "You might want to take this thing seriously." Garrett tapped the table several times.

"I won't be intimidated, threatened, or prodded down any particular path. You know me well enough to know that. People didn't think Bishop Jones was capable of what he was accused of, either. Throughout that investigation his die-hard believers thought the accusations were unfounded, as well. How many people shouted his innocence until the prison doors slammed shut?" Maxwell drained the last bit of coffee from his cup. "I've got a meeting to get to."

"We've got to check and double-check any and everything associated with this case. If this thing festers and gets out of control, other investigations and possibly convictions could be questioned as well."

"If I thought that was a possibility, I'd be as concerned as you. The reality is, I'm a winner, and that doesn't sit well with everyone. It's not by chance that I've won every case." Maxwell stood. "Some delusional reporter digging around won't make a guilty party innocent. The work we've done and the cases we've won were all solid."

Garrett fished cash from his pocket and tossed it onto the table. "Does that include the case with Deacon Burton?"

"You know what? I'm past being tired of your references to the case against Deacon Burton and his innocence. If your skin has gotten too thin for what we do"—Maxwell waved his hand back and forth between them—"just let me know. I can discontinue the use of your services at any time." Maxwell walked away and headed to his office.

"I'll be sure to do that," Garrett barked as the annoyed attorney widened the distance between them with every step. Maxwell might have other folks shaking in their boots with his superman persona, but Garrett's name wasn't on that list. Did the attorney really think he was invincible? Maxwell had better pay attention to what he was telling him. There was a storm brewing in the distance, and the winds might very well blow pretty hard.

Chapter 40

Upstairs in his office, Maxwell paced the floor, fretting over his strife with Garrett. Annoyance swept over him, on the brink of maturing into anger as he paced faster. Why was Garrett willing to destroy a winning formula? They made a good team and were alike in many ways. Both of them were hardworking, diligent, the best at what they did, and committed to making a difference. Maxwell was grieved as he watched his trusted investigator become more disaffected. Garrett was getting soft, and there was no room in their world for a man to let a case run him into the corner of remorse.

Maxwell stopped in the middle of the floor. The cabinet door beckoned. Once the door was open, he pulled out the storage box and dug inside. When he'd tucked the obituary away in the box, he had had no intention of later disturbing its resting place. Yet the obituary was now in his hand. The man might be dead, but he was still stirring up folks on this side of the grave. Wasn't an obituary the last voice for that person? Couldn't the deacon just rest in peace?

He slammed the lid down on top of the box. Sounds of the deacon's wife screaming in the courtroom at the guilty verdict filled his head. *He's not guilty. Oh my God. You can't do this. It's not right. It's just not right.*

The screeching sound of his cell phone drowned out her words. After the second ring, Maxwell snatched the phone from his side and offered an abrupt greeting. "Maxwell Montgomery."

Only silence spoke back to him.

"Maxwell Montgomery. How can I help you?" Maxwell inspected the screen on his phone. The call was from a restricted number.

"How can you *help* me? Well, you could put a gun to your head and blow your brains out. That would help me and a lot of other folks that you have wronged." The voice was deep and muffled. He thought for sure it was a man.

"Hmm. Blow my brains out, huh? Since that's not going to happen, what else can I do for a coward like you?" Maxwell hustled to his desk to grab a pen and paper. He jotted down the time, the noises he heard in the background, and what was being said.

"Oh, you've left a trail of bodies in your personal crusade. You don't care who you hurt. You destroy churches and the lives of good people."

"I hold church leaders accountable."

"Since you're big on accountability, I'll be the one holding *you* accountable."

"Are you one of the people I've supposedly wronged?"

"You're not slick, Montgomery. You'll know who I am when I'm ready for you to know. I suggest you pay attention to your surroundings. You might soon be standing in the face of this coward."

Then the line went dead. Maxwell tossed the pen. His mind was whirling more from curiosity than fear. Who was this person? Did the random calls and the obituary come from the same person? Was this the nut he'd seen on the street, pointing the imaginary gun? He wasn't sure. He wasn't going to hide out, but wisdom suggested that he needed to be more cautious and to take the threats seriously.

Chapter 41

The car engine growled as Maxwell shifted gears. He slowly glided his car into the barbershop parking lot. Glad to see only four other cars there, he shifted the car into park. A quick haircut before the shop got too crowded meant he would get home and back to work well before noon. It was Saturday, but it was a workday for him.

Maxwell ambled down the sidewalk and past the wide picture window that offered a full view into the barbershop. He glanced up at the red, white, and blue barber's pole that hung over the door as he entered.

"Maxwell, there's one person ahead of you. I'll be ready for you in about fifteen minutes," the barber assured him.

Maxwell was glad he didn't have to wait long. There were eight barber chairs, and he knew none of them would be empty in the next hour. He gave the barber a nod and took a seat facing the door. Every hour of his time was precious, and he wanted to get in and out. The busy attorney snagged the morning paper. TV screens blasted the news, sports updates, and two different ball games. Uninterested and intent on avoiding conversation, Maxwell shielded himself with the newspaper.

He'd turned to the sports section when the door chimed, announcing more patrons. A woman strolled in with two young boys.

"Both boys need a cut?" the barber asked.

"Yes, please," she replied, rubbing her hand across one boy's head.

The familiar voice caught Maxwell's attention. He was dazed when he saw that Sonya was standing a few feet away. It couldn't be her. There was no reason for her to be in his barbershop way across town. She didn't even have children. Maxwell kept his face shielded by the newspaper. Yet he felt her intense gaze burning right through the paper, daring him to show himself. He snatched the paper down into his lap to find a laser-like stare waiting for him.

"Well, Mr. Montgomery. What a surprise to see you here." Sonya gave him a smirk as she stepped closer.

He didn't believe her. She had to have noticed his car and his personalized plates in the lot.

"I brought my two cousins to get a haircut," she stated, with her hands on both boys' shoulders. "I'm trying to help my aunt out. You know she's got a lot on her plate, now that her husband is gone."

Maxwell met her stare with a firm glare of his own. Was she for real? What kind of game was she playing? He'd never run into her at this barbershop before. There were plenty of barbershops much closer to where the boys lived. He was sure she'd planned the run-in.

"Aren't they handsome boys? They look so much like their dad." She gave both boys a gentle shove toward Maxwell.

Being that close, he was forced to consider their dark brown eyes and their facial features, which definitely bore a resemblance to Deacon Burton's. Maxwell wanted to tell Sonya, "Stop the games and grow up. This battle is already over." Using those boys as pawns to antagonize him was low, even for Sonya, but Maxwell wouldn't give her the satisfaction of him making a scene. His voice slinked up out of his throat. "They are nice-looking boys." They bored through to his soul and urged him up from his seat. "Excuse me." He maneuvered around the boys standing in front of him, and bathroom bound he was.

In the bathroom, behind closed doors, he kicked at the air and loudly grunted, "Ugh." Suddenly, he bent down to check for feet in either of the stalls. Thankful he was alone, Maxwell attempted to calm himself. He paced the floor from one end of the bathroom to the other. No way could he let Sonya see the frustration that had welled up inside him. He needed to get his hair cut and to execute a smooth exit. Maxwell gnawed at the inside of his cheek, then trekked to the sink. Standing in front of the mirror, he considered the man peering back at him. Whatever was not in his control, he would have to accept. This encounter was one of those things.

He inhaled, taking a slow breath that filled his lungs, and then allowed the breath to escape between his lips. He marched out of the bathroom and back to what might become a battlefield, confident that Sargent Sonya would be waiting on the front line to launch her next attack on him. As he reached the end of the hallway, he searched the barbershop for his adversary. Several more people were now in the room, but Sonya and the boys were gone.

"I'm ready for you, Mr. Montgomery," the barber said.

"Where's the young lady with the two boys?" Maxwell inquired while climbing into the barber chair.

"She said she didn't have time to wait."

Maxwell surveyed the parking lot through the window. No sign of Sonya or the car she'd driven while working for him, but he acknowledged to himself that she might have gotten a new car. "Does she bring those boys here often?"

"No. I've never seen her before."

So she had purposely shown up to taunt him. No surprise. Sonya knew where he got his hair cut. She'd made and canceled enough appointments for him. What was wrong with her? Why couldn't she move on? Nothing she did or said would bring her uncle back. Maxwell clutched both arms of the chair so tightly, the veins in his hands protruded. What if she was the one making those crazy calls? He had to really think about it. She wouldn't go that far, would she?

Sonya pulled into a strip mall a few blocks away from the barbershop and parked. She could have stayed and let Maxwell wallow in the awkwardness, but Sonya had to put the boys first. They didn't know their father's killer like she did. They were innocent and had to be shielded from the truth.

For now Sonya had to be content with random encounters, but one day, she was absolutely certain that the big and bad heartless Attorney Maxwell Montgomery would get what was coming to him.

Chapter 42

The Bible class was over, and the room buzzed with voices while several inmates crowded the podium. They waited their turn to speak with Pastor Harris. The last inmate approached the pastor and latched on to his hand, shaking it vigorously.

"Thanks so much for coming here every week. I look forward to Tuesdays," he said. "You've encouraged me to do something different with my life. I will not come back to jail again. I absolutely will not let this jail sentence turn into hard time in prison." He shook his head as he glanced down and tugged at his tan overalls. "My ninety-day sentence is up next week. You can count on me being in your church next Sunday."

Pastor Harris's face blossomed: his eyes were bright, and a pearly white grin parted his lips. "You *can* change your life, and it sounds like you plan to take a good first step."

"Time's up. Let's go," the guard urged the inmate talking with Pastor Harris.

"Call me at the church when you get out," the pastor said, giving the inmate a thumbs-up. Pastor Harris watched the young man, who appeared to have gang tattoos on the back of his neck, shuffle from the room. The pastor gave a thick cough. His throat burned, so he rubbed it, swallowed two big gulps of water from the bottle on the podium, and tossed a lozenge in his mouth. He wasn't well, but it wouldn't prevent him from teaching Bible class at the jail. He hadn't missed a week in three years. The ailing pastor was glad he'd shown up today and been consistent. Had he chosen not to come, that young man might have decided to go back to selling drugs. *Why not?* With limited education and no job prospects, hustling was what the young man had known to survive.

If only I could do more, the pastor thought. There were so many young men who needed help.

Where were some of the other church leaders? More people needed to get involved; perhaps there was something he could do to drive that effort too. He considered the possibilities while he headed toward the parking lot. Glad to reach his car, he got in and blasted the heat, feeling slightly chilled. As he backed out, his phone squalled. He took a quick peek at the screen. It was the investigator he called last week. The eager pastor zipped his car back into the parking stall and answered quickly.

"Mr. Harris. This is David, with Remington Investigation."

The pastor sat up straight, with all ten fingers planted deep into the grooves of the steering wheel. He waited for the investigator to continue.

"I sent my findings to your home address in an overnight package yesterday. You should receive it around three p.m. today. A thorough investigation was done. I think you will find the information interesting reading. Let me know if you need anything else."

"I will, and I appreciate your time." After the call ended, the pastor just sat there, paralyzed by the conversation. What information could possibly be in the package that was on its way to him? Maybe Maxwell Montgomery did have a sketchy past. Had he done something worthy of disbarment? Could the attorney have his law license revoked? Wouldn't that be ironic?

The heel of his hand flew up to massage his left temple. He had a dull headache and it was growing stronger. Pastor Harris's attention darted to the dashboard clock. Two thirty-five. He didn't have long to wait for answers. He had to get that overnight package. The inquisitive pastor thrust the gearshift into reverse and zoomed out of the lot. His planned stop at the bank and the flowers he usually picked up each week for his wife would have to wait until later. He was homebound, with a fierce determination.

Home was at least thirty-five minutes away with the midday traffic. Each light seemed to turn red right when he approached it. He could feel his pulse beating in his fingertips, thanks to his cement grip on the steering wheel. Traffic lights, a train that held him up for ten minutes, and slow drivers each hindered him as he raced to get home. Finally, his street was two blocks away. Suddenly, he realized his headache was gone. His curiosity poked at him. Who was Maxwell Montgomery? What had the investigator uncovered?

As he pulled up to his house, the pastor couldn't wait to grab the mail. He stopped the car in front of the driveway, climbed out, left the car door ajar, hurried to the mailbox, and yanked it open. It was empty. He shoved his hand inside, all the way to the back. Nothing. He returned to the car, pulled into the driveway, and pressed a button that lifted the garage door. His wife's car was there. She was home; maybe she had the package. The car door swung open, he slung one foot out of the car, and lunged forward. He felt something gripping his body and preventing him from exiting the car. He'd forgotten to take off his seat belt. He unbuckled it and dashed inside the house.

As soon as he opened the door, his gaze landed right on his target. A stack of mail rested on the kitchen counter. His hand ravished each envelope as he looked for the package with his name and an Illinois postmark. It wasn't there. Where was it? His head whipped around to the clock on the wall, which told him it was 3:40 p.m. The package had to be there somewhere. He couldn't wait another day.

"Hi, honey. I thought I heard you come in," his wife said.

"Did I get a package of some kind or a large envelope?" He moved closer to her.

"Yes, I signed for it and put the package on the desk in your office."

His body turned quickly, like a spinning top.

"Renaldo, what's wrong? You seem edgy, and where's my hug and kiss?" She rested her hand on her hip and tilted her head to the side.

Her words stopped his movement instantly. Pastor Harris stepped back over to her and folded her in his embrace, with a quick peck on her lips. "Sorry, hon. I'm anxious to get to that package. It's very important."

"Well, I'm off to the grocery store. I ran late with my last couple of patients and didn't leave work as early as I was hoping."

"Be careful. Traffic is crazy." He placed another soft peck on her lips and trotted off to his office. His eyes searched his desk before he reached it. A large flat shipping envelope caught his attention. The pastor scooped it up, tore into it, and freed the contents from the envelope. He stepped backward without looking and collapsed into the chair in front of his desk.

He pulled out an eight-by-ten photo of Maxwell Montgomery. That was definitely him. The right man had been investigated. Next, out came a black folder, which contained a background report and a several-page narrative. Pastor Harris removed the background report and read it thoroughly. Nothing there, no arrests or legal matters. That wasn't surprising. Quickly, he flipped the page over to be sure he wasn't missing anything on the back side. It was completely blank, so it sailed to the floor.

He opened the black folder again, took out the narrative, and began to read. *Maxwell Montgomery is from Chester, Pennsylvania. He has only one sibling, a sister, Christine, and he grew up with both parents in the home for the majority of his childhood.* Pastor Harris read two pages, which gave him the details of Maxwell's family life. What his parents did for a living, the challenges he faced when he left his parents' home at seventeen, and Maxwell's stellar success in school weren't of interest to him. *He graduated from law school at the top of his class.* No surprise there, either. Maxwell was obviously smart and persistent. Pastor Harris didn't need a report to tell him that. However, a sense of shock snaked through him, creating a prickling sensation underneath his skin, when he read the next line. *Maxwell Montgomery was born Paul Montgomery, Jr.* What? His name wasn't even Maxwell. He read the sentence a second time. Pastor Harris licked his lips, hungry for more information, wondering what had prompted the name change.

The pastor turned the third page and found an aged newspaper clipping stapled to it. His eyes moved faster across the typed lines. *Paul Montgomery, Sr., served faithfully as the deacon and treasurer of his local church for decades. The pastor of the church at the time engineered a get-rich-quick scheme that failed. It cost Paul Sr. his home, his life savings, his retirement fund, and the college funds he'd set aside for his two children.* Pastor Harris rose from his chair, took two steps, and wiped away the beads of sweat that had formed on his nose.

The next page he read with his finger slowly moving across the page as he digested every word. *Paul Sr. was arrested and spent three years in prison on fraud and embezzlement charges associated with the pastor's get-rich-quick scheme. His wife, Ethel, was the church secretary, and she did not escape the scandal unscathed. She served six months in prison due to the same scheme.* He hungrily sucked up the entire backstory to Maxwell's life.

Pastor Harris read the last section of the narrative. *The pastor who engineered the get-rich-quick scheme, lost millions of dollars of his church members' money, and did not serve one day in prison was. He is the same Bishop Ellis Jones whom Attorney Maxwell Montgomery later built a case against, a case that sent him to federal prison and shut the doors of his mega-ministry.* "What? It can't be," the pastor said aloud. He read that last section again.

Pastor Harris paced the floor of his office with the narrative in his hand. He came to a sudden stop by the window. Leaning against the windowsill, he squeezed his eyelids shut tight. He rubbed at the knot in the back of his neck, which partnered with a dull pain over his right eye, hinting that his headache would reappear, strong and powerful. His eyelids opened, and he peered out across the housetops and off into the distant sky.

Finally, Maxwell's motivation was becoming clearer. It was vengeance that drove his relentless pursuit of clergy and the personal war he was waging against churches. The pastor stared at the photo of Maxwell. Now that he had information that probably no one else knew, what should he do with it? Pastor Harris raked his teeth over his bottom lip and stared at Maxwell's picture. Now he knew exactly who this wounded soul was.

Chapter 43

Maxwell stood on the balcony outside his bedroom, winding down from another hectic Saturday. Exhausted, Maxwell was grateful to have a full plate of work to keep him occupied. Too much idleness might leave him vulnerable to deal with his family, Garrett, second-guessing, or mixed feelings about Nicole. Admittedly, her engagement affected him in a way he wouldn't have expected. She had him worried. He toyed with his cell phone, flipping it over repeatedly in his hand, wanting to call her. Maybe a call would be well received, or maybe she was still mad at him for interfering. He peered at the lights lining his swimming pool and allowed himself to drift away temporarily. His reminiscing took him back to some of the cool summer nights he and Nicole had spent out by the pool gobbling down that pizza she liked with the feta cheese, pine nuts, and caramelized onions. A simple slice of pepperoni was his preference, but he didn't mind taking a bite of hers every now and then.

Enough, he decided. Being indecisive was unacceptable in his line of work. Making a bad decision was better than wasting time fretting and not making any decision. He was done with worrying. Nicole was getting a call. Besides, what was the worst that could happen? She'd hang up on him. After pressing the CALL button, he leaned against the balcony railing and waited for a series of rings. As he pulled the phone away from his ear, giving up, Nicole finally answered.

"Hey. How are you?" he said.

"I'm good."

"Really, how are you doing? I know I dropped a bombshell on you about your fiancé, and I really am sorry if I caused you any pain." He stumbled over his words, wanting to be considerate, but he didn't have much practice in that area. "Uh, is there anything I can do?"

"You've done enough."

Maxwell turned his back to the pool and searched for the right words to smooth the tension between them. "Are you angry with me for having him investigated?"

"I'm not just angry at you. I'm angry, period. I'm angry because he lied to me. Walking around, talking about how he's never been married and didn't have any children." Her voice faded out for a few seconds; then she offered her confession. "I guess I'm angry at myself too."

The sound of glass crashing against something rang out in the background.

"What was that?" Maxwell questioned. He got no response. "Nicole, do you hear me?" He stood up straight and scrambled to keep his phone from hitting the balcony floor. "Answer me. What's going on? Is he there?"

"No. I'm here alone."

"What happened?"

"It was my champagne glass. Let's leave it at that," she told him.

Maxwell planted himself in one of the cushioned chairs on the balcony. "Are you sure you're good? You don't sound too good if you're breaking up stuff."

"No big deal. It's just glass. Good thing I'm not as fragile."

"How about grabbing a bite to eat?" he suggested.

"I don't really feel like getting dressed to go out," she quickly replied.

"Not a problem. I can pick up something and bring it to you." He tapped his hand against his leg, waiting for her answer, and peered down at the empty pool.

"Okay. Give me about an hour."

Maxwell ended the call and stood to face the night sky. He was glad she'd said yes. He actually felt his excitement rising. He even snickered. The Nicole he knew had probably kicked James out by now and vowed never to see him again. Maxwell knew what that felt like. He'd seen her in action. When his relationship ended with her, she was finished. Not one subsequent phone call, text, or e-mail. There was nothing. James was bound to get the same cold shoulder, not that Maxwell felt an ounce of sympathy for the liar. Besides, Nicole deserved better, a lot better.

Maxwell entered his bedroom and shut the balcony door. He was greeted by a batch of documents, notes, and files sprawled across his bed. Maxwell grinned and grabbed his keys from the dresser. With his keys in hand, he eagerly bounced down the stairs and out to his car. The work he left behind tried to pursue him as he drove, but he refused to be taunted. Nicole needed a friend, and he would be there for her. Who was he kidding? This was as much about him as it was about Nicole. The voice of his conscience was getting louder, and the faces in his dreams were too hard to shake off. The truth was that he needed a friend too.

Just then he was startled by a call coming in. The caller ID on the dashboard console told him it was Garrett. Maxwell eagerly answered.

"We need to talk about the Faith Temple investigation when you have time tomorrow," Garrett said.

"What's up? Did you find something?" Maxwell asked.

"I'll have a better handle on things by midday tomorrow. Let's talk then."

Maxwell's phone beeped, informing him Nicole was on the other line. "Okay. I will be in all day tomorrow. Stop by at whatever time works for you. I have to go." He quickly clicked over to answer the other line before she hung up.

"Hey, Nicole. I'm on my way."

"I was thinking we should just get together another day," Nicole suggested.

"Nope. Too late for that. I'm almost there. See you in a few minutes."

Maxwell whipped into a fast-food shop, eager to get back on the road. Twenty minutes later, he was ringing Nicole's doorbell with Chinese food in hand. He tugged at the collar of his dress shirt. He almost felt uncomfortable without a tie on. He put his hand in his pants pocket, located a single quarter, and twirled it between his fingers. What was taking her so long to come to the door? He didn't want to seem anxious. He waited a bit before ringing the bell a second time. Seconds seemed like minutes until Nicole opened the door.

"I was about to leave and take the food home and eat it myself," Maxwell teased as he followed Nicole through the foyer and into the living room. "Should we camp out here and eat?"

"You're not funny, and you know where the kitchen is." Nicole took one of the bags of food from him. She led him into the kitchen, where she had plates and silverware ready. Three steps up the marble platform, and they were at her beveled-glass table.

"I hope you still like egg foo yung and extra spicy kung pao shrimp," Maxwell said as they took the food out of the bags and opened the containers.

"Yep, still two of my favorites," Nicole confirmed.

They both sat down and served themselves. For several uneasy moments, Maxwell listened to the sound of their forks clanking against their plates. Nicole looked healthy, but the bright, cheery glow that usually adorned her face wasn't there. Surely that was his fault. Maybe he should have left well enough alone. She didn't seem to be head over heels in love with James, but at least Nicole had the experience of being engaged. She was on her way to getting married. Maybe that was enough for her. However, now the relationship appeared to be in trouble. He felt awful, but his curiosity didn't diminish. He wanted to know, without asking, what had happened between James and Nicole.

Nicole glanced up from her plate at Maxwell. She was glad for the company. Maxwell's considerate approach and his insistence that he bring her dinner told her he cared. Yet talking about her ex-fiancé with her ex–significant other wasn't appealing. Hopefully, if she kept quiet, Maxwell would eat, get the hint, and go home.

"Before you wouldn't let me come over, out of respect for your fiancé. How come you let me come over tonight?" Maxwell dabbed at his mouth with the linen napkin and swallowed some water without taking his eyes from Nicole's or blinking even once.

Her hopes that he would take the hint were dashed. She should have known his questioning nature wouldn't take a backseat. Her fork clanked against the plate when she dropped it. She swept her hair from the side of her face and tucked it behind her ear.

"James is history. I've closed that door. Now, will you leave it shut?"

Maxwell felt an unexpected sense of joy. "Not a problem. If you want to talk, I'll listen."

Nicole had thought she knew everything about the man she was prepared to marry. Unfortunately, she had had no idea that he had two faces. Either way, she was ready to move on. "So, what's going on with your big case against Pastor Harris? I keep reading about it in the newspaper. It seems you're having a hard time trying to prove the man is a fraud. That's surprising for you."

Not a topic Maxwell wanted to discuss. His eyes shot up from his plate and met Nicole's. He stopped chewing, and his fork clinked against the plate when it dropped from his hand. His appetite had fled, and he had no desire to pursue it.

Chapter 44

The bright sunlight filled Maxwell's car, only intensifying his growing headache. Monday wasn't starting well. He kept one hand on the steering wheel while he rubbed his forehead with the other. Maxwell struggled to drive. His eyelids were heavy with pain, and he had to squint. He'd never been late to court. He considered the clock on the dash and abandoned his route to the courthouse. His squealing tires and the loud honking car horns behind him admonished him for his illegal U-turn. He snagged the open parking space in front of the nearest drugstore. Inside, he searched the aisles for a painkiller to provide some relief. As he stood there with a bottle of Extra Strength Tylenol in hand, a voice called out to him from the other end of the aisle.

Maxwell recognized the voice as it stung him. Why would Pastor Harris want to talk to him? They had nothing to discuss. The case he was busy preparing against the pastor and Faith Temple would do his talking. Maxwell ignored him, turned, and headed toward the opposite end of the aisle.

"Maxwell Montgomery," the pastor called out again as he closed in. Footsteps with a rushed rhythm sounded behind Maxwell. "Mr. Montgomery, just a minute please."

Maxwell couldn't ignore the man any longer. The pastor's insistence wouldn't allow it. He stopped and bit down on his bottom lip. Maxwell gasped and faced the man who was pursuing him. Though he didn't feel like engaging in any type of confrontation, Maxwell was prepared to ignore his pounding headache long enough to come out swinging.

"Good morning," the pastor said and extended his hand, standing less than a foot away.

Maxwell reluctantly obliged, not sure which was more painful, shaking the pastor's hand or his crippling headache. Both were a pain he'd rather not have. The good news about his headache was that it would be gone after he knocked back a few pills. Pastor Harris wouldn't be so easy to get rid of.

"I wanted to ask about your father. He's been on my mind and in my prayers."

"Are you serious?" The puzzled attorney's forehead sprouted wrinkles, and his eyelids dipped down low over his eyes. "Why would you be praying for my father? That's a joke, right?" Maxwell smothered his snicker with the fist he pressed against his mouth. "I fully expect a long list of charges to be brought against you and Faith Temple. Instead of worrying about my father, you might want to use those prayers for yourself." A sharp pain shot through Maxwell's head. "Ow." His hand flew up to soothe the pain that streaked through his head and landed above his right eye.

"Are you in pain?"

"I got a powerful headache." It was a good reason for not wanting to chitchat with the pastor. Maxwell was beyond ready to go.

Pastor Harris immediately placed one hand on Maxwell's shoulder and the other on the back of his head and began to pray.

Maxwell wanted to refuse his prayer, but the pastor did not give him a chance. He could have pulled away from Pastor Harris and declared that he didn't believe in prayer. More importantly, he didn't believe in the pastor.

But making a scene probably wasn't wise. So he shut his eyelids tightly, hoping to shut off the pain and ignore the pastor's voice.

The strong voice of the praying pastor demanded the pain that plagued Maxwell to cease.

Did this guy really think his hocus-pocus would work?

Pastor Harris's voice lowered as he ended the prayer and patted Maxwell on the shoulder. "I'm trusting God for your headache to be completely gone very shortly. You won't be bothered by it again."

"You think I trust you to help me?"

"Why not? I'm a man of God. That's my job, even if you're trying to come after me. I don't even blame you. I actually pity you."

"Huh? I definitely don't need your pity."

"How about my forgiveness?"

"I need that even less, preacher man."

Pastor Harris responded to Maxwell's bitter words. "I wouldn't be so sure about that. Forgiveness is a gift that we all need to receive in our life at some point. Maybe it's time for you to forgive your father. Over twenty years ago he trusted a young Pastor Ellis Jones, who might have made mistakes. Bishop Jones is a different man now. He's grown in his faith and matured into his calling as a pastor. What happened back then in Chester is done. Let it go. You can't live today while holding on to hurts from yesterday."

Maxwell's eyelids widened. How did Pastor Harris know about the Montgomery family's connection with the bishop? His throat dried up, and the words zipping around in his head would not take the form of coherent statements. His whole body felt like it was about to shut down. What else did Pastor Harris know? Maxwell's mind was swirling.

"Paul Montgomery, Jr., don't be ashamed of where you came from. We all make mistakes and have to be forgiven. We also have to be able to forgive ourselves, Brother Maxwell." Pastor Harris strolled down to the end of the aisle and exited the building.

Maxwell stood there, speechless, unable to process fully what had occurred. How was it remotely possible that this man knew his past and his name? His head was spinning. Maxwell hurled the bottle of Tylenol down the long aisle. It crashed into the wall and bounced on the floor. With clenched fists, he surveyed his surroundings. *Good.* No one had seen him. He briskly hiked out of the store to his car, got behind the wheel, and sped off, with a pounding headache riding along with him.

Traffic lights, cars, buildings, pedestrians, nothing registered in Maxwell's mind on his drive to the courthouse. He drove on complete autopilot. His thoughts did battle, one against the other, the entire drive. He zipped into the parking garage and yanked a ticket from the automated slot. With his car parked and the engine off, he heard Pastor Harris's voice in his head. *Paul Montgomery, Jr., don't be ashamed of where you came from.* What would Pastor Harris do with the information about his true identity? Who would he tell? Had he already told someone? Not even Garrett knew that his name was Paul, and he was also unaware of Maxwell's connection to Bishop Ellis Jones.

Maxwell slammed the heels of both hands into the steering wheel multiple times. His chest rose and fell with the weight of his heavy breathing. A couple of minutes passed. He squeezed his eyelids together tightly, latched on to the steering wheel with both hands, and counted to ten to gain his composure. He needed more time, but there wasn't any left. He had fifteen minutes to get to court. Maxwell had to maintain control. He couldn't allow

Pastor Harris's discovery to make him come unglued. He needed to be 100 percent in court. He shook his head from left to right, massaged his temple, and realized his headache was completely gone. Not a minute too soon. Pastor Harris's prayer came to mind, but Maxwell refused to link the prayer to his headache vanishing.

After peering into the rearview mirror and tugging at his tie, Maxwell reclaimed his confidence. He stepped from the car and grabbed his briefcase. Maxwell knew who he was and didn't need a self-righteous pastor to tell him. He was an attorney who had enjoyed undeniable success in the courtroom. Maxwell would find out what Pastor Harris knew and would figure out how to deal with him. He had to. There was no other option.

Chapter 45

Maxwell's car glided through his neighborhood and onto his street. It was quiet, and the blanket of night had just begun to cover the sky. A few scattered stars offered a dim glow way up high. He pressed the button over his visor to open the garage door, drove in, and then headed inside the house. He immediately unbuttoned his shirt collar, ripped the tie from his neck, and flung it across the sofa. He headed upstairs and wound up in the open loft space, an area Maxwell didn't often frequent. There sat his shiny black baby grand piano. Maxwell struggled to remember the last time he'd touched it. He did remember how calming the music was.

He ran his finger across the top of the piano. Not a speck of dust was present. His cleaning lady kept every corner of his house spotless. Even the rooms he rarely visited. She was worth every dollar he paid her and more. A song came to mind. It was his mother's favorite. He sat down on the piano bench and raised the fallboard. Although the melody was hazy in his head, somehow his fingers performed every keystroke perfectly. The second time Maxwell played the song, he could feel his mother sitting next to him on the bench. He could almost smell the fresh baked cookies after school, the ones she'd give him with milk before his piano lesson when he was seven years old. Maxwell shook off the cloak of nostalgia that attempted to embrace him by lowering the fallboard down over the ivory keys and abandoning the rarely visited space.

There was at least a couple hours' work awaiting him in his briefcase. After a quick perusal of the newspaper, he would get right on it. Maybe he'd get four hours of sleep tonight. That wouldn't be bad, considering that the night before he'd gotten only three. He made a sandwich, nabbed the *Philadelphia Tribune* and a bottle of water, and planted himself on the sofa. Two bites into his sandwich, he swallowed hard. He'd discovered yet another article about himself. Maxwell wasn't alarmed, since he had been constantly in the news lately. So much for his plan to have Pastor Harris tormented by the media. From what Maxwell could see, that approach had backfired and landed him in the spotlight, alone. Although he savored his victory over Greater Metropolitan, Maxwell was concerned about the negative publicity affecting his business. He couldn't let that happen.

Maxwell read the first paragraph under his picture on the front page. *Is Maxwell Montgomery on trial? The court of public opinion is in session and doesn't appear to be leaning favorably toward the local attorney. There are mounting sentiments within the community that probes into Pastor Harris and Faith Temple amount to no more than a witch hunt. A similar witch hunt led to the imprisonment of five church leaders and the collapse of Greater Metropolitan, a church with roughly three thousand members located in Philadelphia. Many believe that one of those church leaders, Deacon Steve Burton, was wrongly accused and convicted with Attorney Montgomery's assistance. The deacon was found guilty by association in the charges brought against Greater Metropolitan Church. He received a ten-year federal prison sentence and was recently murdered in prison, after serving a little over a year of his sentence.*

The infuriated attorney leapt off the sofa. Having the media continuously portray him as the bad guy had to stop. He paced the floor from the sofa to the double doors of the formal dining room and back to the sofa as his newspaper dangled from his hand. He came to a jerking stop as he flung the paper up to his face and read more of the article. *Attorney Montgomery has brought down many mega-ministries and major church leaders who were found guilty of a litany of charges. He has won every case and is estimated to have won over two hundred and thirty million dollars in civil cases for his clients. But, as they say, there's a first time for everything. The once thorough and sure shot Maxwell Montgomery seems to have missed his target with Deacon Steve Burton. Will this case mean that an asterisk must be placed on his undefeated winning streak? Could this be the first in Montgomery's list of mistakes?*

Maxwell flung the newspaper across the room, and it knocked over a John-Richard original sculpture he'd acquired for a small fortune. He didn't care. His reputation, which was more valuable, was taking a beating in the media. With the remote in hand, he turned on the TV and caught the tail end of a news broadcast that questioned why no formal charges had been brought against Pastor Harris. "Attorney Maxwell Montgomery has been unable to provide any supporting documentation against the admired leader of Faith Templo, Pastor Harris." He couldn't flick the TV off fast enough. Weren't there more newsworthy events happening in Philadelphia? Surely there had to have been a robbery, an accident, or something an elected city official had promised and failed to keep their word about. Maxwell's story shouldn't be a lead story, or at least he preferred it not to be.

Maxwell schlepped past his briefcase and the work inside it that waited. He dragged himself upstairs, peeled off his clothes, and retreated to the shower. Hot water beat down on his shoulders and his neck. The beads of water were like tons of weight holding him down. His head hung low and his palms pressed against the shower wall while steam engulfed him. If the media was riding his back now, what would happen if they found out about his connection to Bishop Ellis Jones? His reputation and his law firm would be ruined. The heat of public scrutiny was uncomfortable.

He jerked his head backward, allowing the cleansing water to rain down on his face. Maxwell pounded reassurance into his mind. He held fast to the belief that Pastor Harris was a con artist, just like the rest. He wholeheartedly believed it. Why couldn't anyone see it but him? He was more compelled to get the necessary proof. The naysayers would see who was right. He could already envision the media's apology and the revised headlines: ANOTHER CHECK IN THE WIN COLUMN FOR ATTORNEY MAXWELL MONTGOMERY.

After stepping out of the shower, Maxwell dried his body and slipped on a T-shirt and a pair of shorts. *Whew*, he thought. He determined that a shave was required after running both hands along his jawline while peering in the mirror. That same reflection challenged him. Would he deserve it if Pastor Harris held a press conference and unveiled his cloudy past? Would that be Maxwell's just reward for sacrificing his personal life in the name of securing justice for others? The man in the mirror glared back at him, without answers to his questions.

Just then Maxwell's phone squealed and snapped him out of the trance. When he got across the room, the noise had stopped. The call had ended. *Great*. He wasn't up for a conversation, anyway. Before he could walk away, the phone rang again. He took the call.

"Hey, I'm sure you've probably read the newspaper or seen the news reports by now. This kind of press is bad for business, yours and mine."

"Look, Garrett, I can weather the storm with the sharks. I just need you to come through on your end. Find something on this guy. It's time to put the plan that we talked about in play. Let's see if the good pastor can resist a beautiful young woman who is willing to throw some serious cash at the church. You've got everything set up now, right?"

Garrett grunted into the phone. "There are still just a couple of details to nail down."

"Let's get this thing sewn up. In the next day or two, that pawn needs to be in motion. You'll need to stop by tomorrow evening to pick up the cash needed to make this thing happen."

"Okay. I'll stop by your office after five. Let's wrap this up." Garrett slung his phone across the counter, glad the call was over. He peered at the newspaper. The sight of Pastor Harris's and Maxwell's photos side-by-side poked at him. Hopefully, there was not a storm brewing in the distance that would leave Garrett and Maxwell swinging alone in the wind. Maxwell's law firm might be able to handle the fallout, but Garrett was certain his investigation service wouldn't. *Might be time to cut ties*, he thought. He'd soon see.

Chapter 46

Maxwell squeezed the stress ball in his hand and released it, then repeated the process. He tossed it against the wall a few times, then slung the ball into his desk drawer. It had to happen, and he was bold enough to do it. He pressed the speed dial on his phone.

"It's almost five. Are you on your way?"

"I'll be there in ten minutes," Garrett assured Maxwell.

"See you then."

Maxwell hung up, and his pen flew across the paper as he wrote notes that he wanted to cover with Garrett. This was a delicate project, and everything had to be planned out carefully. He reached into the top drawer of his desk and pulled out a thick white envelope. He slipped the money out of it, fanned the bills like a deck of cards, and then slapped them against the palm of his hand. He returned the money to the envelope, sealed it, and placed the money back in the drawer. Then he punched down hard on the keypad of the phone he'd purchased especially for this occasion. His foot tapped the floor rapidly. After the fourth ring, there was still no answer. By the sixth ring, Maxwell was standing.

"What took you so long to answer?"

"Relax. Everything is cool," declared the man on the other end of the line.

"She needs to be on a plane tomorrow," Maxwell insisted as the wrinkles across his forehead faded.

"Why does she have to be from Belize, anyway?" The man's voice was thick and raspy.

The guy was asking too many questions. Did he think Maxwell was going to tell him that the seduction plan required a woman who was far removed from the media in Pennsylvania? Anywhere in the United States was too close. Maxwell would have gotten a woman from Antarctica had there been a viable contact on the underground hotline that he used for special cases like this.

"Just be sure she's on the plane," Maxwell demanded, pressing his knuckles against his desk.

"She'll be ready. Don't worry. I'll get back to you tomorrow with her travel details."

"Don't bother. My guy will contact you. He'll take care of your fee for making the connection."

"Whatever you say. Just have my money before the girl gets on the plane."

"You'll get your money." Maxwell terminated the call, removed the back of the cell phone, and plucked out the SIM card. He broke it in half, tossed the disposable phone into the trashcan next to his desk, and flushed the card pieces down the toilet. He was satisfied, having eliminated anyone's ability to link that call to him.

He made a trip to the bathroom and on the way back into his office, Maxwell's eyes shifted to a bookshelf housing silver scales of justice mounted on a marble base. It drew him closer. He picked up the heavy symbol and was instantly encouraged. The countless long nights spent working and the personal sacrifices made had been worth it. He'd enjoyed a flawless record and a stellar reputation . . . until Greater Metropolitan. Maxwell was certain the negative attention would dissipate, but he had to question his upcoming move. Was it worth it? In the past, the end result had consistently justified whichever route he'd taken to win. Somehow this didn't settle as well. Was he being a defender of justice, or was he about to tip the scales? The heavyhearted attorney placed the scales back on the bookshelf, next to one of his bar association plaques.

A strong gust of wind slammed against the tall window behind Maxwell. He turned his back to justice as another loud gust of wind crashed into the window. Maxwell dashed to the window to check out the ruckus. He examined the sky, and dark clouds were forming. The leaves on the trees were swaying with the wind. It appeared that a storm was brewing. Maxwell was on the brink of facilitating a storm of his own. He was about to set an act in motion that mirrored nothing he'd done in all his years as an attorney. Yet it was necessary. He couldn't allow Pastor Harris to slip through the cracks of justice.

A shrilling phone in his jacket pocket demanded attention. Maxwell was debating whether to answer when he realized it was his sister. Why was she calling? He didn't have time for arguing but was compelled to answer. She would get only a couple minutes of his precious time. He trudged into his office, took a seat behind the desk, prepared himself, and answered the call.

"I want to thank you for paying Dad's hospital bill. I had Mom call to get the total for his last stay so we could set up payments, and the bill was already paid."

"No big deal."

"It is. It really is. You say you don't care about us. You pretend not to be interested in how Dad is doing. Yet anytime there's a medical bill to be paid, you snag it and pay it before it's barely been processed."

"I paid a bill, Christine. I didn't operate on him."

"It says you care. Stop being so hard and just let your family back into your life. You walked away from us so many years ago. You can't possibly want this distance between yourself and your family. Aren't you lonely? Don't you feel like something is missing? No wife, no kids, no family. Is that really what you want?"

"You know what? I am really getting tired of these lectures every time I talk to you. I've got to go." He pressed his thumb against the END button hard, held it there a few seconds, until the phone powered off, then tossed the phone onto his desk. He didn't need a psychoanalyst. He didn't need anybody waiting for him when he got home. Whatever this thing between him and the Montgomerys was, it wasn't a relationship. That was definitely not a picture he'd painted. He'd just framed it.

A moment later his assistant's voice broke through on the intercom. "Mr. Montgomery, I'm about to leave, unless there is something else you need."

"No. Thank you. Go on home."

"Garrett just arrived."

"Send him right in."

"I'll lock up. See you tomorrow," his assistant told him.

Maxwell met Garrett at the door and ushered him into his office. "Thanks for coming over."

"Sure. I'll take the money and get out your way."

"Shhh. Not yet." Maxwell scurried to the security panel on the wall behind his desk and watched the light turn red, signaling that his office alarm was engaged. Maxwell plopped down in the chair behind his desk and swiveled. "We're alone. Now we can talk."

"You're sure you want to do this? You are actually going to set Pastor Harris up by paying a woman to see if he will cheat on his wife?" Garrett stood near the front of the desk, with his car keys in hand.

A cryptic, snicker slipped past Maxwell's tight lips. "Absolutely. If his character is as clean and straitlaced as you keep telling me, he should pass the test of infidelity with no problem. But if he cheats, you can best believe he's fallen prey to other shady dealings."

"I still don't think this is the right move to make. And I can definitely tell you I won't be a part of doctoring evidence in any way. If Pastor Harris turns the woman down, then that's it. We pull the plug on this crazy mission and put the woman back on a plane out of here."

"I'm fine with that." Maxwell removed from the drawer a four-by-six photo of a woman with olive-colored skin, coal-black eyes, and a short, sassy haircut. He pulled out a second photo. This one was a body shot of the woman. He passed both photos to Garrett. "Nice, right? I believe she is just the bait we need."

As Garrett examined the photos, his gaze bounced back and forth between Maxwell and the images of the woman. "So what's next?" Garrett's burning stare bore directly into Maxwell's eyes.

"All you need to do is get in touch with our contact. Once he gets paid, he'll put the woman on the plane tomorrow. Finalize the details and meet her at the airport when she arrives. Give her the instructions on how she is to meet Pastor Harris and what to do from there." Maxwell reached across the desk and handed the unenthusiastic investigator a thick white envelope. "That will cover the contact's fee, yours, plus a bonus. There's extra in there to compensate the woman, cover her hotel expenses, and pay her flight back to Belize. If you need more, just let me know."

Maxwell scooped up a pen and crossed items off the checklist in front of him. "Oh, and the contact's number is in there. Of course, my name is not to be mentioned to the woman." He dropped the pen and snapped his fingers on both hands. "It's that simple."

"Simple? Are you kidding me? This is crazy and risky. You have to admit this is over the line, and I'm not sure I want to be a part of it." The right side of Garrett's mouth twitched.

Maxwell clutched the arm of his chair to prevent himself from leaping up. He needed Garrett to make this thing happen. There was no one else he could trust. The woman could never see Maxwell's face and be able to identify him. Garrett had to stay in the game. "Look, this is no big deal. Think of it as a way to prove whether Pastor Harris is the real deal or not. You keep saying he appears to be. Well, here is a way to prove it."

Garrett shook the envelope of money and aimed it toward his determined employer. "Don't work me, Maxwell. I know what this is, and I'd be willing to bet this will come back to bite us both." He shoved the envelope into his jacket pocket.

A blank four-by-six manila envelope on the desk distracted Maxwell. His assistant must have placed it there earlier. "Give me a second, Garrett. Let me check this out." There was no return address and no postmark. *Now what?* What was some knucklehead sending him in the mail? He tapped the envelope with his middle finger. He considered whether he should open it. The mystery item in his hand dared him, and he took the bait. *Why the heck not?* Maxwell tore into the end of it. He slipped the item out and unfolded it. He was stunned seeing a copy of his legal license. It had his name, the correct dates, and an official seal from the state of Pennsylvania. The yellow sticky note attached to it read, *Enjoy. You won't have it much longer.*

Maxwell became more irritated than worried. His conscience was hounding him. The media was hounding him, and then were was this clown sending threatening notes and making prank calls. He'd had enough.

"I need one more favor."

"What else could you possibly want me to do?"

Maxwell disregarded Garrett's tone and stayed on task. "I'm tired of this wannabe stalker wasting my time. Could you do me a favor and look into this nonsense?" He lifted the contents of the envelope in his hand as he spoke to Garrett.

"I'm glad you're finally taking the threat serious."

"Does that mean you'll find this person for me?"

"Of course, I'll look into it. I might not agree with your tactics lately, but I'm not going to let anything happen to you."

"Cool," Maxwell replied. "I'm stuffing the notes into an envelope as we speak. I'll drop it off at the courier service on my way out the building tonight. The package will be at your office early tomorrow." Maxwell hesitated and then uttered, "Thanks for your help. I know you didn't have to say yes. Regardless of our differences, I respect you and that's for real."

"Just be careful."

Chapter 47

Maxwell's office door swung open and pulled both his and Garrett's attention. Maxwell's head whipped toward the door. His assistant entered without knocking and started talking immediately in a rapid and a stern tone.

"You need to check out the news broadcast, right now."

"Where did you come from? You left and I put the alarm on the door."

"I saw the news when I got to the lobby and came right back up. You have to see this. Turn your TV on."

"This better be good since you barged in on my meeting," Maxwell demanded. He pressed the power button, and his assistant took the remote from him and selected the channel that he needed to watch. He glared at her with squinted eyelids. The news broadcast snatched his attention from her.

"Maxwell Montgomery, the prominent attorney with a perfect win record, attempted to build a case against Pastor Renaldo Harris of Faith Temple Church with a witness who was discovered to have lied. Mr. Layne accused Pastor Harris of infidelity, being a womanizer, and stealing money from the church. After a thorough investigation, it was discovered that Mr. Layne was simply a disgruntled member and a paid staff member at Faith Temple who had been fired and was determined to discredit Pastor Harris in retaliation."

Garrett and Maxwell stared at each other for a few seconds. Garrett dropped his head for a few seconds then looked up and shot a stern look at Maxwell. "I told you this would happen."

"I knew that attorney was wrong about Pastor Harris. If he had done the right kind of investigating, he would have discovered the man was innocent before he tried to build a case against him. Shoot, most of these lawyers are dishonest and crooks themselves," said an older man who was being interviewed.

"I don't want to hear any 'I told you so' speeches. I've worked too hard for my reputation to be dragged through the mud. This case isn't over yet."

Maxwell's assistant retreated to the office door. She was met by reporters herding toward her.

Reporters with cameras flashing, microphones being shoved at Maxwell. His assistant attempting to ward off the reporters was suddenly the circus of events in his office.

"Do you have a comment on the recent discovery that your witness, Mr. Layne, lied about Pastor Harris's infidelity and misappropriation of church funds?" a thick male voice demanded.

"Mr. Montgomery, why did you think Mr. Layne would be a credible witness against Pastor Harris?" Another male reporter asked.

"What evidence did he provide against the pastor that made his accusations seem credible?" Maxwell heard another reporter shout out.

Then a female voice taunted him with a question. "Will your error tarnish your perfect win record? Will this be the case that you lose?"

Maxwell looked to his right and noticed that the question came from the same female reporter that had been in his office before, asking if he was feeling guilty about Deacon Burton's death. His office was crowded, and the air was suddenly thick. "Here's a comment for you. A guilty and corrupt man cannot be fully exonerated simply because one witness may not have been reliable. It will take more than that to stop the case against Pastor Harris and Faith Temple. The truth will be uncovered. And this case will not be tried in the media and not in my office. Get out, or I will call security and have you removed from the premises."

He turned to his assistant and said, "Call security and get these reporters out of here or you'll be looking for a job in a matter of minutes."

Garrett shook his head again at Maxwell and pressed his way through the reporters that were starting to file out of the office.

Maxwell grabbed the now warm bottle of water on the corner of his desk and chugged it down. This case would not be derailed, and his reputation would not be damaged. Maxwell would make sure of that. *Defeat was not an option.* Maxwell crushed the plastic water bottle between both hands and continued to squeeze it hard as he watched the last reporter leave his office.

Chapter 48

The sun was approaching the horizon. A sliver of light attempted to break through the early Saturday morning darkness. Chirping birds were still able to hide themselves in the shadows of the trees as Maxwell jogged past. It had been a seventy-hour workweek, but that didn't hinder him from getting up at the crack of dawn to get in his usual five-mile run. His running companion was the realization that he had nothing concrete against Pastor Harris.

He didn't have an individual client calling a foul against the pastor. When all else failed, Maxwell was generally able to get a small group of people to join in on a class-action lawsuit. He'd never fallen short on getting people to sign up and lie under oath when there was money involved. In fifteen years, he'd only been turned down once, by Jill Winston. While he had nothing concrete on the pastor, he did have a solid plan in place. The attractive, sexy woman the perfect pastor was about to meet would uncover his true character and expose his sins for sure. Maxwell was drenched in optimism.

The encounter with Pastor Harris in the drugstore came to mind when Maxwell ran by a man seated on a bench, with a bandage on his forehead. The fact that Maxwell hadn't suffered a headache since Faith Temple's senior pastor had prayed for him didn't make him a believer for one second. He pushed the prayer out of his mind and chased the possibility of building an airtight civil case that would stick once Pastor Harris met the woman whom Maxwell was paying good money to perform her magic. He chuckled within. Pastor Harris didn't know it, but he'd better be loading up on prayers for himself.

Maxwell was energized by thinking about the fallout. Garrett needed to get the plan under way and wrapped up. The woman couldn't be in town too long. The fewer people she was around, the less chance of anything going wrong. The only person she needed to know in Philadelphia was Pastor Harris. Garrett was a professional, but he hadn't facilitated anything like this before, as far as Maxwell knew. This thing had to be handled with caution, or it could blow up in their faces, and even take him down, instead of his intended target.

The sting in his legs and his dry mouth encouraged Maxwell to notice the mile marker on the running path. He'd run five miles in one direction, instead of going his usual two and half miles and then heading back. He turned around and hurried home to hit the shower. His body pressed forward, and so did his worries as he considered what waited for him at the office. His office would be quiet, and there were a few things he wanted to knock out.

In an efficient management of time, he showered, dressed, and had a cup of coffee before he left the house. The sun was fully awake, but clouds had begun to form when he got into his car. After stopping at the gas station and the bank, he headed to the barbershop before going to the office. The rain found its way to his windshield as Maxwell stopped at a red light. He noticed a man sitting in the drizzling rain. *Why would he sit there and not attempt to shield himself?* His cardboard sign read: LOST MY JOB, MY HOME, AND MY FAMILY. I'M HUNGRY. SOMEBODY HELP ME.

Maxwell had seen plenty of panhandlers on street corners. He'd never stopped or been moved by words on a sign previously. He'd always figured that most of them were con artists and were just looking for a handout, instead of working. He didn't get that feeling about this particular man. Instead, the man yanked Maxwell back to the day his family was forced to move out of their home. He could vividly see the moving van, the empty rooms, and the boxes of things they gave away, since a four-bedroom house wouldn't fit into a tiny apartment. As a birthday gift, his father had had a mural painted on his bedroom wall of every Supreme Court justice, including his hero, Thurgood Marshall. It was gone too. Maxwell lost a home that day and his family along with it.

The traffic light had turned green, red, and back to green again. Cars had blown their horns while zooming around him. Maxwell's car was still sitting at the corner. The last honking car horn behind him got his attention. He eased his foot off the brake, turned the corner, and pulled over to the side of the road. He removed several bills from his wallet and got out of the car, ignoring the rain. Maxwell walked up to the man and held the money out in front of him.

The man did not reach for the money.

"Take it. You can have it." The man looked up at him. He appeared to be close to Maxwell's age and hid behind a hedge of wild, bushy hair. Maxwell leaned over and stuffed the money into the man's empty tin can.

A raspy voice spoke through the bushy hair on the man's face. "Thank you."

"Get out of the rain. You should get somewhere dry," Maxwell suggested.

The man held his gaze and responded, "Thank you. Maybe I will."

Maxwell was perplexed. Why wouldn't he get out of the rain? He had some money now. He'd given him more than enough for a meal and a room, if the man wanted to get one. Maxwell examined the man's dirty nails, torn clothes, mangy hair, and beard. What situations in life would take a man to such a low point? Unfortunately, he knew the answer, thanks to the bishop. Maxwell went back to his car. He wiped the rain from his face and couldn't help but look back at the man in his rearview mirror.

And the great Pastor Harris wanted him to let go of the past. *No way*, Maxwell thought. The past was his true source of motivation. He pulled onto the road and drove a little faster, putting some distance between himself and what could have been his life. His father could have been the man sitting on the corner. Heck, *he* could have been that man. There had to be consequences for the wrong done in life. Even for those who used the pulpit as a shield. If Maxwell got his way, every man who deserved it would have his day in court.

A few minutes later, Maxwell parked the car on the street and entered the barbershop. He claimed a seat in the corner, pleased to see there wasn't a swarm of folks waiting for their turn.

"I'll get to you in just a bit, Mr. Montgomery," his usual barber told him.

He replied with a quick nod. He'd been using the same barber for several years. He'd be in and out quickly, which was just what he needed. No time to socialize or shoot the breeze with the fellas in the shop. He was there for a haircut and nothing else. Hopefully, Sonya wasn't going to disrupt his plan, like she'd tried to during his last visit.

An older man with a cane on his lap watched Maxwell. Out of the corner of his eye, Maxwell noticed the man shifting his attention between him and the TV. Their eyes met. They examined each other, neither willing to lift his gaze.

The old man lifted his cane and pointed it at Maxwell. "You're that attorney who's going around, tearing down the good pastor's name. Pastor Harris is a good man. Son, don't you have something better to do with your time, money, and fancy car?" He took a glimpse over his shoulder at Maxwell's car sitting out front. "Looks like you've made enough money digging around in people's lives to keep you satisfied. Why don't you go somewhere and sit down? You're wasting your time, anyway, with Faith Temple. You're going to come up dry when it comes to Pastor Harris." He shook the cane in Maxwell's direction and then turned his attention back to the TV.

The man's speech seemed to have a profound effect on the other patrons. A hush had claimed the room. Maxwell struggled to hold his tongue in his own defense. That old man didn't know him. He had probably read or heard some of the garbage about him in the media. Instead of giving him the tongue-lashing someone else would have received, Maxwell fell prey to words his father had often repeated: "Son, respect your elders." Maxwell picked up the newspaper next to him. He would let that one slide and wouldn't come out with both barrels loaded and blast the man out of his business. But the old guy had better know that this was a one-time pass. Seconds weren't free.

Chapter 49

Garrett glanced at the monitor for the fifth time in less than thirty minutes. The inbound flight from Belize would be arriving late. There was a buzz of people scurrying around the airport, searching for their departure gate, and others waiting to see a familiar face near the baggage terminal. He needed to meet the woman as soon as possible terminal and get out of that very public place. Maxwell didn't want to be seen with the woman or have his name mentioned. That was understandable. However, Garrett didn't want to be sucked down into the abyss of destruction, either, if the dirty deed went south. He inspected the picture of the woman again and refreshed his memory of her face. He would have to identify her in a sea of folks who would be searching for their baggage on the carousel.

Garrett hustled to the window and huddled in a corner. He took out a small flip phone and punched in a number that he read from a slip of paper. The phone rang several times, with no answer. Garrett's contact had better pick up, and the woman had better be on the flight. The phone continued to ring. There was no answer and no voice mail. He flipped the phone shut and squeezed it hard in the palm of his hand. His eyes latched on to the monitor that displayed the inbound flights. The plane from Belize had landed. The phone in his hand rang, and Garrett jammed it to his ear.

"What going on? Is she on the plane?" Garrett demanded.

"Calm down. She's on the plane," the contact replied.

"She had better be. You got a lot of money to make sure she landed in Philadelphia."

"She will be there."

"You'll hear from me if she isn't." Garrett snapped the phone shut.

Swarms of people engulfed the baggage carousel. Garrett clenched the picture of Colita between his fingers, meticulously examining every slim woman who looked to be about five-eight with a curvy build and a mole on the side of her right eye. A woman fitting that description approached the baggage carousel. It wasn't long before she retrieved a designer garment bag and a matching roller bag. The investigator watched her survey the crowd, her head moving back and forth. She appeared to be paying close attention to the men who came near her.

Garrett inched a bit closer, his gaze shifting from the woman's face back to the picture. Was it her? He didn't have time for a wild-goose chase. He approached the woman, who was dressed in a royal blue, formfitting dress and a lightweight black jacket. She was attractive, all right.

"Excuse me. Are you Colita?"

"Yes," she sang out, her island accent apparent.

"You can call me Nathan."

"What do other people call you?" she asked in a flirtatious way.

"Doesn't matter. Let's get to your hotel."

Garrett relieved Colita of her luggage and guided her through the airport and out to the rental car he'd secured for their short trip. No time for any pleasantries, like a handshake. She needed to be tucked away behind the closed door of a hotel room as quickly as possible. He tossed the luggage in the trunk, opened the passenger door for Colita, hopped in the car, and sped away from the airport, feeling better with each mile traveled.

Colita sat quietly during the ride. Garrett was glad she didn't initiate any conversation, and he happily returned the same courtesy. He drove to a nearby little town, found the hotel, entered the lobby, and paid the desk clerk for a week's stay. One week was all Colita had to get Pastor Harris tangled up in her web of deceit. After that, Garrett was done.

Once they were behind closed doors, Garrett was free to talk.

"What did your contact in Belize tell you about the job you're here to do?"

"That it paid well and all expenses would be covered," she said in broken English. She winked at Garrett, licked her lips, and allowed her head to move up and down to access his tall frame.

"I'll make this quick," he offered, ignoring her gaze and her actions. "You're here to play a practical joke on a friend. He's a local pastor." Lying about the job, characterizing it as a practical joke, couldn't be avoided. He had to give the impression that the task would cause no one a problem. "My friends and I would like for you to call him and act interested in his church. Say you're new in town, and you've heard good things about his ministry. Set up an appointment to meet with him at the church."

Garrett crossed his ankles as he leaned against the wall, dictating more details to Colita. "Once you get there, show an interest in the church and compliment him on the building." A quick hard knock at the door pushed Garrett to an upright position, with both feet planted solidly on the floor. He rushed to Colita and whispered, "Ask who it is, but don't open the door."

She followed his instructions. "Who is it?"

"The maid, ma'am. You dropped your room key here, outside the door."

Garrett looked up toward the ceiling, then back at Colita. He hustled to the other side of the room. Once he was out of view from the doorway, Garrett motioned for her to open the door.

Colita thanked the maid as she accepted the room key and shut the door.

Garrett moved from his hiding place and stepped closer to Colita. "Okay, so the objective is for you to seduce Pastor Harris. Make the offer subtle and smooth. Flatter him, and you can figure out the rest, since I was told you do this for a living."

"Actually, I don't seduce men for a living. I get paid for a service. That's not seduction. That's supply and demand."

He ignored her jazzy response. "Whatever you call it, remember that I'm paying you for results."

"I bet you'd be surprised if I told you most of my clients are rich women who pay me to get their husbands in compromising situations. I guess it's the easiest way to get more in their divorce settlements. Rich men don't want such choices in their personal life to be made public." Colita winked at Garrett. "And you said this pastor is a friend, huh?"

Garrett's gaze dashed away from hers and returned. "You can say that." He reviewed the final details of the plan and removed an envelope from his inside jacket pocket. He shoved it at her. "There's enough money to take care of any incidentals you might need. You can order room service or have food delivered. Eat or don't eat, so long as you stay in the room."

"Stay here?" she questioned, with pinched eyebrows and a tilted head.

"Yes. One of the requirements for you to be paid is that you stay out of sight. The practical joke won't work if you're seen around town."

Colita shook her head and peeked inside the envelope. "How much is in here?"

"Count it." Garrett crossed his arms across his body.

"I see that you're concerned. Would you like for me to give you a sneak preview of my skills?" She stepped within inches of him, licked her full red lips, and squeezed the thick bicep muscle that bulged through Garrett's jacket.

He flicked her hand from his arm. "I'm not the target." He then handed her several pictures of Pastor Harris, his wife, his church, and his automobile. "The pastor's contact information is there also." Garret's phone buzzed. A quick check told him Maxwell wanted an update. "I've got to get going. I'll talk with you in the morning, and you will need to contact the pastor by early afternoon. Call me if you need anything." He slipped her a piece of paper with the number of his throwaway phone and made a dash for the door.

"What I need is walking out the door," she teased.

He ignored her and let the door closing behind him act as his response. The elevator ride back down to the lobby was much too slow. Colita was a piece of work, and that whole situation was too close to the line he drew. Garrett wanted to make a quick call to Maxwell and get home. He needed a shower to wash off traces of the pile of crap surrounding him.

Chapter 50

The traffic was thick, and the morning had already slipped away. Bright rays of sun broke through the windshield and impeded Garrett's vision. He shielded his eyes with his hand and then remembered his shades in the console. *Enough with the piercing sunlight,* Garrett thought, realizing he had twenty minutes to get to his meeting on time. The problem was that he hadn't heard back from Colita. She should have been up and working. He was annoyed that she hadn't given him an update by now. Several days had already passed, and she was still working on arranging a meeting with Pastor Harris. He needed her to pick up the pace. The sooner she did the deed, the sooner she could get out of town and let him breathe easier.

A wide yawn overtook Garrett. More sleep was a necessity, but it wasn't in sight. Restless nights had haunted him since the day he agreed to Maxwell's crazy scheme to set up Pastor Harris. This entire idea had stunk from the beginning. Against his better judgment, he'd agreed to go through with it. Doubts were creeping. This had to end quickly. He'd call again. Colita had better answer before he arrived at his destination.

Garrett pressed the SEND button on his phone. Five rings later, there was still no answer. What was she doing? He didn't have time to race over and babysit her. Determined, he ended the call and tried again. Still no answer. *Dang.* Where was she? His fingers tapped rapidly against the steering wheel. He tried the number once more out of sheer desperation. Colita answered on the second ring.

"Where have you been?" he barked, lashing out, unable to harness his fear about the scheme backfiring. I've been calling you all morning."

"I was in the shower."

"For an hour?" To avoid getting peeved, Garrett kept his focus. "Never mind about the shower. Do you have an appointment with Pastor Harris yet?" His fingers stopped moving, and he clutched the steering wheel with a clawlike grip.

"I'm meeting him at the church in an hour."

"Good." He gulped. "Be sure to use cash for meals and your travel. Also, remember not to keep receipts. I will contact you this evening. Oh, and there might be a nice bonus in this for you, depending on how well you do." He hung up. The call was over, but Garrett's fretting was not, and probably wouldn't be until Colita was on a plane destined for Belize. That flight couldn't come soon enough.

In the meantime, he'd look into Maxwell's stalker problem. The amount of controversy his client had stirred in the past year created a long list of candidates. He'd start with the biggest cases and the angriest defendants. He had work to do, but Garrett was confident in his abilities when it came to finding a real culprit.

Colita painted her lips with the ruby-red lipstick, smacked them together tightly, and then smiled at her reflection. Her bright white teeth sparkled. She approved of her appearance. He'd have to be dead not to respond to her and not to be enticed by what she had planned for the pastor. She scooped up her purse and the room key, left the room, then sashayed to the elevator. During the taxi ride to the church, she examined the pictures of Pastor Harris and his wife. *Nice looking guy with strange friends,* she thought. She didn't know any friends who would pull such a prank. But as long as she got paid with a shot at an extra bonus, too, the underlying reason for them pulling the prank didn't matter to her.

The taxi stopped in front of Faith Temple. Colita paid the driver. "There's a fifty-dollar tip if you'll wait for me," she said, putting extra effort into masking her accent. "I need to leave quickly when I'm finished here. This shouldn't take very long."

"Fifty bucks? You bet I'll wait," the taxi driver responded.

Colita slung her long legs out of the taxi and planted her pointed heels on the pavement. She climbed the steps to the wooden double doors of Faith Temple. She tugged at her jacket and the bust line of her dress as she strutted by the large cross that hung over the archway. *Wow.* She hadn't seen the inside of a church since she was eight years old and living with her mother in Trinidad.

When her mother died, Colita had picked up with a cruise line, which landed her in Central America. It hadn't taken long for her to find a way to make much more money than she could from serving people on a ship for tiny tips. Admittedly, her innocence was gone once she embraced the new profession, and so was the need to attend church.

The sign over the door she entered said MAIN OFFICE.

"Good morning," greeted Martha with a kind voice as she peered over her glasses. "How may I help you?"

"I'm here to see Pastor Harris. He's expecting me. I'm Colita."

"Your last name please."

"It's not necessary," Colita informed her.

The lady stared at Colita and hesitated, like she wasn't accepting such an answer.

There is no reason to cause a problem, Colita thought, being that she was this close to meeting Pastor Harris. She quickly changed her tune. "I'm sorry. Where are my manners? I'm Colita Smith." She didn't feel bad about telling a fib in the church. This was, after all, some strange hoax, and dishonesty was acceptable, or so she preferred to believe.

Just as Colita had figured, the receptionist resumed beaming and speaking in her kind voice. "I will let him know you're here. Have a seat." Martha sealed her statement with a quick glance over the top of her glasses to take in Colita's tall frame.

Colita couldn't figure out why the receptionist kept looking at her. She took the seat near the wall, the one farthest from the lady. Ten minutes meandered by as Colita counted the pictures, certificates, and awards that adorned the walls. The uneasiness she felt wasn't expected. Perhaps the pastor would pass her test quickly, figure out this was a prank, and send her packing. She could then report that the unsuspecting pastor hadn't fallen for the prank. She didn't quite know what that meant to his friends, but her pay wouldn't be impacted one way or the other.

Pastor Harris entered the outer office, and Martha made the introductions. "Glad you could make it," Pastor Harris said as he shook Colita's hand vigorously.

He led her into his office. She sat down in a chair in front of Pastor Harris's desk. Colita swung her right leg over her left and allowed her red toenails to sparkle in the sunlight that streamed through the window. She made sure Pastor Harris got an eyeful of her golden-toned thighs.

The pastor didn't seem to react. "How long have you been in Philadelphia?" he asked.

"Not long at all," she offered in a soft, sultry tone after delicately rolling her tongue around her lips.

"I understand that you were in a battered women's shelter and recently relocated here."

"Oh, uh, yes, that's me," she said, suddenly feeling awkward. Nathan had suggested she use the shelter story, although she wondered if that was really his name. He'd said that a vulnerable, needy woman had a much better chance of capturing the pastor's attention. Since she wanted to please her employer, Colita had gladly agreed with the strategy. She'd confidently recited this story to the lady over the phone. But sitting this close to a minister and telling a fib wasn't the same. Prank or not, she wasn't comfortable.

"Do you have any family in town?"

"No. I'm all alone," she muttered.

"Okay . . . well, let me tell you a little bit about the church." He spent the next ten minutes talking about Faith Temple, then followed this up with a tour of the building. They talked as she trailed behind him. The tour started in the sanctuary and concluded in the social hall.

"You have a beautiful church," Colita said while she rubbed her hand across the top of her bosom at the end of the tour. The tour had allowed her to push her awkwardness to the side and get back to work. This was her business, and she did it well. "May I have some water, please?"

"Certainly. There should be some bottles of water in the kitchen." He darted into the nearby kitchen and came back with a cold bottle of water and held it out to her.

Colita stroked his hand with hers when she reached for the water. She batted her thick eyelashes and pitched him a subtle smile, barely turning up the corners of her mouth. Pastor Harris's hand opened wide, and he released the bottle. Colita struggled to prevent the bottle from hitting the floor.

"I'm sorry. I didn't mean to do that," the pastor stated.

She winked and untwisted the cap on the bottle. She wrapped her lips around it, toying with him. Her stare held his until he shifted his eyes away.

"If you're interested in learning more about our church or becoming a member, I'll put you in touch with one of the ladies on our membership board."

"Really? Can't you help me with a membership?" she said, batting her eyelids.

"No. They're much better at the new member intake process than I am. Normally, you would have met with them today, but I was told you insisted on meeting with me first. So, I wanted to accommodate your request."

"I'd prefer to talk with you," the temptress insisted and moved closer to him. The toes of their shoes were inches away from touching. "You smell delicious." She inhaled his cologne and released a whisper of air between her lips. Suddenly, Colita reached up and traced his jawline with her finger.

Pastor Harris seized Colita's hand and pulled it away from his face. "Look, young lady, I don't know what you're trying to do, but I'm married." He stretched his left hand out so that it came close to her face and tapped the gold band that embraced his finger.

"I know. That doesn't mean anything. Besides, she doesn't have to know." She tugged at the tip of his tie.

"I would know, and God would know. That's more than enough." The pastor shook his head at her with squinted eyes.

"You might want to take the time to listen to my proposition. I'm offering more than it appears. I have a way that your ministry could make a lot of money tax free," she said and rubbed her fingertips together. "What ministry couldn't use some extra money, right?"

"Miss . . . ," he said, trying to recall her name.

"Colita," she stated.

"Right. Miss Colita, I appreciate your interest in Faith Temple, but your actions are inappropriate."

Colita tried unsuccessfully to dissuade him of that notion.

"No, now wait. I'm not judging you, but I am convicting you. I'm the senior pastor of this church. I'm here to help you strengthen your walk with the Lord, not to tear you down and contribute to your sinning."

Colita didn't say anything, actually feeling convicted, until she remembered this was all a prank. *Thank goodness.*

A young man entered the social hall. "Excuse me, Pastor. The youth group meeting will be starting in here in about fifteen minutes. Do you need me to move my meeting to another area of the church?"

"No, not at all. I'm finished here. Can you please see Miss Colita to her car?" Pastor Harris exited the room swiftly without speaking another word to her.

Colita followed the young man to the reception area, not sure what to think. That was a first. No man had ever turned her down. Two facts were true: Pastor Harris didn't fall for the hoax, and she wasn't getting the bonus. Hopefully, the prank had turned out the way the pastor's friends expected. Regardless, she was getting paid. *Money should come so easily every day*, she thought.

Chapter 51

The gray sky and the dark clouds concerned Maxwell, since he'd had his car detailed the day before. Maybe he could make it to the courthouse parking garage before the downpour started. His hands-free device signaled a call coming in just as Maxwell's foot pressed the gas pedal harder. The display on his dashboard read Christine. What did she want? He didn't have time to bicker with her about anything. She'd have to call him another day. Within a few minutes, she'd called two more times. He began worrying. It was always bad news when she called him repeatedly. When he decided to answer, it was too late. Maxwell gave a voice command and dialed her right back. There was only one ring, and then he heard sobbing and words laced with whimpers that he couldn't understand.

"Christine, what is it? What's wrong?"

Her voice cracked, and she managed to reply, "My baby got hit by a car while riding his bike."

Maxwell whipped his Porsche to the side of the road and slammed his foot down hard on the brake. The sound of screeching tires accompanied his abrupt stop. "What? No, no, don't tell me that. Where is he? Where is Tyree?"

More sobbing and muffled whimpers saturated the phone line before an understandable word broke through. "We're at Wilmington Hospital. He's being prepared for surgery right now. I haven't been able to reach Mom and Dad yet."

"I'm on my way. I'll be there as soon as I can."

Maxwell checked his rearview mirror and saw the line of cars barreling down on him. He ignored the NO U-TURN sign, and his tires spat out a trail of dust and gravel as he peeled off. He punched the gas pedal and jerked the steering wheel as he sped across two lanes of traffic, dodging the cars that were in his way. His high-performance engine sucked up the miles as he zoomed down the highway. This couldn't be happening. He had bought Tyree that bike for his birthday. He'd purchased knee pads and a helmet too. He intended for Tyree to be safe, but he hadn't been.

Maxwell was dying inside. He aggressively fought off doubts and fears. He couldn't lose that little boy. He hadn't spent enough time with him. Maxwell had missed birthdays, Christmas, and basically every holiday since Tyree was born. He had always showered him with gifts. Regrettably, Maxwell hadn't rewarded his nephew with the time he'd constantly begged for with his uncle Max. Maxwell drove faster, wishing remorse and mistakes would move to the backseat or get out of the car completely.

His tires squealed as he charged into the hospital parking lot and slid into a stall. He climbed out of the car, slammed the door shut, and ran across the parking lot, toward the emergency room doors. He stormed inside, dashed to the counter, and demanded an answer.

"Where is Tyree—" He couldn't finish his question before Christine's frazzled voice grabbed him. He turned toward her.

"Thank God, you came," she exclaimed as she eliminated the distance between them and flung her body into his. "What am I going to do? What if he doesn't make it?"

He felt the weight of her body and her pain. He guided her to the row of seats behind them, and they both sat down. "Take a deep breath," he directed, and then he did the same. "One more," he directed, and he exhaled along with her. "Now, tell me what happened."

"Tyree was riding his bike on the sidewalk. I was sitting in the yard, watching him. A drunk driver flying through the neighborhood drove onto the sidewalk and hit my baby." Her swollen eyelids fluttered. The red lines that streaked across the whites of her eyes were clouded by another downpour of tears. "I saw it happen. I watched that man hit my child, and there was nothing I could do. I couldn't get to him in time."

With a clenched fist, Maxwell punched his thigh twice. "A drunk driver." He bit down hard on his bottom lip as his gaze rose toward the ceiling. "How bad is it?"

"There is a lot of internal bleeding. He has a broken leg and a collapsed lung. The doctors are concerned about the bleeding in his brain." Christine pressed her nails into Maxwell's hand. "I can't believe this. It's too much. It's just too much." Her head dropped onto his shoulder.

He stood up, holding on to her and forcing her to stand with him. "Where is he now?"

"Upstairs. They're doing a CAT scan before taking him into surgery." She dabbed the tears streaming down her cheeks. "Oh, and I finally got ahold of Mom and Dad. They are on their way."

In that moment, Maxwell didn't care about his issue with their parents. Nothing was more important than Tyree, nothing. "Let's get upstairs and see about my little man."

The elevator ride was quiet, with the exception of Christine's muffled whimpers. When the doors opened, Maxwell and Christine stepped off the elevator and walked down the hallway, their steps in sync. They stopped at the nurses' station for an update. The surgery was about to begin. There was nothing they could do but wait. They headed to the waiting room, moved past several people, and found seats across the room, in front of a large window. Christine slumped down into a chair. Maxwell trekked from the seats to the window and back again. Those had better be the best doctors Wilmington Hospital had to offer, or they'd be dealing with a highly motivated attorney, the kind they'd never encountered previously. Nothing could go wrong with the surgery. He halted his steps in front of his sister.

"Who is the doctor performing the surgery? I assume he's a brain trauma specialist."

Christine lifted her head, and tears streamed down both cheeks. Emotion choked her words. Then she croaked out, "I don't know. Oh my God. What if he's not a specialist? Is Tyree going to be all right?" Her hand flew up to her mouth as she gasped.

Her brother slipped his hand in hers and latched on with a viselike grip. "Don't you worry. Anything he needs, I'll make sure Tyree has it. A specialist, a different hospital, anything . . . It doesn't matter."

Christine clutched his hand and nodded her head. "I know you will, and I can't thank you enough. That little boy is crazy about his uncle Max, and you've always loved him. Even though you weren't around a lot, I know how much you love him." She rose slowly from her seat and threaded her arms around Maxwell's neck. She held her embrace for a few moments and then released her hold on him. "Excuse me for a few minutes. I need to go to the ladies' room."

He paced to the window and glanced down at the people scurrying through the parking lot and along the sidewalk. The phone on his hip rang out loudly. He yanked it from his belt and pushed it to his ear.

"Just wanted you to know the deed is done. He didn't take the bait. We can meet, and I'll give you the details about this project and the stalker situation."

"Garrett, I can't deal with either right now. My nephew is in the hospital. I've got to give him my full attention."

"Oh, man. Sure, sure. Do what you have to. I'll get the package returned to sender, and we can close that chapter. Let me know if there's anything I can do for you."

"I'll catch up with you when I can."

Maxwell ended that call and made one to his office. When his assistant was on the line, he spoke rapidly. "Cancel everything for me today. My nephew was hit by a drunk driver, and I'm in Delaware."

"I'm so sorry to hear that. I hope he'll be all right."

"Me too," Maxwell echoed.

"Do you have any idea how long you'll be gone?"

"As long as it takes. For now, I'm out for the rest of today and tomorrow for sure. I'll give you a call later to let you know if it's going to be longer."

His assistant offered more kind words before they concluded the call.

Maxwell was done with work for now. He silenced the ringer on his phone and let his energy be spent on positive thoughts for Tyree. He needed the surgery to be over, and he desperately needed to hear that the prognosis was favorable. If he didn't like what he heard, he'd fly in the best doctor from anywhere in the world. Cost wasn't a factor. His millions had no value if they couldn't be used to save the one person on earth he loved the most.

Chapter 52

The hospital waiting room, a makeshift home, had remained occupied by the Montgomery family on and off for several days. Ethel paced the room and periodically slipped into the restroom to pray. When she returned this last time, Christine handed her a phone.

"Who is it?" Ethel asked, not appearing very pleased.

"It's Auntie. She wants to talk to you."

Ethel took the phone. "I appreciate you calling. Tyree had another seizure, so we can sure use your prayers. I'll talk to you later." Ethel shoved the phone into Christine's hand. "Take this thing. All that chirping and buzzing in my ear while I was trying to talk was so annoying."

"That's why I'm getting you a cell phone for Christmas. I want to watch you try to figure out how it works," Paul Sr. told his wife and chuckled. Christine and Ethel snickered along with him.

Maxwell had claimed a corner of a two-seat sofa. His arms were folded across his body, and his chin was pinned to his chest. If he kept his eyes closed, they'd think he was asleep. He wouldn't have to interact with anyone. He heard his dad grunt and announce that he was thirsty.

"I'm going on a coffee run. I'll be right back," Paul Sr. informed them.

Christine tagged along with him.

Good. He was leaving the room right on time. Maxwell could get some fresh air and not have to walk past his dad to leave the room. He performed a fake stretch, arms and legs elongated, as if he had just awakened.

"You're up?" his mother said. "Do you want coffee? Your dad went to grab some."

He didn't want anything from that man. "I'm going to step outside for a minute."

"You're not leaving, are you?" Ethel laced her fingers together and wiggled them back and forth.

"No. I just need some fresh air. I'm going back to the same stores I went to yesterday to pick up another change of clothes and a razor." The complimentary razor provided by the hotel didn't provide the kind of close shave that Maxwell sought. "Tyree won't know me with a forest growing from my face."

"I'm so glad you're here." Ethel cradled his face between her hands. "You're a handsome man with or without a scraggly beard."

Her touch was unsettling. He had to get out of there. That mushy, emotional stuff felt like a suit that was too tight. He stood and quickly left the waiting room. Maxwell was halfway down the hallway and turning the corner when he saw his self-appointed adversary, Pastor Harris, approaching. Before a syllable could escape Maxwell's mouth, the pastor shoved his hand at Maxwell and gave him a firm handshake.

"What are you doing here?"

"I called your office to set up an appointment. Your assistant told me you might be out for a while due to your nephew's accident."

"And you decided to come down here?"

"Of course. I'm a pastor. That's what I do. I help people when they're in need."

"But y—you know we have a . . . ," Maxwell stammered. "Well, a situation between us."

Pastor Harris spoke boldly. "Like I told you before, my calling goes way beyond our differences. I'm here as a man of God who wants to support your family in any way that I can, if you'll let me."

Maxwell cleared his throat and tugged at the skin on his neck after he swallowed down his slice of humble pie. He had to acknowledge the pastor's presence. He didn't want to, but the man had driven forty-five minutes to an hour from Philadelphia to Wilmington. The pastor didn't have to go out of his way. Yet he had. Maxwell was stunned. Why should he care anything about a little boy he didn't know?

"I appreciate you coming down here," Maxwell said. "My family is in the waiting room." They headed that way.

"How is your nephew doing?" Pastor Harris asked as they approached the waiting room.

"He's had several seizures over the past couple of days. It doesn't look good. I wish there was more we could do." Maxwell's volume dipped. "I'm accustomed to being in control. I guess it's difficult for me when I'm not."

"We all have our moments, but know that God is always in charge, whether we believe it or not."

Maxwell wasn't going to argue religion. He wasn't in a state of mind to argue with anyone.

Ethel eased up close to them as they entered the waiting room. "Pastor Harris, it's good to see you again." She took the pastor's hand. "I appreciate you coming to pray for my husband last year."

"My pleasure, Mrs. Montgomery."

"I've seen you in the newspapers quite a bit lately. I wouldn't have expected to see you here." Her eyes darted to Maxwell and then back to the pastor.

"I hope you don't believe everything you read."

"I sure don't." She patted Maxwell on the shoulder as she glanced up at him. "I'm sorry to interrupt, Paul. I need to talk with you a minute."

Maxwell glanced at Pastor Harris when his mother called him by his birth name. *Not now*, he thought. He didn't want his mother echoing his past in front of the one man who might use it against him.

Ethel and her son stepped away from the pastor. She questioned Maxwell in a whisper. "Why is he here? Aren't you investigating him?"

Just then Christine and Paul Sr. returned. On their heels, a doctor entered the waiting room, and with him came a sense of dread, which abruptly ended Ethel's questioning.

"What is it? What's going on?" Christine demanded.

"We're rushing Tyree into surgery. He's bleeding internally again," Tyree's doctor informed them. "We have to get that under control and relieve the swelling on his brain. I'll give you an update as soon as I can."

"Oh no, not another surgery," Christine cried out.

"My poor grandbaby." Ethel's voice and body shook as she thrust her hands into the air. She grabbed her head and swung it back and forth.

Ethel held her daughter. Fear gripped the room. Christine cried. Paul Sr. went to his wife and daughter, folded them both in his arms, then quickly glanced at Maxwell, his eyes deserting his son in a split second.

A hush fell over the room. Maxwell was frozen in his spot. There was nothing he could do. He had control of nothing, and for him, that was unbearable. His arms felt like cement blocks hanging from his shoulders.

Pastor Harris corralled the fragmented family into a circle. Their differences didn't matter; nor did their past. Didn't they realize they needed each other? He understood that all things happened for a reason. This situation, too, had a purpose. Perhaps, due to the very pain the young boy's accident had brought to his family, a healing would come. "I need everyone to hold hands," the pastor directed.

Maxwell found himself between Pastor Harris and his dad. How did he end up in such an uncomfortable position? He was humbled, being so far from his comfort zone. He chalked his predicament up to the power of love. It had to be, because Tyree's well-being was the only reason Maxwell Montgomery willingly stood hand in hand with the two men whom he despised.

Pastor Harris considered each face in front of him, instructed them to close their eyes, and began to pray. "Lord, in this time of crisis, this family needs you. Only you." He prayed for healing. Pastor Harris clearly understood that the healing they sought was needed for more than Tyree's injuries. Pastor Harris wasn't worried. God was able.

Chapter 53

Maxwell tried to adopt a worry-free mindset, but Tyree's surgery was entering the second hour.

"Pastor Harris, we appreciate you being here," Christine said. "I don't know how long my son will be in surgery. They said three to four hours, but you never know."

"We understand if you have to get back to your church," Ethel interjected.

Pastor Harris reached over Paul Sr. and touched Ethel's hand. "I'm exactly where God wants me to be. I'd like to stay until the young man gets out of surgery."

Maxwell wasn't as receptive to the pastor's intervention. He wasn't opposed to support. It was the kind of support that bugged him. "They're right. Don't feel like you have to stay, if you have something else to do. We can handle it here."

"Speak for you," Christine said. "Anybody who can pray like he did and get through to God, I want them right here. My son needs a miracle, and I'm not kicking anybody out who can help me get it."

Maxwell wanted to rebuke her, except she was right. He certainly wasn't the person to trust in the empty hallelujah jabber of a Bible-thumper, at least not until Tyree went into surgery again. His sister and his parents were scared. He got that, and he wouldn't squelch the encouragement that Pastor Harris brought to the family. Maxwell sank into his seat. He'd grit his teeth and tolerate a few more hours with Mr. Healing Hands for their sake.

The tension in the room hovered, taunting Maxwell to make his exit.

About twenty-three minutes shy of the three-hour mark, Tyree's doctor entered the waiting room. Maxwell popped up first, followed by Christine and Pastor Harris.

"How's he doing?" Maxwell asked.

Christine latched on to Maxwell's arm, shivering heavily. Ethel stood nearby. Paul Sr. kept his seat but inched to the edge.

"The surgery went well. We were able to relieve the pressure and stop the internal bleeding."

"What does that mean? Is he going to be okay?" Christine asked, her words running out like a high-speed train.

"He's stable. We've done all that we can do medically. Now we'll have to wait and see." The doctor gazed at their somber faces. "Let's hope for the best."

"Can I see him?" Christine asked.

"He'll be in recovery for about an hour. Then you can see him. Don't be alarmed if he stays asleep throughout the day and into the night."

Christine was in no shape to respond. Maxwell thanked the doctor and consoled his sister as she cried aloud.

Ethel rested her hand on Christine's back. "Baby, there isn't much we can do. We have to trust God on this."

"I know, Mom, but it's hard," Christine replied.

Ethel nodded. "I know."

"She's right, Christine," Pastor Harris added. "No matter what this looks like, God is able."

"Don't make any promises that God can't keep," Maxwell said. He was grieved too and didn't want his family to be swayed by a fictitious hope in the supernatural. Tyree needed the best medical treatment, not a bunch of fluffy words.

"Paul Jr., stop this foolishness," his father said so loudly it made everyone turn in his direction. "Whether you agree or not, God is able."

Maxwell broke the grip his sister had on him. "Or so you say, coming from the man who sold out his family for the church."

"Stop it," Ethel shouted and whacked Maxwell on the arm. "You stop this right now. My grandson is fighting for his life. I won't have you disrespect the name of God in my presence."

Christine sniffled.

Ethel went on. "I've let you go on and on for years, but it stops here. If you're going to be in this hospital, with this family, you will respect me, your father, and the man of God standing here—"

"No, Mrs. Montgomery. I'm okay," Pastor Harris interrupted.

"You're not. My son has gone too far," Ethel said, burning a stare into Maxwell that was hard to ignore. "He is using the gift that God gave him to hurt good people, and it has to stop."

Maxwell was reeling. His natural reaction was to defend his actions. Yet lashing out at his mother while they stood in a surgical waiting room didn't feel appropriate. He'd have to acquiesce.

Once tempers mellowed and they were seated, Pastor Harris broke the silence. "I hate to leave you, but I must get back to Philadelphia."

"We understand. You have no idea how grateful we are to have you take the time out of your busy schedule for us. May God bless you," Ethel said, clasping both her hands around one of his and shaking it intensely.

"I'll be praying for you," the pastor said.

Christine and Paul Sr. thanked him.

"Attorney Montgomery, can you please step outside with me?"

Maxwell wasn't expecting the request. He didn't have to look at his three family members to know that they were glaring at him. Turning the pastor down wasn't an option, not with the heat that was sure to come from his family. He'd avoid the disturbance.

"Sure. Why not?"

The men strolled into the hallway and walked down a ways without an utterance. Pastor Harris stopped not too far from the elevator.

"You have a wonderful family, and my heart goes out to them."

Maxwell pressed his hand against the wall and peered at the floor. This preacher man wasn't equipped to rate the Montgomery family. "That's because you don't know them like I do."

"That's true, which is why I can accept them for who they are."

"Why did you have me come out here?" Maxwell asked, somewhat annoyed.

"I wanted to let you know I'm available if you need me. Let's set aside the other stuff that's going on between us."

"You mean the investigation? Is that what this is about? You're offering a helping hand to my family in order for me to ease up on you?" With this revelation, Maxwell was definitely annoyed.

"Is that what you think?" the pastor fired at Maxwell.

"I don't know what to think."

"Is it this difficult for you to accept help when you genuinely need it? Have you been that wounded?"

Maxwell's defenses kicked in. "I don't need your kind of help."

"If your nephew needs help, your family needs help. That means you need help."

Maxwell couldn't argue the point. He hated that Pastor Harris was making good sense. He didn't reply.

"Know that I will be fasting and praying for your nephew, your family, and for you."

"For me?"

"Yes, you. To be honest, I'd prefer to be miles from you. Lord knows, I don't want to have anything to do with you."

"So, why are you here?" Maxwell asked sharply.

"Because God said so. Don't ask me, but there's some kind of anointing or calling on you, Attorney Maxwell."

"What? Get out of here with that nonsense," Maxwell said, with his face scrunched up.

"You don't have to believe me. I get it. You're blind about God's purpose for your life, but don't you worry. When He's ready, God will open your eyes. That's why I'm praying for you."

Maxwell didn't have the stamina to wage a fight in the hallway. He was worn out. "Any praying you do should be for Tyree. Like you said, he's the one who needs it."

"Already done. He's been on the tarrying prayer chain since this morning."

"What's that?"

"Fifty people are assigned to pray on a matter every day for however long it takes for God to move."

Maxwell was intrigued. "What if it takes a month?"

"What if?"

"Yeah, like fifty people are going to keep praying for a stranger."

"That's what we do at Faith Temple."

Maxwell desperately wanted to discount Pastor Harris, but there seemed to be an element of sincerity in what he said.

"You've probably heard that my church has a reputation for getting people healed."

Not only did Maxwell know about this reputation, but he'd also hoped to use it as a basis in the developing civil case.

"What people don't realize is that prayer is the key to our healing ministry. We stay prayed up at the church. There's prayer going on twenty-four hours a day."

"That's a lot of praying." Maxwell couldn't recall any ministry which he'd battled that had made the same claim.

"It works. There is truly power in prayer," the pastor said and chuckled.

"Hopefully, it will work for my nephew."

The pastor pointed his index finger in the air, with his arm raised. "He loves for us to hand Him our challenges." Pastor Harris grinned slightly. "The doctors have done what they were supposed to do. Now watch God do what He's going to do."

Maxwell didn't fully embrace the pastor's message of hope, but a large part of him wanted to, which caught him off guard. He'd never been close to trusting in prayer or religion to fix a real problem. In his experience, religion caused more problems than it solved.

Pastor Harris took several steps and pressed the elevator button. "Call me when your nephew wakes up and makes a miraculous recovery in the next few days."

"That will be a call I'll gladly make."

The elevator beeped, signaling that it was approaching their floor.

"I'll expect your call."

"So confident. Why?"

"When you trust in the Lord and let Him lead you, why not be confident?" Pastor Harris chuckled again as the elevator door opened. "Who knows? Maybe one day

I'll see you in one of my services. And it won't be as an attorney looking to build a case against me." He stepped on the elevator.

"If you believe in miracles, I guess it's possible."

"I do," Pastor Harris said as the elevator door closed.

Maxwell was speechless. He'd established a lucrative law firm based on not trusting religious leaders. For Tyree's sake, just this once, Maxwell wished he could.

Chapter 54

Maxwell languished in the hallway, alone. Loneliness swept in and stole his solace. Being on his own was a familiar concept, one he'd mastered. He lived alone, he'd built his practice single-handedly, and he enjoyed life on his terms. His model had worked flawlessly until lately. Maxwell rested his head against the wall, his hands in his pockets. He shut his eyes and reflected on his accomplishments.

To the average person, his success was a dream come true, a shot at the good life. Maxwell clutched his fist as tightly as he could. What good was his success when it counted? He couldn't wave his bar association membership over Tyree's bed and have him recover. He couldn't line the room with hundred-dollar bills until his multi-million-dollar account was drained. He couldn't wrap his nephew in his collection of awards. His winning court record wasn't going to keep the swelling down in Tyree's head. Maxwell sulked. He'd spent his entire adulthood building his impenetrable world, and for what? Who was he? Maxwell opened his eyes, took in his surroundings, and sighed. The answer was surreal. He raised his foot and pressed his shoulder against the wall with his hands still in his pockets. He was alone, and he didn't have to be.

Maxwell ripped the phone from his side and dialed Nicole. It was after two o'clock. She might be at the office, but with her traveling, he wasn't sure. When she didn't answer the office phone, Maxwell hastily retrieved her cell number from his mobile directory and hit SEND. He wanted her to answer badly, and thank goodness she did.

"You have no idea how glad I am to catch you," he said, sighing in relief.

"Maxwell, I wasn't expecting a call from you. What's going on?" she asked in a calm manner.

"I'm in Delaware. Tyree was in an accident. He's pretty bad off."

Anxiousness laced Nicole's reply. "Your nephew? The one you always talk about?"

"That's the one," Maxwell said as the clarity in his voice faded.

"I'm so sorry. When did it happen?"

"A few days ago."

"Is there anything I can do?"

He paused, reluctant to reply truthfully. Maxwell wasn't accustomed to needing anyone or anything. During his early teenage years, he'd needed to be a priority in his parents' life, but they had let him down. The hurt had stayed with him. In his late teens he'd discovered the best way to mask the pain was to cut his family out of his life. He'd dealt with the pain once and planned never to bother with it again. His plan had worked for years. He'd taken meaningful emotions out of every relationship, except for the one with Tyree. What he hadn't realized until recently was that his relationship with Nicole had penetrated his emotional barrier too, putting him in unfamiliar territory.

"Did you hear me?" she repeated.

"I did," he said, tapping his index finger on his cell phone. He was in a bind. He wanted to see her but didn't want to need her. Maybe she wouldn't come, since he'd never introduced her to his parents the entire time they'd dated. How could he? He was estranged from them. He contemplated the matter some more and finally came to a decision. To heck with strategizing. He'd come clean. "There *is* something you can do for me."

"What?"

"Come down to Wilmington for me."

"Did you say Wilmington?"

He wasn't shocked at her reaction. He was more shocked that the words had come from his mouth. "Yes. It's been tough these past few days. I could really use a friend."

"You sure?"

"Positive." Maxwell couldn't be more certain. He needed her.

"Okay. Where should I meet you?"

"Wilmington Hospital. I'm here with my family . . . my sister, mother, and father."

"You're with your family? I thought you didn't get along with them."

"That's true, but we're here for Tyree. That's what's important."

"Maybe I can finally meet them."

"I don't see why not."

"I wasn't expecting that answer," Nicole replied in a playful way. "Well, if you're sure, I'll take off early and see you around six."

"Perfect. Hit me on my cell and let me know when you get to the parking garage."

"Did you need me to stop by your office and bring anything?"

"No, thank you. I've taken a leave of absence for the rest of the week."

"Are you serious?" she shouted. "This is not the Maxwell Montgomery I know. I thought you'd never turn your back on work for anybody."

Maxwell grunted. "Never say never. Given the right set of circumstances, anything and anybody can change. I'll see you this evening, and I appreciate you coming down."

"No problem. It's what friends do."

They disconnected the call. Maxwell was energized. He bounced back to the waiting room to find Christine sprawled out across a sofa and his parents sitting in a pair of chairs.

"You were gone a long time. I thought you'd left," Christine said.

"I hope you didn't get into an argument with Pastor Harris," Ethel said, chiming in.

"No, I didn't, Mom." Maxwell wasn't offended. He was feeling too hopeful to be dragged into a disagreement. He chose to stay positive and to send good vibes to Tyree.

"Thank the Lord, because he's a good man. He didn't have to drive all the way down here," Ethel stated.

"And wait with us for three hours," Christine added.

"Sure didn't," Paul Sr. commented.

Maxwell was outnumbered, with all three family members, including his father, singing the praises of Pastor Harris. What they didn't know was that Maxwell might be inclined to agree. Experience forced him to hold off on joining the Pastor Harris praise team based on one upbeat encounter. It would take more to convince him that the pastor was indeed a "good man." However, Maxwell had to admit that the pastor's rating was climbing. His family didn't have to know.

The seat next to Paul Sr. was empty. Maxwell sat there, drawing puzzled looks from his mother and sister. *Why not?* Maxwell figured. When Tyree got better, he'd want to see his family together. There was a long bridge to cross, in Maxwell's mind, before he could embrace the Montgomery clan. For Tyree's sake, Maxwell was willing to take a few steps today. *Never say never* was the motto of the day.

Maxwell saw his father flipping through the sports pages. "Pops, can I get some of that paper?"

"Sure can," his father replied and handed Maxwell several pages of the newspaper.

"You still a Phillies fan?"

"Until the day I die," his father answered.

Maxwell eased back in his seat.

"We don't plan on that day coming anytime soon," Ethel said, grinning at her husband.

"Maybe I can get a couple of tickets and we can go to a game, if you're interested," Maxwell suggested.

Ethel shot up from her seat. "Yes, he's interested."

"I can speak for myself." Paul Sr. turned to Maxwell. "I'm not turning down seats at a Phillies game. You get the tickets. I'll go."

Ethel smiled; Christine, too, although not as wide.

Maxwell was relieved that his father hadn't turned him down. It actually felt better than he'd anticipated.

"You look tired, probably because you've been in this hospital practically around the clock. You haven't been home in a few nights. I appreciate you being here, but I understand if you want to go home tonight and get a good night's sleep in your own bed," Christine told him.

"I'm not leaving. My room down the road in Brandywine is perfectly fine. I'll be there until we get some good news about Tyree."

Christine clearly mouthed the words "Thank you."

"You don't have to waste money on a hotel suite when we have an extra bedroom," Ethel told him.

Maxwell heard her but wasn't eager to answer. Staying in their house was a bad idea. The Montgomery family might be in the midst of reconciliation, but it was going to be a slow process. Rushing through the steps would be detrimental. Staying at the hotel was wise.

"I get a discount the longer I stay." It wasn't a great answer, but he didn't want to hurt his mother with the truth.

"Oh, well, I guess you know what you're doing," Ethel said, sounding disappointed.

He wasn't happy about hurting her, but he wasn't changing his mind. She'd thank him later. "I have a feeling Tyree's going to have me down here quite a bit. So, I will take a rain check on the room."

His mother's countenance glistened.

Maxwell was pleased with his gesture. Maybe there was hope for them, after all.

Chapter 55

Nicole waited patiently at the entrance to the Green Room, a restaurant in the Hotel du Pont. She hadn't been in downtown Wilmington in years, and she had never been there with Maxwell. She was oddly giddy, as if they were on their first date.

"You're here," Maxwell said, bopping into the lobby. "Sorry I'm late," he said and kissed her on the cheek without making a big deal of the gesture. "I could have been here sooner, but I got a text from your office, saying you were running behind," he told her. "That's why I figured it was easier to meet here instead of at the hospital."

"I didn't want to keep the great attorney Maxwell Montgomery waiting too long. So, I shifted my schedule around and got down here as soon as I could." She snickered.

"I'm glad you're here."

"Me too."

Maxwell approached the podium so that they could be seated. "We have a reservation for two under Montgomery."

"Please follow me," the maître d' said and took the lead.

Maxwell eased his hand around Nicole's waist as they went to their table. After they were seated, the maître d' placed thick linen napkins across their laps and handed them each a menu.

"Mr. Montgomery, is this table to your liking?"

"It's fine."

"Very well, sir. I will send the wine steward."

"Give us a few minutes," Maxwell said.

"Certainly. Let us know when you're ready."

When the two of them were alone, Nicole reached across the table and touched Maxwell's hand. "How's your nephew?"

"He's stable."

"I hope he gets better soon," she said, patting his hand and hoping to provide a comforting presence.

"Me too."

"I hated not getting here early enough to meet your family. Ever since you mentioned my meeting them this afternoon, I've thought about it constantly. I really hope to get another chance to meet them."

"I can make it happen, that is if you can carve time into your busy schedule," he said, glancing at the menu.

"Look who's talking. You know only one way, and that's working around the clock."

Maxwell rested his menu on the table. "True, but I might be changing."

"And the sky is green," she replied, checking out the menu.

"Seriously, Tyree's accident has caused me to reassess my priorities."

Nicole was captivated by such a comment coming from Maxwell. He was a bona fide workaholic. She didn't see him changing.

"I'm thinking about extending my leave for another month or two."

"Not happening, and you know it. What would happen to your open cases?"

Maxwell hadn't figured out the details, but pulling back seemed feasible. Ironically, he didn't have too many active cases, given that 80 percent of his time was dedicated to Faith Temple and Pastor Harris.

"This might be a good time to expand my practice and add a few more attorneys. That way I can take time off and not worry about my practice."

"That will be the day,"

"You don't think I'm capable of making changes in my life?"

"You're capable but not willing to change," she said, resting her left hand on top of his.

Maxwell noticed her engagement ring was gone. He didn't want to get too cocky before confirming that James was history. However, if he was gone, Maxwell figured one man's misfortune could be another's great opportunity.

"I see you're doing some changing too," he said, touching her naked finger.

"Let's not talk about my failed engagement. I want to enjoy our dinner." She took another quick glance at the menu. "I could use a nice glass of wine."

"It has been a tough day. I could use one too. Better get a bottle." He beckoned the wine steward.

"Between a four-course meal and a bottle of wine, you're not getting out of here for less than three hundred dollars before the tip."

Maxwell grinned. "It's only money."

At least he could get some use from his money. He'd found out the hard way that his money had limitations when it came to matters of the heart. Tyree's accident would be a permanent reminder.

"I'm grateful that you came," Maxwell said, peering at Nicole. "I need you here, more than you know."

Her radiance captured his attention, reminding Maxwell that he wasn't alone. He'd let Nicole slip away once without the slightest resistance. His recent brush with loneliness indicated that might not have been a wise decision. Sitting across the table from Nicole, he found that it was difficult admitting he'd made a mistake.

Yet there she was. He caressed her hand. He'd learned relationships might not be as disposable as he'd once believed. If he got another chance, Maxwell was determined not to waste it. He wouldn't be as foolish this time.

Not every mistake could be fixed, but some deserved the effort.

Chapter 56

Maxwell had limited his libations at dinner last evening to two glasses of wine. Waking up without a headache or a full-fledged hangover was his reward. He sat on the side of his bed, contemplating the whirlwind of events over the past couple of days as a myriad of feelings consumed him. He went from Tyree to his relaxing dinner with Nicole. His father and Pastor Harris rattled around in his mind too. How could they not? Twenty-four hours ago both men had been on his "despise" list. Maxwell swallowed hard and let his neck rock backward.

Thick blinds had fought aggressively to keep sunlight from shining into Maxwell's hotel room and brightening his morning. He raised the blinds and let the light chase the darkness away. With a small effort from him, the fight was over quickly. Maxwell pondered his new reality a little longer and then got into gear. He'd developed a routine of getting to the hospital by 8:00 a.m. and making a day of it. He was particularly eager to get to the hospital today since Tyree still hadn't awakened as of last night. Maybe one of those prayers on Pastor Harris's chain would work. It was a long shot for Maxwell to consider remotely the possibility that a distant God could heal a sick little boy in Wilmington based on the requests of a bunch of strangers in Philly. Yet he was desperate enough to believe it might work. He couldn't handle the alternative.

Maxwell wasn't familiar with the traffic patterns on a Friday morning in Wilmington, Delaware. It was close to seven o'clock. She hadn't asked, but Maxwell knew Christine was counting on seeing his face every morning. He wouldn't be late. He'd hustle in case there was a slowdown along his four-mile stretch on I-95.

Fortunately, traffic wasn't an issue. Maxwell arrived at the hospital a few minutes early. Since Tyree was in the ICU, only two visitors were allowed to see him at once. Maxwell went to the family's central meeting spot in the waiting room and looked for his mother or father in order to get an update. He was surprised when he did not to see them there. He began worrying.

Christine darted into the room. "Maxwell, come quickly," she shouted and tugged at his arm. She spoke so fast, it was difficult to understand her.

Maxwell's heart beat rapidly, and sweat beads formed on his brow. He had to ask but didn't want to know. "What is it, Christine?" Maxwell prepared as best he could for the bad news.

Tears began streaming down Christine's cheeks.

Maxwell couldn't take the ax hanging over his head any longer. "Is he gone?" Maxwell asked, suppressing his own tears.

"No, he's awake and asking for you," she said and paused long enough to hug her brother tightly around his neck.

"Oh, Christine, thank God," Maxwell shouted before realizing what he was saying.

"I know. Can you believe it?" Christine grabbed Maxwell's hand and briskly maneuvered him through the hallways, en route to Tyree's room. "Yesterday he was in bad shape. Wait until you see him now." Her tears transformed into glee as they approached the room situated across from the nurses' station.

"Are Mom and Dad here?" he asked.

"Dad wasn't feeling well last night. I sent them home, and I told them to sleep in this morning. I called them when Tyree woke up. They're on the way."

A pediatric nurse met them at the doorway to Tyree's room.

"Is he still awake?" Christine asked.

"He most certainly is," the nurse replied in a warm tone. "Talking and asking for food."

Christine clasped her hand across her mouth as tears began flowing again.

"Considering his condition last night, this is nothing short of a miracle," the nurse added. "Your family is very fortunate. That little guy in there must have a very special angel looking out for him."

"I guess he does," Maxwell replied, anxious to get inside the room.

The nurse pushed the door open. Christine and Maxwell rushed in.

"Uncle Max," Tyree cried out.

Maxwell scooted to his nephew's side. Tyree was trapped by tubes, a needle taped to his arm, and a plethora of machines. None of this dampened Maxwell's enthusiasm. Tyree was alive, awake, and talking.

"You came," Tyree said.

Maxwell was overcome. He couldn't recall experiencing such raw emotion and that uncontrollable feeling of caring about the welfare of someone before himself. He figured this must be what true love felt like.

"Of course, I came," Maxwell said and gently rubbed Tyree's shoulder. "You're my little man. Where else am I going to be if you need me?"

Tyree smiled. "Does that mean you're going to visit more?"

Maxwell glanced at Christine and then back at Tyree. "It does," Maxwell said, bending down closer to Tyree's eye level. "As a matter of fact, I'm going to be here so much that you'll get tired of seeing me. How about that?"

"No, I won't," Tyree replied as his joy oozed out. "Mommy, Uncle Max is going to come see me a lot now."

"So I hear," Christine said, giving Maxwell another look. "Does that make you happy?"

"Uh-huh, because we can play football and baseball and soccer. Oh, and basketball." Tyree became very animated. He sat up in the bed and began making sports gestures.

Maxwell eased him back on the pillow. "We'll see about basketball and soccer later. For now, let's get you better and out of this hospital. Okay?"

"Okay," Tyree responded, with a dramatic dip in his level of excitement.

Maxwell wasn't bothered by his nephew's disappointment about having to settle down. Once Tyree was at home, Maxwell would make it up to him.

Christine pulled Maxwell to the side. "You see he's doing well. You can take a break and go home," she said, gripping his wrist.

"Don't worry about me. I can stay."

"No, please go home and take care of your business. You've gone above and beyond. You deserve a break. Plus, if you stay, Tyree will want to talk, and he's not ready for too much exertion."

"You're probably right." There was some unfinished business waiting for him at the office that couldn't be avoided. Perhaps it was time to go. "I'll definitely be back tomorrow."

Christine thanked her brother and hugged him again. "Can you do me a favor?"

"Sure, anything."

"Please thank Pastor Harris for coming down and praying with us. I know he helped us get a miracle."

Maxwell stood motionless. He'd broken the basic rule of law: never agree to a deal without understanding the terms. There he stood, having agreed to do his sister a favor without first asking her what it entailed. Of course he hadn't imagined that she would ask him to thank Pastor Harris. Why couldn't she have asked him to do a simple task, like pay a hundred-thousand-dollar hospital bill or buy her a new house, something within his abilities? Instead, she had asked him to contact Pastor Harris, the man Maxwell was out to get, and to thank him for the contribution he'd made to Tyree's recovery. Christine was oblivious to the gravity of her request.

"I'm going home, little man, but I'll see you tomorrow."

"You promise?"

Maxwell hesitated, understanding that by promising to see Tyree, he was also opening up a door to the rest of his family. It wasn't a small feat. Despite the unpleasantness that might come with frequent family encounters, there was only one answer. "I promise."

Chapter 57

The ride from Wilmington whizzed by, owing to the fact that Maxwell was in a state of euphoria. Tyree was going to recover. Maxwell didn't care if it was the result of medical treatment, prayers, or well wishes. He was grateful for each contributing piece of the puzzle. That was why his mind drifted to Pastor Harris and Faith Temple. It would be simple to block out the pastor and return to business as usual, but Maxwell had promised to call Pastor Harris if and when Tyree's condition improved. Maxwell hadn't forgotten about his promise to Christine either. However, some promises were too difficult to keep. He was sure the pastor understood that.

Maxwell reached downtown Philadelphia and went straight to the office. He had a ton of work to shove into a ten hour day. He'd start with his top priority, the Faith Temple case.

"Good morning, Mr. Montgomery," his assistant said, jumping up to greet him. "I wasn't expecting to see you. How's your nephew?" she inquired.

"He's awake and doing very well." He was glad to share the good news.

"I'm glad to hear that. Thank goodness. I know how worried you've been."

Maxwell unlocked his private office. His assistant followed him inside.

"Now that you're back, where do you want to start? You have phone messages, appointments to be rescheduled, stacks of mail, and a set of new client inquiries."

"Let's start with finding the best headhunting firm in the country. I'm going to hire two or three attorneys, and I want the best talent out there."

"What about the mail and messages?"

"What about them?" Maxwell said, sitting in his high-back chair and dropping his key ring on the desk.

His assistant must have detected the annoyance in his voice. "Usually, you want me to keep you updated on the correspondence. I figured—"

Maxwell cut her off. "I'm sure you've done a great job with managing the office in my absence." She appeared to relax slightly. "We'll have a chance to catch up later. Right now, I'd like you to find Garrett and see if he can come in this morning."

"Anything else?"

"Not for now."

As his assistant was leaving, Maxwell called out to her. "By the way, I appreciate you holding the office together during my absence." He rested his elbows on his desk. She seemed pleased with the compliment. "Expect to find a little extra in your paycheck."

"Thanks, Mr. Montgomery, but I just did my job. The extra pay isn't necessary."

"Don't let your pride get in the way. You earned the money. Take it."

She thanked him again and closed the door on her way out.

Maxwell rubbed his chin. He was back in his office, his sanctuary. It should have been comforting, but it wasn't. Maxwell was about to pull out his box of memories but decided not to. He had at most ten hours before nightfall to get some serious work done.

His Faith Temple folder sat on top of his pile. He opened the folder and read some notes he'd taken last week. He glanced at a few articles criticizing his attack on the church and flung them to the side. Maxwell peeked at the tax documents and the background data Garrett had provided. Maxwell stared at the wealth of information. He was certain the makings of a civil case, and possibly a criminal case, lay among those pages. He'd built lucrative cases on much less. He didn't have the famous "smoking gun," that one piece of evidence Pastor Harris couldn't refute. Maxwell wasn't bothered. Smoking guns rarely existed with any case. He had over one hundred wins as proof, and only a few had ironclad evidence. Faith Temple was his for the taking.

Less than an hour passed, and there was a knock on the door. Maxwell closed the folder. "Come in." He hadn't expected to see Garrett so soon.

"Good to see you back. Your assistant gave me the news about your nephew. That's great, man." Garrett shook Maxwell's hand and then took a seat.

"Yeah, you can imagine how relieved I am. That's my little man, and he means the world to me."

Garrett nodded.

"So, what were you up to while I was out?" Maxwell asked.

"What else? Working the Faith Temple case."

"Where does it stand?"

"I can tell you up front that it's not what you'd hoped to hear."

"Try me."

"Let's start with Colita. As I told you on the phone, the seduction ploy flopped."

"Is she gone?"

"Heck, yeah. I couldn't wait to get her on the plane and out of town."

Maxwell took a pen and flipped open the Faith Temple folder again. "What else?"

"Well, I wasn't going to tell you, because it's not a big deal, but Faith Temple had a brush with insider trading."

Maxwell sat up. "Really?"

"Don't get excited. Bottom line is the church used an investor who made some questionable investments. Apparently, the church wasn't aware of the impropriety. Once they found out, the financial director sold off the questionable shares and reported their actions to the trade commission. They were cleared. End of story."

"But you know the media can put a different spin on the story and paint this in another light," Maxwell said.

"Maybe, but it would be grasping at straws. You tried that once with Layne, and what a disaster. There's nothing there."

"Then where does that leave us?"

"With no leads."

"I hate to say it, but I agree."

Garrett was puzzled by the response. "Sounds like you might finally be thinking rationally about this investigation."

Maxwell's neck stiffened. "I'm always rational," he said, with an extra dab of bass so Garrett was certain to get the message.

"Okay. Then you'll quit reaching for evidence that isn't materializing?"

"Let's be clear. There is *always* evidence. I can build a case against anybody. You know that I can." He snickered. "If I wanted, I could build a case against you."

"If you wanted to make up stuff, I guess you could." Garrett stood. "I'm done, Maxwell. I've done too many dirty deeds for you." He tossed his hands into the air. "I'm done with Faith Temple and Pastor Harris. That's it, no more. The man is clean, and I'm not carrying the guilt of putting him in jail or worse. Did it once," he said and approached Maxwell's desk. Garrett slammed his fist on the Faith Temple folder. "I won't do it again."

Maxwell stood up to face Garrett. "You don't have to." He wiggled the folder from underneath his investigator's fist. "This case is closed."

"Say what?" Garrett said, pumping his fist into the palm of his other hand.

"It's closed. I'm done too."

"Yeah, right."

"I mean it."

Garrett pressed his knuckles against the desk and let his gaze plummet. "So, you think he's clean too?"

"I don't know if he's completely clean. I can't go that far."

"Then I'm confused. Why are you willing to close the case?"

"Because I owe him, and I pay my debts."

"I'm lost."

Maxwell sighed and twirled the pen he was still holding between his fingers. Recounting the highs and lows of the past several days wasn't pleasant. He'd spare Garrett the sorrowful moments and cut to the happy ending.

"Pastor Harris came down to the hospital and sat for three or four hours with my family while my nephew underwent his second surgery."

"Really? Even with you investigating him?"

"Can you believe that?" Maxwell was humbled. "At first, I thought he was doing it as a way to suck up to me, hoping I'd give him a pass on the investigation."

"I guess it's possible."

Maxwell shook his head. "Nope. Don't think so. As much as I hate admitting it, Pastor Harris seems to be a decent guy."

"What?"

"Yes, he just might be, and I owe him. He prayed for my nephew at the hospital, and then—check this out—he had fifty church members pray for Tyree around the clock."

"That's deep."

"Who does that?" Maxwell scrunched up his face.

"You think those prayers helped your nephew get better? I mean, that would be a big claim."

"I'm honestly not sure, but just in case, I'm giving him the benefit of the doubt and leaving him alone."

Garrett roared with laughter.

"What's so funny?" Maxwell asked.

"You think we've found the first honest minister? And what if there are more out there?"

Maxwell chuckled lightly. "I hope this isn't a trend, or I'll be out of business."

Garrett reached out to shake Maxwell's hand. "On a serious note, you're doing the right thing. I'm proud of you for taking the high road. It takes a real man to do this."

"I'm making either a really smart move or a very dumb one. Either way, it's done."

"So, what are you going to do with the information we've collected?"

"Shred it all. That way nothing will end up in the media or in a prosecutor's hands. If I'm not going after Pastor Harris, nobody else is using my information to go after him."

"Cool. I'm out."

Before Garrett got to the door, Maxwell spoke again. "I know we've made mistakes that can't be fixed, but hopefully, this will move us in the right direction."

"It's a good start," Garrett replied. "You want me to let the pastor know you're dropping the case?"

Maxwell stared at the Faith Temple folder. "No thanks. I owe him a call. I'll do it myself."

Garrett was almost through the doorway when he abruptly turned to Maxwell. "I forgot the other piece of information that I wanted to tell you."

Maxwell couldn't imagine what it was.

"Remember you asked me to check into the stalking thing?"

Maxwell's curiosity rose and his heart beat rapidly. "What about it?"

"You, my friend, have a lot of enemies."

"Tell me something I don't already know." Maxwell was disappointed if that was all Garrett had to share. He was looking for a name.

"Wait now, this is good. Having enemies isn't new for you, so why would you just now start getting threats? I figured this much attention had to do with the Greater Metropolitan case. Of course, Reverend Simmons was my first suspect."

"No doubt. He was very angry at his sentencing. I can see him doing this, although it would take some effort, since he's in prison for a long time."

"Exactly. That's why I got a list of relatives of Reverend Simmons and Bishop Jones, for starters. I cross-checked to see if any had records."

Maxwell's curiosity was piqued. "And what did you find?"

"Bishop Jones's grandson got out of jail about five months ago."

"That's right, he did have a grandson in and out of trouble. I even think the bishop was trying to help him."

"You got it. Bishop Jones went to prison before he was released, and now word on the street says that he blames you."

"Yeah, okay, but that doesn't make him a stalker."

Garrett chuckled. "It's him. I had one of my buddies from the phone company pull up the call log. And guess what?" Garrett asked without letting Maxwell answer. "Your cell phone number is all over the log. It's him for sure."

Maxwell blew out a heavy sigh. "Hmm, nothing is easy these days."

"You want me to get some more evidence so you can take it to the police?"

Maxwell mulled over the situation. Finally he said, "No, you've done enough. I'll take it from here."

"But you are going to the police, right?"

"I'm not sure." Maxwell wasn't crazy. He believed the man could be dangerous. He also knew that sending the bishop's grandson back to jail wasn't going to help the kid in the long run. Maxwell had to consider his options, with going to the police being the very last route. Maxwell wasn't delusional. He couldn't mentor the young man personally, but there were others who could. Everybody deserved a chance to correct their mistakes, including Bishop Ellis Jones's grandson. The young man didn't know that clinging to anger and revenge was costly. Maxwell knew that better than anyone.

Chapter 58

Maxwell sat in the Faith Temple parking lot, meditating on what he'd say to Pastor Harris. Saying they'd been at odds was an understatement. A week ago, Maxwell had been out for blood. The more people seemed to adore Pastor Harris, the more Maxwell committed himself to his mission of exposing him. Maxwell had wholeheartedly believed that followers had a right to know the character of their leaders. He accepted that some didn't want to know, but ignorance wasn't a warm shelter for responsible adults. Maybe the general public wouldn't agree with Maxwell's tactics or mission, but many had benefited from his tireless efforts. Maxwell opened the car door and climbed out, unashamed of the career he'd pursued. He'd taken a few questionable turns. Maxwell realized that, and he was willing to correct what he could.

He stepped sharply to the church's office. He hadn't called ahead intentionally. A random visit didn't allow the pastor to script a conversation ahead of time. Maxwell wanted an unrehearsed and open dialogue. Since Pastor Harris had nothing to hide, Maxwell was certain he wouldn't mind.

"Oh, it's *you* again," Martha said, with a mean look.

"I come in peace," Maxwell said, grinning.

His charm fizzled on this trip.

"The only kind of peace you're getting is a piece of my mind," she said, flipping her glasses up on the bridge of her nose and tinkering with the computer keyboard. "I'm getting my password on here this time, and don't you be eyeballing what I'm typing."

Maxwell was amused. He had to refrain from laughing openly. Instead, he chuckled quietly. Before he could ask a question, Pastor Harris emerged from his study.

"Attorney Montgomery, I didn't expect to see you."

"Pastor, don't worry. I have my password on this computer. He's not getting any information from me." Martha stood, shaking her finger in Maxwell's direction, a scowl plastered on her face.

Maxwell raised his arms in the air. "I'm here to give you an update on my nephew. That's it."

Martha's cutting stare stayed on Maxwell. He wasn't going anywhere in that office without her watchful eye on him. He understood and wasn't offended.

"Can I get you anything to drink? Coffee, water, a soft drink?" the pastor offered.

"No, I'm good," Maxwell replied. He acknowledged the gesture, but he wasn't there for a social visit. He had business to handle quickly, and hopefully, he would leave unscathed.

Pastor Harris beckoned Maxwell into his study.

"How's your nephew?" the pastor asked, motioning for Maxwell to have a seat.

Maxwell didn't sit. "Actually, he's alert, and the doctor's prognosis is good."

"Amen," the pastor exclaimed, clapping his hands.

"The nurse said it was a miracle."

"Aha. What did I tell you, Mr. Montgomery? God is able."

"Maxwell."

"What?" Pastor Harris asked.

"Please call me Maxwell."

"If you'll call me Renaldo." The pastor's countenance lit up. "Please sit."

"No, that's okay. I'm not going to be here long." Maxwell took a rapid glance at the ceiling, as if words were lining up for him there. He drew in a breath and exhaled. The best way to handle an uncomfortable conversation was to hit it head-on. "My sister and I want to thank you and your church members for the prayers made on behalf of my nephew."

"I told you prayer works. God is good and faithful."

"Something worked, and although I'm not saying it was or wasn't your prayers, Tyree is awake and doing well. So I have to say thank you."

"Thank the Lord, not me. He's the one who deserves the praise."

Maxwell slid his hands into his pockets and let his head bop up and down several times. "Maybe one day I will."

"This Sunday would be as good a time as any."

"This weekend isn't good. I'm taking time off and spending it in Delaware with Tyree."

"Good for you. We all need a break from the office."

"I suspect I'll be taking quite a bit of time off in the next couple of months."

"Humph. And what about your active cases, like the one against me and Faith Temple?" the pastor asked.

"As of today, that case is closed, and the files will be shredded."

"Right. Just like that you're dropping the case? That's a little difficult to believe."

"Seriously," Maxwell said, swinging his arms like an umpire calling a runner safe. "I'm done."

Pastor Harris hunched his shoulders. "If you're telling me the truth, I'm glad."

"It is the truth," Maxwell confirmed, as difficult as it was to believe.

"Why the abrupt change?"

There were several reasons Maxwell could spew, but the real answer was simple. "We didn't have a legitimate claim against you."

"I'm glad to hear it."

"And trust me, we looked," Maxwell said, snickering.

"What about the prosecutor and the media picking up the case?"

"I plan to destroy all my records related to you and the church. Don't worry. The prosecutor is too lazy to pull together a meaningful case against you. And the media likes hype. If I'm not pushing the story, they'll drop it and move on to the next headliner. When I say this is done, it is."

"Then I guess we both got a miracle today. Thank the Lord," the pastor bellowed. "You sure I can't offer you a seat?"

"I'm sure," Maxwell said and prepared to shake the pastor's hand. "Thanks again, and I won't forget your kindness toward my family. But there is something that I'm curious about."

"What is it?" the pastor asked.

"How did you find out about my past and my name change?"

"I had you investigated. You are not the only one who knows how to turn over a stone or two." Pastor Harris offered a slight grin and patted Maxwell on the shoulder.

Maxwell glared directly into Pastor Harris's eyes. Should he ask him? Would he even tell the truth? *Why not?* He'd come this far. "Once you knew about my past and my connection to Bishop Jones, why didn't you tell anyone about it or shout it to the press?"

"For what? Who would that have helped? No one. There has been enough finger-pointing and people hurting. I am in the business of building people up, not tearing them down. You have a good heart, Maxwell Montgomery. You do. Trust that."

"I doubt you'd have many supporters on that one."
Maxwell had one more comment that had to be made;
then he'd go. "Just so you know, I'm not proud about
what went down with Deacon Burton. He deserved
better, and I'll have to live with the guilt."

"You don't have to live with guilt. That's not God's plan
for us. That's why Jesus died on the cross for our sins
and rose again with all power, my brother. No matter
how good you are in the courtroom, nobody can claim
perfection. Life is full of mistakes. You just have to know
how to repent, seek forgiveness, and go on with a wiser
perspective."

"If only it was that easy to fix a mistake."

"Actually, it is."

"Not everybody's going to eagerly accept my apology,"
Maxwell said.

"That's true, but you can't worry about everyone.
Make your atonement and let God mend the broken and
angry hearts. He's the only one who can. Tell you what,
why don't you come to church one Sunday and we'll talk
more?"

"I won't make a promise I can't keep, but I will think
about it."

"Good enough. Oh, and, uh, Maxwell, remember that
God sees your heart, not your past and not your failures.
He's focused on your future, and it's bright in the Lord."

At least someone saw a bright future for him, Maxwell
thought. He said good-bye and walked out. His next call
would be to Nicole. Since today was one of miracles,
perhaps she'd be willing to have dinner with him two or
three nights in a row. If Tyree could be fixed, Maxwell
could too. He was open to the possibilities: marriage,
time off work, and a visit to Faith Temple sooner than
Pastor Harris expected.

Maxwell settled into his Porsche and cranked the raspy high-powered engine. He pressed down on the accelerator, prepared to enjoy the ride, with guilt sitting on the curb. This was a glorious day. Maxwell would sleep well tonight, for the first time in months.

Reading Guide

Makes you go, "Hmmm!"

Now that you have read *Redeemed*, consider the following discussion questions:

1. Did Maxell have Nicole's fiancé investigated because he wanted them to break up? Did he simply want to make sure Nicole was marrying a good guy?
2. Is there a future for Maxwell and Nicole?
3. Did Maxwell commit a crime when he hired a woman to tempt Pastor Harris into adultery? Since Pastor Harris didn't take the bait, does that excuse Maxwell's actions?
4. Maxwell wanted to collect evidence against Pastor Harris by any means necessary. Do you think such drastic measures are taken in real life to reach a guilty verdict in a criminal or civil case? Discuss local and national cases for which there were allegations of misused or abused authority.
5. Maxwell was estranged from his sister and his parents. Yet his sister and his mother called him often. He didn't like it. Do you think they were being pushy or doing the right thing by constantly reaching out to him?
6. Before reaching the conclusion, who did you think was the mystery person behind the threats Maxwell received? Why?

7. Maxwell harbored bitter animosity toward his dad for the devastating choice he made to trust Pastor Ellis Jones, but that was over twenty years ago. Maxwell was successful and financially independent. So why did he struggle so much with forgiving his father?

8. Mrs. Burton was a Christian. Even though her husband was murdered and she was grieving his death, should she have displayed such anger and an unforgiving attitude toward Maxwell? Forgiveness is a foundational truth and a necessity in our Christian walk. How do we forgive in tragic circumstances, such as Deacon Burton's imprisonment and murder?

9. Do you believe that Pastor Harris's prayer and around-the-clock prayer vigil had anything to do with Tyree's recovery? Discuss your faith and the power of prayer.

10. Maxwell seemed to be softening as a result of Tyree's accident. Do you think his change will last? State why or why not.

11. Throughout the story, Maxwell battled with the guilt associated with helping to send an innocent man to prison. At first he denied the implications of his actions. When that didn't work, he tried to justify his actions. When that failed as well, his next step was to make restitution by setting up trust funds for the innocent man's family. Do you think that will resolve his guilt? If not, what will?

Note: The Redeemed Faith-Based Drama Series is loosely based on the biblical leader and apostle Paul. Originally named Saul, he was known as someone who was committed to persecuting the church. It seemed that this would be his legacy, but God had other plans for him. Saul had an encounter with God on the road to Damascus, and this altered his philosophy, and he became a faithful believer. His name was changed to Paul, and he repented. He spent the rest of his life preaching the good news of salvation and deliverance, through the acceptance of Jesus Christ, to a list of struggling churches (New Testament).

Acknowledgments

We are grateful for the readers who have graciously allowed us to entertain them with our drama series, beginning with book one, *Relentless*, and followed by book two, *Redeemed*. We give a special thanks to our incredible editor, Joylynn Ross, who offers the perfect balance of meaningful feedback and encouragement. We thank Smiley Guirand for producing such captivating cover designs from a mere concept. We also thank Valerie Johnson (Visual Sells) for bringing our characters to life in her outstanding video trailers. Many thanks to our agent, Andrew Stuart, and the rest of our Urban Books family.

From Patricia

I want to thank my wonderful family, including my daughter, parents, brothers, sister-cousin nieces and nephews, goddaughters, friends, advanced readers, spiritual parents, church family, prayer warriors, Delta Sigma Theta sorority sisters, booksellers, book clubs, and so many other supporters. I especially wish to thank my dearest husband and soul mate, Jeffrey Glass. Life is a journey filled with purpose. Sharing this ride with my incredible hubby has been sweeter than words can express. I'm truly blessed.

I also want to honor the memory of Mr. Don Bartel (1924-2015), one of my beloved spiritual fathers, who showed me so much love and support over the years, along with his beautiful bride of 67 years, Mrs. Mary Bartel.

Finally, I am grateful and honored to do this project with Gracie Hill, my childhood neighbor, my high school friend, and my sister in Christ. Blessings to you always.

From Gracie

I am thankful to God for all his many blessings, great and small. I am thankful to each person who has joined Patricia and me on the literary journey of the *Redeemed* drama series. You made *Relentless* a number one national best seller. Thank you so much for your support and encouragement. I am so thankful to Joylynn Ross, our editor. She is insightful and easy to work with, and she showers us with a wealth of expertise and direction. I am very excited to be a part of the Urban Christian family of authors and their awesome production team. Much thanks to Smiley Guirand for the fabulous job he did with the covers of both *Relentless* and *Redeemed*.

I also thank my wonderful family, my children, my sisters and brothers, and my husband, Brian Hill. I give a special thanks to my pastor, District Elder Rickey Bates, First Lady Valarie Bates, and my Promise of Life Ministries family. Thank you for your love, support, and prayers.

Authors' Note

Dear Readers:

Thank you for reading *Redeemed*. We hope you were entertained by this second installment in the Redeemed Faith-Based Drama Series. Look for our other titles.

We invite you to join our mailing lists, to drop us a note, or to post a message on our web site. You can also find each of us on Facebook, at Patricia Haley-Glass and Gracie Hill.

As always, thank you for the support. Keep reading and be blessed.

www.patriciahaley.com

www.graciehill.com

UC HIS GLORY BOOK CLUB!

www.uchisglorybookclub.net

UC His Glory Book Club is the spirit-inspired brain-child of Joylynn Ross, an author and the acquisitions editor at Urban Christian, and Kendra Norman-Bellamy, an author for Urban Christian. It is an online book club that hosts authors of Urban Christian. We welcome as members all men and women who have a passion for reading Christian-based fiction.

UC His Glory Book Club pledges its commitment to providing support, positive feedback, encouragement, and a forum whereby members can openly discuss and review the literary works of Urban Christian authors.

There is no membership fee associated with UC His Glory Book Club; however, we do ask that you support the authors by purchasing their works, encouraging them, providing book reviews, and, of course, offering your prayers. We also ask that you respect our beliefs and follow the guidelines of the book club. We hope to receive your valuable input, opinions, and reviews that build up, rather than tear down, our authors.

What We Believe:

—We believe that Jesus is the Christ, Son of the Living God.

—We believe that the Bible is the true, living Word of God.

—We believe that all Urban Christian authors should use their God-given writing abilities to honor God and share the message of the written word that God has given to each of them uniquely.

—We believe in supporting Urban Christian authors in their literary endeavors by reading their titles, purchasing them, and sharing them with our online community.

—We believe that everything we do in our literary arena should be done in a manner that will lead to God being glorified and honored.

We look forward to online fellowship with you.

Please visit us often at:

www.uchisglorybookclub.net.

Many Blessings to You!

Shelia E. Lipsey,
President, UC His Glory Book Club